April 20-1919.

Easter Greeting
to Uncle Annius
from Helen

THE HEART OF THE DESERT

SIDE BY SIDE, THEY RODE OFF INTO THE DESERT SUNSET. *Page 313.*
The Heart of the Desert.

THE HEART OF THE DESERT

(KUT-LE OF THE DESERT)

By HONORÉ WILLSIE

Author of "Still Jim"

With Frontispiece In Colors
By W. HERBERT DUNTON

A. L. BURT COMPANY, PUBLISHERS
114-120 East Twenty-third Street - - New York

PUBLISHED BY ARRANGEMENT WITH FREDERICK A. STOKES COMPANY

Copyright, 1912, *by*
THE RIDGWAY COMPANY

Copyright, 1913, *by*
FREDERICK A. STOKES COMPANY

All rights reserved, including that of translation into foreign
languages, including the Scandinavian

SIXTH PRINTING

September, 1913

CONTENTS

CHAPTER		PAGE
I	THE VALLEY OF THE PECOS	1
II	THE CAUCASIAN WAY	19
III	THE INDIAN AND CAUCASIAN	37
IV	THE INDIAN WAY	53
V	THE PURSUIT	69
VI	ENTERING THE DESERT KINDERGARTEN	83
VII	THE FIRST LESSON	99
VIII	A BROADENING HORIZON	113
IX	TOUCH AND GO	129
X	A LONG TRAIL	141
XI	THE TURN IN THE TRAIL	153
XII	THE CROSSING TRAILS	167
XIII	AN INTERLUDE	181
XIV	THE BEAUTY OF THE WORLD	195
XV	AN ESCAPE	209
XVI	ADRIFT IN THE DESERT	219
XVII	THE HEART'S OWN BITTERNESS	233
XVIII	THE FORGOTTEN CITY	249
XIX	THE TRAIL AGAIN	261
XX	THE RUINED MISSION	271
XXI	THE END OF THE TRAIL	291

The Heart of the Desert

CHAPTER I

THE VALLEY OF THE PECOS

RHODA hobbled through the sand to the nearest rock. On this she sank with a groan, clasped her slender foot with both hands and looked about her helplessly.

She felt very small, very much alone. The infinite wastes of yellow desert danced in heat waves against the bronze-blue sky. The girl saw no sign of living thing save a buzzard that swept lazily across the zenith. She turned dizzily from contemplating the vast emptiness about her to a close scrutiny of her injured foot. She drew off her thin satin house slipper painfully and dropped it unheedingly into a bunch of yucca that crowded against the rock. Her silk stocking followed. Then she sat in helpless misery, eying her blue-veined foot.

In spite of her evident invalidism, one could but wonder why she made so little effort to help herself. She sat droopingly on the rock, gazing from her foot to the far lavender line of the mesas. A tiny, impotent atom of life, she sat as if the eternal why which the desert hurls at one overwhelmed her, deprived her of hope, almost of sensation. There was something of nobility in the steadiness with which she gazed at the melting distances, something of pathos in her evident resignation to her own helplessness and weakness.

The girl was quite unconscious of the fact that a young man was tramping up the desert behind her. He, however, had spied the white gown long before Rhoda had sunk to the rock and had laid his course directly for her. He was a tall fellow, standing well over six feet and he swung through the heavy sand with an easy stride that covered distance with astonishing rapidity. As he drew near enough to perceive Rhoda's yellow head bent above her injured foot, he quickened his pace, swung round the yucca thicket and pulled off his soft felt hat.

"Good-morning!" he said. "What's the matter?"

Rhoda started, hastily covered her foot, and looked up at the tall khaki-clad figure. She never had seen the young man before, but the desert is not formal.

"A thing like a little crayfish bit my foot," she answered; "and you don't know how it hurts!"

"Ah, but I do!" exclaimed the young man. "A scorpion sting! Let me see it!"

Rhoda flushed.

THE VALLEY OF THE PECOS

"Oh, never mind that!" she said. "But if you will go to the Newman ranch-house for me and ask them to send the buckboard I'll be very grateful. I—I feel dizzy, you know."

"Gee whiz!" exclaimed the young man. "There's no time for me to run about the desert if you have a scorpion sting in your foot!"

"Is a scorpion sting dangerous?" asked Rhoda. Then she added, languidly, "Not that I mind if it is!"

The young man gave her a curious glance. Then he pulled a small case from his pocket, knelt in the sand and lifted Rhoda's foot in one slender, strong, brown hand. The instep already was badly swollen.

"Hold tight a minute!" said the young man.

And before Rhoda could protest he had punctured the red center of the swelling with a little scalpel, had held the cut open and had filled it with a white powder that bit. Then he pulled a clean handkerchief from his pocket and tore it in two. With one half he bound the ankle above the cut tightly. With the other he bandaged the cut itself.

"Are you a doctor?" asked Rhoda faintly.

"Far from it," replied the young man with a chuckle, tightening the upper bandage until Rhoda's foot was numb. "But I always carry this little outfit with me; rattlers and scorpions are so thick over on the ditch.

Sombody's apt to be hurt anytime. I'm Charley Cartwell, Jack Newman's engineer."

"Oh!" said Rhoda understandingly. "I'm so dizzy I can't see you very well. This is very good of you. Perhaps now you'd go on and get the buckboard. Tell them it's for Rhoda, Rhoda Tuttle. I just went out for a walk and then—"

Her voice trailed into nothingness and she could only steady her swaying body with both hands against the rock.

"Huh!" grunted young Cartwell. "I go on to the house and leave you here in the boiling sun!"

"Would you mind hurrying?" asked Rhoda.

"Not at all," returned Cartwell.

He plucked the stocking and slipper from the yucca and dropped them into his pocket. Then he stooped and lifted Rhoda across his broad chest. This roused her.

"Why, you can't do this!" she cried, struggling to free herself.

Cartwell merely tightened his hold and swung out at a pace that was half run, half walk.

"Close your eyes so the sun won't hurt them," he said peremptorily.

Dizzily and confusedly, Rhoda dropped her head back on the broad shoulder and closed her eyes, with a feeling of security that later on was to appall her. Long after she was to recall the confidence of this moment with unbelief and horror. Nor did she dream how many weary days and hours she one day was to pass with this same brazen sky over her, this same broad shoulder under her head.

Cartwell looked down at the delicate face lying against his breast, at the soft yellow hair massed against his sleeve. Into his black eyes came a look that was passionately tender, and the strong brown hand that supported Rhoda's shoulders trembled.

In an incredibly short time he was entering the peach orchard that surrounded the ranch-house. A young man in white flannels jumped from a hammock in which he had been dozing.

"For heaven's sake!" he exclaimed. "What does this mean?"

Rhoda was too ill to reply. Cartwell did not slack his giant stride toward the house.

"It means," he answered grimly, "that you folks must be crazy to let Miss Tuttle take a walk in clothes like this! She's got a scorpion sting in her foot."

The man in flannels turned pale. He hurried along beside Cartwell, then broke into a run.

"I'll telephone to Gold Rock for the doctor and tell Mrs. Newman."

He started on ahead.

"Never mind the doctor!" called Cartwell. "I've attended to the sting. Tell Mrs. Jack to have hot water ready."

As Cartwell sprang up the porch steps, Mrs. Newman ran out to meet him. She was a pretty, rosy girl, with brown eyes and curly brown hair.

"Rhoda! Kut-le!" she cried. "Why didn't I warn her! Put her on the couch here in the hall, Kut-le. John, tell Li Chung to bring the hot-water bottles. Here, Rhoda dear, drink this!"

For half an hour the three, with Li Chung hovering in the background, worked over the girl. Then as they saw her stupor change to a natural sleep, Katherine gave a sigh that was almost a sob.

"She's all right!" she said. "O Kut-le, if you hadn't come at that moment!"

Cartwell shook his head.

"It might have gone hard with her, she's so delicate. Gee, I'm glad I ran out of tobacco this morning and thought a two-mile tramp across the desert for it worth while!"

The three were on the porch now. The young man in flannels, who had said little but had obeyed orders explicitly eyed Cartwell curiously.

"You're Newman's engineer, aren't you?" he

asked. "My name's DeWitt. You've put us all under great obligations, this morning."

Cartwell took the extended hand.

"Well, you know," he said carefully, "a scorpion sting may or may not be serious. People have died of them. Mrs. Jack here makes no more of them than of a mosquito bite, while Jack goes about like a drunken sailor with one for a day, then forgets it. Miss Tuttle will be all right when she wakes up. I'm off till dinner time, Mrs. Jack. Jack will think I've reverted!"

DeWitt stood for a moment watching the tall, lithe figure move through the peach-trees. He was torn by a strange feeling, half of aversion, half of charm for the dark young stranger. Then:

"Hold on, Cartwell," he cried. "I'll drive you back in the buckboard."

Katherine Newman, looking after the two, raised her eyebrows, shook her head, then smiled and went back to Rhoda.

It was mid-afternoon when Rhoda woke. Katherine was sitting near by with her sewing.

"Well!" said Rhoda wonderingly. "I'm all right, after all!"

Katherine jumped up and took Rhoda's thin little hand joyfully.

"Indeed you are!" she cried. "Thanks to Kut-le!"

"Thanks to whom?" asked Rhoda. "It was a tall young man. He said his name was Charley Cartwell."

"Yup!" answered Katherine. "Charley Cartwell! His other name is Kut-le. He'll be in to dinner with Jack, tonight. Isn't he good-looking, though!"

"I don't know. I was so dizzy I couldn't see him. He seemed very dark. Is he a Spaniard?"

"Spaniard! No!" Katherine was watching Rhoda's languid eyes half mischievously. "He's part Mescallero, part Pueblo, part Mohave!"

Rhoda sat erect with flaming face.

"You mean that he's an Indian and I let him carry me! Katherine!"

The mischief in Katherine's brown eyes grew to laughter.

"I thought that would get a rise out of you, you blessed tenderfoot! What difference does that make? He rescued you from a serious predicament; and more than that he's a fine fellow and one of Jack's dearest friends."

Rhoda's delicate face still was flushed.

"An Indian! What did John DeWitt say?"

"Oh!" said Katherine, carelessly, "he offered to drive Kut-le back to the ditch, and he hasn't got home yet. They probably will be very congenial, John being a Harvard man and Kut-le a Yale!"

Rhoda's curved lips opened, then closed again. The look of interest died from her eyes.

"Well," she said in her usual weary voice, "I think I'll have a glass of milk, if I may. Then I'll go out on the porch. You see I'm being all the trouble to you, Katherine, that I said I would be."

"Trouble!" protested Katherine. "Why, Rhoda Tuttle, if I could just see you with the old light in your eyes I'd wait on you by inches on my knees. I would, honestly."

Rhoda rubbed a thin cheek against the warm hand that still held hers, and the mute thanks said more than words.

The veranda of the Newman ranch-house was deep and shaded by green vines. From the hammock where she lay, a delicate figure amid the vivid cushions, Rhoda looked upon a landscape that combined all the perfection of verdure of a northern park with a sense of illimitable breathing space that should have been fairly intoxicating to her. Two huge cottonwoods stood beside the porch. Beyond the lawn lay the peach orchard which vied with the bordering alfalfa fields in fragrance and color. The yellow-brown of tree-trunks and the white of grazing sheep against vegetation of richest green were astonishing colors for Rhoda to find in the desert to which she had been exiled, and in the few days since her arrival she had not ceased to wonder at them.

DeWitt crossed the orchard, quickening his pace when he saw Rhoda. He was a tall fellow, blond and well built, though not so tall and lithe as Cartwell. His dark blue eyes were disconcertingly clear and direct.

"Well, Rhoda dear!" he exclaimed as he hurried up the steps. "If you didn't scare this family! How are you feeling now?"

"I'm all right," Rhoda answered languidly. "It was good of you all to bother so about me. What have you been doing all day?"

"Over at the ditch with Jack and Cartwell. Say, Rhoda, the young fellow who rescued you is an Indian!"

DeWitt dropped into a big chair by the hammock. He watched the girl hopefully. It was such a long, long time since she had been interested in anything! But there was no responsive light in the deep gray eyes.

"Katherine told me," she replied. Then, after a pause, as if she felt it her duty to make conversation, "Did you like him?"

DeWitt spoke slowly, as if he had been considering the matter.

"I've a lot of race prejudice in me, Rhoda. I don't like niggers or Chinamen or Indians when they get over to the white man's side of the fence. They are well enough on their own side. However, this Cartwell chap seems all right. And he rescued you from a beastly serious situation!"

"I don't know that I'm as grateful for that as I ought to be," murmured Rhoda, half to herself. "It would have been an easy solution."

Her words stung DeWitt. He started forward and seized the small thin hands in both his own.

"Rhoda, don't!" he pleaded huskily. "Don't give up! Don't lose hope! If I could only give you some of my strength! Don't talk so! It just about breaks my heart to hear you."

For a time, Rhoda did not answer. She lay wearily watching the eager, pleading face so close to her own. Even in her illness, Rhoda was very lovely. The burnished yellow hair softened the thinness of the face that was like delicately chiseled marble. The finely cut nose, the exquisite drooping mouth, the little square chin with its cleft, and the great gray eyes lost none of their beauty through her weakness.

"John," she said at last, "why won't you look the truth in the face? I never shall get well. I shall die here instead of in New York, that's all. Why did you follow me down here? It only tortures you. And truly it's not so bad for me. You all have lost your realness to me, somehow. I shan't mind going, much."

DeWitt's strong face worked but his voice was steady.

"I never shall leave you," he said simply. "You are the one woman in the world for me. I'd marry you tomorrow if you'd let me."

Rhoda shook her head.

"You ought to go away, John, and forget me. You ought to go marry some fine girl and have a home and a family. I'm just a sick wreck."

"Rhoda," and DeWitt's earnest voice was convincing, "Rhoda, I'd pass up the healthiest, finest girl on earth for you, just sick you. Why, can't you see that your helplessness and dependence only deepen your hold on me? Who wants a thing as fragile and as lovely as you are to make a home! You pay your way in life just by living! Beauty and sweetness like yours is enough for a woman to give. I don't want you to do a thing in the world. Just give yourself to me and let me take care of you. Rhoda, dear, dear heart!"

"I can't marry unless I'm well," insisted Rhoda, "and I never shall be well again. I know that you all thought it was for the best, bringing me down to the desert, but just as soon as I can manage it without hurting Katherine's and Jack's feelings too much, I'm going back to New York. If you only knew how the big emptiness of this desert country adds to my depression!"

"If you go back to New York," persisted DeWitt, "**you** are going back as my wife. I'm sick of seeing you dependent on hired care. Why, Rhoda dear, is it nothing to you that, when you haven't a near relative in the world, I would gladly die for you?"

"Oh!" cried the girl, tears of weakness and pity in her eyes, "you know that it means everything to me! But I can't marry any one. All I want is just to crawl away and die in peace. I wish that that Indian hadn't come upon me so promptly. I'd just have gone to sleep and never wakened."

"Don't! Don't!" cried DeWitt. "I shall pick you up and hold you against all the world, if you say that!"

"Hush!" whispered Rhoda, but her smile was very tender. "Some one is coming through the orchard."

DeWitt reluctantly released the slender hands and leaned back in his chair. The sun had crossed the peach orchard slowly, breathlessly. It cast long, slanting shadows along the beautiful alfalfa fields and turned the willows by the irrigating ditch to a rosy gray. As the sun sank, song-birds piped and lizards scuttled along the porch rail. The loveliest part of the New Mexican day had come.

The two young Northerners watched the man who was swinging through the orchard. It was Cartwell. Despite his breadth of shoulder, the young Indian looked slender, though it was evident that only panther strength could produce such panther grace. He crossed the lawn and stood at the foot of the steps; one hand crushed his soft hat against his hip, and the sun turned his close-cropped black hair to blue bronze. For an instant none of the three spoke. It was as if each felt the import of this meeting which was to be continued through such strange vicissitudes. Cartwell, however, was not looking at DeWitt but at Rhoda, and she returned his gaze, surprised at the beauty of his face, with its large, long-lashed, Mohave eyes that were set well apart and set deeply as are the eyes of those whose ancestors have lived much in the open glare of the sun; with the straight, thin-nostriled nose; with the stern, cleanly modeled mouth and the square chin, below. And looking into the young Indian's deep black eyes, Rhoda felt within herself a vague stirring that for a second wiped the languor from her eyes.

Cartwell spoke first, easily, in the quiet, well-modulated voice of the Indian.

"Hello! All safe, I see! Mr. Newman will be here shortly." He seated himself on the upper step with his back against a pillar and fanned himself with his hat. "Jack's working too hard. I want him to go to the coast for a while and let me run the ditch. But he won't. He's as pig-headed as a Mohave."

"Are the Mohaves so pig-headed then?" asked DeWitt, smiling.

Cartwell returned the smile with a flash of white teeth.

"You bet they are! My mother was part Mohave and she used to say that only the Pueblo in her kept her from being as stiff-necked as yucca. You're all over the dizziness, Miss Tuttle?"

"Yes," said Rhoda. "You were very good to me."

Cartwell shook his head.

"I'm afraid I can't take special credit for that. Will you two ride to the ditch with me tomorrow? I think Miss Tuttle will be interested in Jack's irrigation dream, don't you, Mr. DeWitt?"

DeWitt answered a little stiffly.

"It's out of the question for Miss Tuttle to attempt such a trip, thank you."

But to her own as well as DeWitt's astonishment Rhoda spoke protestingly.

"You must let me refuse my own invitations, John. Perhaps the ditch would interest me."

DeWitt replied hastily, "Good gracious, Rhoda! If anything will interest you, don't let me interfere."

There was protest in his voice against Rhoda's being interested in an Indian's suggestion. Both Rhoda and Cartwell felt this and there was an awkward pause. This was broken by a faint halloo from the corral and DeWitt rose abruptly

"I'll go down and meet Jack," he said.

"We'll do a lot of stunts if you're willing," Cartwell said serenely, his eyes following DeWitt's broad back inscrutably. "The desert is like a story-book if one learns to read it. If you would be interested to learn, I would be keen to teach you."

Rhoda's gray eyes lifted to the young man's somberly.

"I'm too dull these days to learn anything," she said. "But I—I didn't used to be! Truly I didn't! I used to be so *alive*, so strong! I believed in everything, myself most of all! Truly I did!" She paused, wondering at her lack of reticence.

Cartwell, however, was looking at her with something in his gaze so quietly understanding that Rhoda smiled. It was a slow smile that lifted and deepened the corners of Rhoda's lips, that darkened her gray eyes to black, an unforgetable smile to the loveliness of which Rhoda's friends never could accustom themselves. At the sight of it, Cartwell drew a deep breath, then leaned toward her and spoke with curious earnestness.

"You make me feel the same way that starlight on the desert makes me feel."

Rhoda replied in astonishment, "Why, you mustn't speak that way to me! It's not—not—"

"Not conventional?" suggested Cartwell. "What difference does that make, between you and me?"

THE VALLEY OF THE PECOS

Again came the strange stirring in Rhoda in response to Cartwell's gaze. He was looking at her with something of tragedy in the dark young eyes, something of sternness and determination in the clean-cut lips. Rhoda wondered, afterward, what would have been said if Katherine had not chosen this moment to come out on the porch.

"Rhoda," she asked, "do you feel like dressing for dinner? Hello, Kut-le, it's time you moved toward soap and water, seems to me!"

"Yessum!" replied Cartwell meekly. He rose and helped Rhoda from the hammock, then held the door open for her. DeWitt and Newman emerged from the orchard as he crossed to Katherine's chair.

"Is she very sick, Mrs. Jack?" he asked.

Katherine nodded soberly.

"Desperately sick. Her father and mother were killed in a railroad wreck a year ago. Rhoda wasn't seriously hurt but she has never gotten over the shock. She has been failing ever since. The docter feared consumption and sent her down here. But she's just dying by inches. Oh, it's too awful! I can't believe it! I can't realize it!"

Cartwell stood in silence for a moment, his lips compressed, his eyes inscrutable.

Then, "I've met her at last," he said. "It makes me believe in Fate."

Katherine's pretty lips parted in amazement.

"Goodness! Are you often taken this way!" she gasped.

"Never before!" replied Cartwell serenely. "Jack said she'd broken her engagement to DeWitt because of her illness, so it's a fair war!"

"Kut–le!" exclaimed Katherine. "Don't talk like a yellow-backed novel! It's not a life or death affair."

"You can't tell as to that," answered Cartwell with a curious little smile. "You mustn't forget that I'm an Indian."

And he turned to greet the two men who were mounting the steps.

CHAPTER II

THE CAUCASIAN WAY

WHEN Rhoda entered the dining-room some of her pallor seemed to have left her. She was dressed in a gown of an elusive pink that gave a rose flush to the marble fineness of her face.

Katherine was chatting with a wiry, middle-aged man whom she introduced to Rhoda as Mr. Porter, an Arizona mining man. Porter stood as if stunned for a moment by Rhoda's delicate loveliness. Then, as was the custom of every man who met Rhoda, he looked vaguely about for something to do for her. Jack Newman forestalled him by taking Rhoda's hand and leading her to the table. Jack's curly blond hair looked almost white in contrast with his tanned face. He was not as tall as either Cartwell or DeWitt but he was strong and clean-cut and had a boyish look despite the heavy responsibilities of his five-thousand-acre ranch.

"There," he said, placing Rhoda beside Porter; "just attach Porter's scalp to your belt with the rest of your collection. It'll be a new experience to him. Don't be afraid, Porter."

Billy Porter was not in the least embarrassed.

"I've come too near to losing my scalp to the Apaches to be scared by Miss Tuttle. Anyhow I gave her my scalp without a yelp the minute I laid eyes on her."

"Here! That's not fair!" cried John DeWitt. "The rest of us had to work to get her to take ours!"

"Our what?" asked Cartwell, entering the room at the last word. He was looking very cool and well groomed in white flannels.

Billy Porter stared at the newcomer and dropped his soup-spoon with a splash. "What in thunder!" Rhoda heard him mutter.

Jack Newman spoke hastily.

"This is Mr. Cartwell, our irrigation engineer, Mr. Porter."

Porter responded to the young Indian's courteous bow with a surly nod, and proceeded with his soup.

"I'd as soon eat with a nigger as an Injun," he said to Rhoda under cover of some laughing remark of Katherine's to Cartwell.

"He seems to be nice," said Rhoda vaguely. "Maybe, though, Katherine *is* a little liberal, making him one of the family."

"Is there any hunting at all in this open desert country?" asked DeWitt. "I certainly hate to go back to New York with nothing but sunburn to show for my trip!"

THE CAUCASIAN WAY 21

"Coyotes, wildcats, rabbits and partridges," volunteered Cartwell. "I know where there is a nest of wildcats up on the first mesa. And I know an Indian who will tan the pelts for you, like velvet. A jack-rabbit pelt well tanned is an exquisite thing too, by the way. I will go on a hunt with you whenever the ditch can be left."

"And while they are chasing round after jacks, Miss Tuttle," cut in Billy Porter neatly, "I will take you anywhere you want to go. I'll show you things these kids never dreamed of! I knew this country in the days of Apache raids and the pony express."

"That will be fine!" replied Rhoda. "But I'd rather hear the stories than take any trips. Did you spend your boyhood in New Mexico? Did you see real Indian fights? Did you—?" She paused with an involuntary glance at Cartwell.

Porter, too, looked at the dark young face across the table and something in its inscrutable calm seemed to madden him.

"My boyhood here? Yes, and a happy boyhood it was! I came home from the range one day and found my little fifteen-year-old sister and a little neighbor friend of hers hung up by the back of their necks on butcher hooks. They had been tortured to death by Apaches. I don't like Indians!"

There was an awkward pause at the dinner table. Li

Chung removed the soup-plates noiselessly. Cartwell's brown fingers tapped the tablecloth. But he was not looking at Porter's scowling face. He was watching Rhoda's gray eyes which were fastened on him with a look half of pity, half of aversion. When he spoke it was as if he cared little for the opinions of the others but would set himself right with her alone.

"My father," he said, "came home from the hunt, one day, to find his mother and three sisters lying in their own blood. The whites had gotten them. They all had been scalped and were dead except the baby, three years old. She—she—my father killed her."

A gasp of horror went round the table.

"I think such stories are inexcusable here!" exclaimed Katherine indignantly.

"So do I, Mrs. Jack," replied Cartwell. "I won't do it again."

Porter's face stained a deep mahogany and he bowed stiffly to Katherine.

"I beg your pardon, Mrs. Newman!"

"I feel as if I were visiting a group of anarchists," said Rhoda plaintively, "and had innocently passed round a bomb on which to make conversation!"

Jack Newman laughed, the tension relaxed, and in a moment the dinner was proceeding merrily, though Porter and Cartwell carefully avoided speaking to each

THE CAUCASIAN WAY

other. Most of the conversation centered around Rhoda. Katherine always had been devoted to her friend. And though men always had paid homage to Rhoda, since her illness had enhanced her delicacy, and had made her so appealingly helpless, they were drawn to her as surely as bee to flower. Old and young, dignified and happy-go-lucky, all were moved irresistibly to do something for her, to coddle her, to undertake impossible missions, self-imposed.

Porter from his place of vantage beside her kept her plate heaped with delicacies, calmly removed the breast of chicken from his own plate to hers, all but fed her with a spoon when she refused to more than nibble at her meal.

DeWitt's special night-mare was that drafts were blowing on her. He kept excusing himself from the table to open and close windows and doors, to hang over her chair so as to feel for himself if the wind touched her.

Katherine and Jack kept Li Chung trotting to the kitchen for different dainties with which to tempt her. Only Cartwell did nothing. He kept up what seemed to be his usual fire of amiable conversation and watched Rhoda constantly through inscrutable black eyes. But he made no attempt to serve her.

Rhoda was scarcely conscious of the deference showed

her, partly because she had received it so long, partly because that detached frame of mind of the hopeless invalid made the life about her seem shadowy and unreal. Nothing really mattered much. She lay back in her chair with the little wistful smile, the somber light in her eyes that had become habitual to her.

After dinner was finished Katherine led the way to the living-room. To his unspeakable pride, Rhoda took Billy Porter's arm and he guided her listless footsteps carefully, casting pitying glances on his less favored friends. Jack wheeled a Morris chair before the fireplace—desert nights are cool—and John DeWitt hurried for a shawl, while Katherine gave every one orders that no one heeded in the least.

Cartwell followed after the others, slowly lighted a cigarette, then seated himself at the piano. For the rest of the evening he made no attempt to join in the fragmentary conversation. Instead he sang softly, as if to himself, touching the keys so gently that their notes seemed only the echo of his mellow voice. He sang bits of Spanish love-songs, of Mexican lullabies. But for the most part he kept to Indian melodies—wistful lovesongs and chants that touched the listener with strange poignancy.

There was little talk among the group around the fire. The three men smoked peacefully. Katherine and

Jack sat close to each other, on the davenport, content to be together. DeWitt lounged where he could watch Rhoda, as did Billy Porter, the latter hanging on every word and movement of this lovely, fragile being, as if he would carry forever in his heart the memory of her charm.

Rhoda herself watched the fire. She was tired, tired to the inmost fiber of her being. The only real desire left her was that she might crawl off somewhere and die in peace. But these good friends of hers had set their faces against the inevitable and it was only decency to humor them. Once, quite unconscious that the others were watching her, she lifted her hands and eyed them idly. They were almost transparent and shook a little. The group about the fire stirred pityingly. John and Katherine and Jack remembered those shadowy hands when they had been rosy and full of warmth and tenderness. Billy Porter leaned across and with his hard brown palms pressed the trembling fingers down into Rhoda's lap. She looked up in astonishment.

"Don't hold 'em so!" said Billy hoarsely. "I can't stand to see 'em!"

"They *are* pretty bad," said Rnoda, smiling. It was her rare, slow, unforgetable smile. Porter swallowed audibly. Cartwell at the piano drifted from a Mohave lament to *La Paloma*.

> "The day that I left my home for the rolling sea,
> I said, 'Mother dear, O pray to thy God for me!'
> But e'er I set sail I went a fond leave to take
> Of Nina, who wept as if her poor heart would break!'"

The mellow, haunting melody caught Rhoda's fancy at once, as Cartwell knew it would. She turned to the sinewy figure at the piano. DeWitt was wholesome and strong, but this young Indian seemed vitality itself.

> "Nina, if I should die and o'er ocean's foam
> Softly at dusk a fair dove should come,
> Open thy window, Nina, for it would be
> My faithful soul come back to thee——"

Something in Cartwell's voice stirred Rhoda as had his eyes. For the first time in months Rhoda felt poignantly that it would be hard to be cut down with all her life unlived. The mellow voice ceased and Cartwell, rising, lighted a fresh cigarette.

"I am going to get up with the rabbits, tomorrow," he said, "so I'll trot to bed now."

DeWitt, impelled by that curious sense of liking for the young Indian that fought down his aversion, said, "The music was bully, Cartwell!" but Cartwell only smiled as if at the hint of patronage in the voice and strolled to his own room.

Rhoda slept late the following morning. She had not,

in her three nights in the desert country, become accustomed to the silence that is not the least of the desert's splendors. It seemed to her that the nameless unknown Mystery toward which her life was drifting was embodied in this infinite silence. So sleep would not come to her until dawn. Then the stir of the wind in the trees, the bleat of sheep, the trill of mocking-birds lulled her to sleep.

As the brilliancy of the light in her room increased there drifted across her uneasy dreams the lilting notes of a whistled call. Pure and liquidly sweet they persisted until there came to Rhoda that faint stir of hope and longing that she had experienced the day before. She opened her eyes and finally, as the call continued, she crept languidly from her bed and peered from behind the window-shade. Cartwell, in his khaki suit, his handsome head bared to the hot sun, leaned against a peach-tree while he watched Rhoda's window.

"I wonder what he wakened me for?" she thought half resentfully. "I can't go to sleep again, so I may as well dress and have breakfast."

Hardly had she seated herself at her solitary meal when Cartwell appeared.

"Dear me!" he exclaimed. "The birds and Mr. DeWitt have been up this long time."

"What is John doing?" asked Rhoda carelessly.

"He's gone up on the first mesa for the wildcats I spoke of last night. I thought perhaps you might care to take a drive before it got too hot. You didn't sleep well last night, did you?"

Rhoda answered whimsically.

"It's the silence. It thunders at me so! I will get used to it soon. Perhaps I ought to drive. I suppose I ought to try everything."

Not at all discouraged, apparently, by this lack of enthusiasm, Cartwell said:

"I won't let you overdo. I'll have the top-buggy for you and we'll go slowly and carefully."

"No," said Rhoda, suddenly recalling that, after all, Cartwell was an Indian, "I don't think I will go. Katherine will have all sorts of objections."

The Indian smiled sardonically.

"I already have Mrs. Jack's permission. Billy Porter will be in, in a moment. If you would rather have a white man than an Indian as escort, I'm quite willing to retreat."

Rhoda flushed delicately.

"Your frankness is almost—almost impertinent, Mr. Cartwell."

"I don't mean it that way at all!" protested the Indian. "It's just that I saw so plainly what was going on in your mind and it piqued me. If it will be one bit pleasanter for you with Billy, I'll go right out and hunt him up for you now."

The young man's naïveté completely disarmed Rhoda.

"Don't be silly!" she said. "Go get your famous top-buggy and I'll be ready in a minute."

In a short time Rhoda and Cartwell, followed by many injunctions from Katherine, started off toward the irrigating ditch. At a slow pace they drove through the peach orchard into the desert. As they reached the open trail, thrush and to-hee fluttered from the cholla. Chipmunk and cottontail scurried before them. Overhead a hawk dipped in its reeling flight. Cartwell watched the girl keenly. Her pale face was very lovely in the brilliant morning light, though the somberness of her wide, gray eyes was deepened. That same muteness and patience in her trouble which so touched other men touched Cartwell, but he only said:

"There never was anything bigger and finer than this open desert, was there?"

Rhoda turned from staring at the distant mesas and eyed the young Indian wonderingly.

"Why!" she exclaimed, "I hate it! You know that sick fear that gets you when you try to picture eternity to yourself? That's the way this barrenness and awful distance affects me. I hate it!"

"But you won't hate it!" cried Cartwell. "You must let me show you its bigness. It's as healing as the hand of God."

Rhoda shuddered.

"Don't talk about it, please! I'll try to think of something else."

They drove in silence for some moments. Rhoda, her thin hands clasped in her lap, resolutely stared at the young Indian's profile. In the unreal world in which she drifted, she needed some thought of strength, some hope beyond her own, to which to cling. She was lonely—lonely as some outcast watching with sick eyes the joy of the world to which he is denied. As she stared at the stern young profile beside her, into her heart crept the now familiar thrill.

Suddenly Cartwell turned and looked at her quizzically.

"Well, what are your conclusions?"

Rhoda shook her head.

"I don't know, except that it's hard to realize that you are an Indian."

Cartwell's voice was ironical.

"The only good Indian is a dead Indian, you know. I'm liable to break loose any time, believe me!"

Rhoda's eyes were on the far lavender line where the mesa melted into the mountains.

"Yes, and then what?" she asked.

THE CAUCASIAN WAY 31

Cartwell's eyes narrowed, but Rhoda did not see.

"Then I'm liable to follow Indian tradition and take whatever I want, by whatever means!"

"My! My!" said Rhoda, "that sounds bludgy! And what are you liable to want?"

"Oh, I want the same thing that a great many white men want. I'm going to have it myself, though!" His handsome face glowed curiously as he looked at Rhoda.

But the girl was giving his words small heed. Her eyes still were turned toward the desert, as though she had forgotten her companion. Sand whirls crossed the distant levels, ceaselessly. Huge and menacing, they swirled out from the mesa's edge, crossed the desert triumphantly, then, at contact with rock or cholla thicket, collapsed and disappeared. Endless, merciless, hopeless the yellow desert quivered against the bronze blue sky. For the first time dazed hopelessness gave way in Rhoda to fear. The young Indian, watching the girl's face, beheld in it what even DeWitt never had seen there—beheld deadly fear. He was silent for a moment, then he leaned toward her and put a strong brown hand over her trembling little fists. His voice was deep and soft.

"Don't," he said, "don't!"

Perhaps it was the subtle, not-to-be-fathomed influence of the desert which fights all sham; perhaps it was that Rhoda merely had reached the limit of her heroic self-containment and that, had DeWitt or Newman been with her, she would have given way in the same manner; perhaps it was that the young Indian's presence had in it a quality that roused new life in her. Whatever the cause, the listless melancholy suddenly left Rhoda's gray eyes and they were wild and black with fear.

"I can't die!" she panted. "I can't leave my life unlived! I can't crawl on much longer like a sick animal without a soul. I want to live! To live!"

"Look at me!" said Cartwell. "Look at me, not at the desert!" Then as she turned to him, "Listen, Rhoda! You shall not die! I will make you well! You shall not die!"

For a long minute the two gazed deep into each other's eyes, and the sense of quickening blood touched Rhoda's heart. Then they both woke to the sound of hoof-beats behind them and John DeWitt, with a wildcat thrown across his saddle, rode up.

"Hello! I've shouted one lung out! I thought you people were petrified!" He looked curiously from Rhoda's white face to Cartwell's inscrutable one. "Do you think you ought to have attempted this trip, Rhoda?" he asked gently.

"Oh, we've taken it very slowly," answered the Indian. "And we are going to turn back now."

"I don't think I've overdone," said Rhoda. "But perhaps we have had enough."

"All right," said Cartwell. "If Mr. DeWitt will change places with me, I'll ride on to the ditch and he can drive you back."

DeWitt assented eagerly and, the change made, Cartwell lifted his hat and was gone. Rhoda and John returned in a silence that lasted until DeWitt lifted Rhoda from the buggy to the veranda. Then he said:

"Rhoda, I don't like to have you go off alone with Cartwell. I wish you wouldn't."

Rhoda smiled.

"John, don't be silly! He goes about with Katherine all the time."

John only shook his head and changed the subject. That afternoon, however, Billy Porter buttonholed DeWitt in the corral where the New Yorker was watching the Arizonian saddle his fractious horse. When the horse was ready at the post, "Look here, DeWitt," said Billy, an embarrassed look in his honest brown eyes, "I don't want you to think I'm buttin' in, but some one ought to watch that young Injun. Anybody with one eye can see he's crazy about Miss Rhoda."

John was too startled to be resentful.

"What do you mean?" he exclaimed. "Cartwell is a great friend of the Newmans'."

"That's why I came to you. They're plumb locoed about the fellow, like the rest of the Easterners around here."

"Do you know anything against him?" insisted DeWitt.

"Why, man, he's an Injun, and half Apache at that! That's enough to know against him!"

"What makes you think he's interested in Miss Tuttle?" asked John.

Porter flushed through his tan.

"Well," he said sheepishly, "I seen him come down the hall at dawn this morning. Us Westerners are early risers, you know, and when he reached Miss Tuttle's door, he pulled a little slipper out of his pocket and kissed it and put it in front of the sill."

DeWitt scowled, then he laughed.

"He's no worse than the rest of us that way! I'll watch him, though perhaps it's only your prejudice against Indians and not really a matter to worry about."

Porter sighed helplessly.

"All right! All right! Just remember, DeWitt, I warned you!"

He mounted, then held in his horse while the worried look gave place to one so sad, yet so manly, that John never forgot it.

"I hope you appreciate that girl, DeWitt. She—she's

THE CAUCASIAN WAY 35

a thoroughbred! My God! When you think of a sweet thing like that dying and these Injun squaws living! I hope you'll watch her, DeWitt. If anything happens to her through you not watching her, I'll come back on you for it! I ain't got any rights except the rights that any living man has got to take care of any white thing like her. They get me hard when they're dainty like that. And she's the daintiest I ever seen!"

He rode away, shaking his head ominously.

CHAPTER III

INDIAN AND CAUCASIAN

DeWITT debated with himself for some time as to whether or not he ought to speak to Jack of Porter's warning. Finally he decided that Porter's suspicions would only anger Jack, who was intensely loyal to his friends. He determined to keep silence until he had something more tangible on which to found his complaint than Billy's bitter prejudice against all Indians. He had implicit faith in Rhoda's love for himself. If any vague interest in life could come to her through the young Indian, he felt that he could endure his presence. In the meantime he would guard Rhoda without cessation.

In the days that followed, Rhoda grew perceptibly weaker, and her friends went about with aching hearts under an assumed cheerfulness of manner that deceived Rhoda least of any one. Rhoda herself did not complain and this of itself added a hundredfold to the pathos of the situation. Her unfailing sweetness and patience touched the healthy, hardy young people who were so devoted to her more than the most justifiable impatience on her part.

Time and again Katherine saw DeWitt and Jack leave the girl's side with tears in their eyes. But Cartwell watched the girl with inscrutable gaze.

Rhoda still hated the desert. The very unchanging loveliness of the days wearied her. Morning succeeded morning and noon followed noon, with always the same soft breeze stirring the orchard, always the clear yellow sunlight burning and dazzling her eyes, always the unvarying monotony of bleating sheep and lowing herds and at evening the hoot of owls. The brooding tenderness of the sky she did not see. The throbbing of the great, quiet southern stars stirred her only with a sense of helpless loneliness that was all but unendurable. And still, from who knows what source, she found strength to meet the days and her friends with that unfailing sweetness that was as poignant as the clinging fingers of a sick child.

Jack, Katherine, DeWitt, Cartwell, all were unwearying in their effort to amuse her. And yet for some reason Cartwell alone was able to rouse her listless eyes to interest. Even DeWitt found himself eagerly watching the young Indian, less to guard Rhoda than to discover what in the Apache so piqued his curiosity. He had to admit, however reluctantly, that Kut-le, as he and Rhoda now called him with the others, was a charming companion.

Neither DeWitt nor Rhoda ever before had known an Indian. Most of their ideas of the race were founded on childhood reading of Cooper. Kut-le was quite as cultured, quite as well-mannered and quite as intelligent as any of their Eastern friends. But in many other qualities he differed from them. He possessed a frank pride in himself and his blood that might have belonged to some medieval prince who would not take the trouble outwardly to underestimate himself. Closely allied to this was his habit of truthfulness. This was not a blatant bluntness that irritated the hearer but a habit of valuing persons and things at their intrinsic worth, a habit of mental honesty as bizarre to Rhoda and John as was the young Indian's frank pride.

His attitude toward Rhoda piqued her while it amused her. Since her childhood, men had treated her with deference, had paid almost abject tribute to her loveliness and bright charm. Cartwell was delightfully considerate of her. He was uniformly courteous to her. But it was the courtesy of *noblesse oblige*, without a trace of deference in it.

One afternoon Kut-le sat alone on the veranda with Rhoda.

"Do you know," he said, rumpling his black hair, "that I think DeWitt has decided that I will bear watching!"

"Well," answered Rhoda idly, "and won't you?"

Kut-le chuckled.

"Would you prefer that I show the lurking savage beneath this false shell of good manners?"

Rhoda smiled back at him.

"Of course you are an Indian, after all. It's rather too bad of you not to live up to any of our ideals. Your manners are as nice as John DeWitt's. I'd be quite frantic about you if you would drop them and go on the war-path."

Kut-le threw back his head and laughed.

"Oh, you ignorant young thing! It's lucky for you—and for me—that you have come West to grow up and complete your education! But DeWitt needn't worry. I don't need watching yet! First, I'm going to make you well. I know how and he doesn't. After that is done, he'd better watch!"

Rhoda's eyebrows began to go up. Kut-le never had recalled by word or look her outburst in the desert the morning of their first ride together, though they had taken several since. Rhoda seldom mentioned her illness now and her friends respected her feeling. But now Kut-le smiled at her disapproving brows.

"I've waited for the others to get busy," he said, "but they act foolish. Half the trouble with you is mental. You need a boss. Now, you don't eat enough, in spite of the eggs and beef and fruit that that dear Mrs. Jack sets before you. See how your hands shake this minute!"

Rhoda could think of no reply sufficiently crushing for this forward young Indian. While she was turning several over in her mind, Kut-le went into the house and returned with a glass of milk.

"I wish you'd drink this," he said.

Rhoda's brows still were arched haughtily.

"No, thank you," she said frigidly; "I don't wish you to undertake the care of my health."

Kut-le made no reply but held the glass steadily before her. Involuntarily, Rhoda looked up. The young Indian was watching her with eyes so clear, so tender, with that strange look of tragedy belying their youth, with that something so compelling in their quiet depths, that once more her tired pulses quickened. Rhoda looked from Kut-le out to the twisting sand-whirls, then she took the glass of milk and drank it. She would not have done this for any of the others and both she and Kut-le knew it. Thereafter, he deliberately set himself to watching her and it seemed as if he must exhaust his ingenuity devising means for her comfort. Slowly Rhoda acquired a definite interest in the young Indian.

"Are you really civilized, Kut-le?" she asked one afternoon when the young man had brought a little white desert owl to her hammock for her inspection.

Kut-le tossed the damp hair from his forehead and looked at the sweet wistful face against the crimson pillows. For a moment Rhoda felt as if his young strength enveloped her like the desert sun.

"Why?" he asked at last. "You said the other day that I was too much civilized."

"I know, but—" Rhoda hesitated for words, "I'm too much civilized myself to understand, but sometimes there's a look in your eyes that something, I suppose it's a forgotten instinct, tells me means that you are wild to let all this go—" she waved a thin hand toward cultivated fields and corral—"and take to the open desert."

Kut-le said nothing for a moment, though his face lighted with joy at her understanding. Then he turned toward the desert and Rhoda saw the look of joy change to one so full of unutterable longing that her heart was stirred to sudden pity. However, an instant later, he turned to her with the old impassive expression.

"Right beneath my skin," he said, "is the Apache. Tell me, Miss Rhoda, what's the use of it all?"

"Use?" asked Rhoda, staring at the blue sky above the peach-trees. "I am a fit person to ask what is the use of anything! Of course, civilization is the only thing that lives. I can't get your point of view at all."

"Huh!" sniffed Kut-le. "It's too bad Indians don't write books! If my people had been putting their internal mechanism on paper for a thousand years, you'd have no more trouble getting my point of view than I do yours."

Rhoda's face as she eyed the stern young profile was very sympathetic. Kut-le, turning to her, surprised upon her face that rare, tender smile for which all who knew her watched. His face flushed and his fine hands clasped and unclasped.

"Tell me about it, Kut-le, if you can."

"I can't tell you. The desert would show you its own power if you would give it a chance. No one can describe the call to you. I suppose if I answered it and went back, you would call it retrogression?"

"What would you call it?" asked Rhoda.

"I don't know. It would depend on my mood. I only know that the ache is there." His eyes grew somber and beads of sweat appeared on his forehead. "The ache to be there—free in the desert! To feel the hot sun in my face as I work the trail! To sleep with the naked stars in my face! To be— Oh, I can't make you understand, and I'd rather you understood than any one in the world! You could understand, if only you were desert-taught. When you are well and strong—"

"But why don't you go back?" interrupted Rhoda.

"Because," replied Kut-le slowly, "the Indian is dying. I hope that by living as a white, I may live. Up till recently I have worked blindly and hopelessly, but now I see light."

"Do you?" asked Rhoda with interest. "What have you found?"

"It isn't mine yet." Kut-le looked at the girl exultantly and there was a triumphant note in his voice. "But it shall be mine! I will make it mine! And it is worth the sacrifice of my race."

A vague look of surprise crossed Rhoda's face but she spoke calmly:

"To sacrifice one's race is a serious thing. I can't think of anything that would make that worth while. Here comes Mr. DeWitt. It must be dinner time. John, come up and see a little desert owl at close range. Kut-le has all the desert at his beck and call!"

Kut-le persuaded Rhoda to change the morning rides, which seemed only to exhaust her, to the shortest of evening strolls. Nearly always DeWitt accompanied them. Sometimes they went alone, though John was never very far distant.

One moonlit night Kut-le and Rhoda stood alone at the corral bars. The whole world was radiant silver moonlight on the desert, on the undulating alfalfa; moonlight filtering through the peach-trees and shimmering on Rhoda's drooping head as she leaned against the bars in the weary attitude habitual to her. Kut-le stood before her, erect and strong in his white flannels. His handsome head was thrown back a little, as was his custom when speaking earnestly. His arms were folded across his deep chest and he stood so still that Rhoda could see his arms rise and fall with his breath.

"It really is great work!" he was saying eagerly. "It seems to me that a civil engineer has tremendous opportunities to do really big things. Some of Kipling's stories of them are bully."

"Aren't they!" answered Rhoda sympathetically.

"There is a big thing in my favor too. The whites make no discrimination against an Indian in the professions. In fact every one gives him a boost in passing!"

"Why shouldn't they? You have as good a brain and are as attractive as any man of my acquaintance!"

The young man drew a quick breath.

"Do you really mean that?"

"Of course! Why shouldn't I? Isn't the moonlight uncanny on the desert?"

But Kut-le did not heed her attempt to change the subject.

"There are unlimited opportunities for me to make good, now that the government is putting up so many dams. I believe that I can go to the top with any man, don't you, Miss Rhoda?"

"I do, indeed!" replied Rhoda sincerely.

"Well, then, Miss Rhoda, will you marry me?"

Rhoda raised her head in speechless amazement.

Kut-le's glowing eyes contracted.

"You are not surprised!" he exclaimed a little fiercely. "You must have seen how it has been with me ever since you came. And you have been so—so bully to me!"

Rhoda looked helplessly into the young man's face. She was so fragile that she seemed but an evanescent part of the moonlight.

"But," she said slowly, "you must know that this is impossible. I couldn't think of marrying you, Kut-le!"

There was a moment's silence. An owl called from the desert. The night wind swept from the fragrant orchard. When he spoke again, Kut-le's voice was husky.

"Is it because I am an Indian?"

"Yes," answered Rhoda, "partly. But I don't love you, anyhow."

"But," eagerly, "if you did love me, would my being an Indian make any difference? Isn't my blood pure? Isn't it old?"

Rhoda stood still. The pain in Kut-le's voice was piercing through to the shadow world in which she lived. Her voice was troubled.

"But I don't love you, so what's the use of considering the rest? If I ever marry any one it will be John DeWitt."

INDIAN AND CAUCASIAN

"But couldn't you," insisted the tragically deep voice, "couldn't you ever love me?"

Rhoda answered wearily. One could not, it seemed, even die in peace!

"I can't think of love or marriage any more. I am a dying woman. Let me go into the mist, Kut-le, without a pang for our friendship, with just the pleasant memory of your goodness to me. Surely you cannot love me as I am!"

"I love you for the wonderful possibilities I see in you. I love you in spite of your illness. I will make you well before I marry you. The Indian in me has strength to make you well. And I will cherish you as white men cherish their wives."

Rhoda raised her hand commandingly and in her voice was that boundless vanity of the white, which is as old as the race.

"No! No! Don't speak of this again! You are an Indian but one removed from savagery. I am a white! I couldn't think of marrying you!" Then her tender heart failed her and her voice trembled. "But still I am your friend, Kut-le. Truly I am your friend."

The Indian was silent so long that Rhoda was a little frightened. Then he spoke slowly.

"Yes, you are white and I am red. But before all that, you are a woman of exquisite possibilities and I am a man who by all of nature's laws would make a fitting mate for you. You can love me, when you are well, as you could love no other man. And I—dear one, I love you passionately! I love you tenderly! I love you enough to give up my race for you. I am an Indian, Rhoda, but first of all I am a man. Rhoda, will you marry me?"

A thrill, poignant, heart-stirring, beat through Rhoda's veins. For one unspeakable moment there swept through her spirit a vision of strength, of beauty, of gladness, too wild and sweet for words. Then came the old sense of race distaste and she looked steadily into the young man's face.

"I cannot marry you, Kut-le," she said.

Kut-le said nothing more. He stood staring at the far desert, his fine face somber and with a look of determination in the contracted eyes and firm-set lips that made Rhoda shiver, even while her heart throbbed with pity. Tall, slender, inscrutable, as alien to her understanding as the call of the desert wind or the moon-drenched desert haze, she turned away and left him standing there alone.

She made her slow way to the ranch-house. Kut-le did not follow. Rhoda went to bed at once. Yet she could not sleep, for through the silence Kut-le's deep voice beat on her ears.

"I love you passionately! I love you tenderly! I am an Indian, but first of all I am a man!"

INDIAN AND CAUCASIAN

The next day and for the three or four days following, Kut-le was missing. The Newmans were worried. The ditch needed its engineer and never before had Kut-le been known to neglect his work. Once a year he went on a long hunt with chosen friends of his tribe, but never until his work was finished.

Rhoda confided in no one regarding her last interview with the Indian. She missed Kut-le, but DeWitt was frankly relieved. For the first time since Porter's warning he relaxed his vigilance. On the fifth evening after Kut-le's disappearance, Jack and DeWitt rode over to a neighboring ranch. Katherine was lazy with a headache. So Rhoda took her evening stroll alone. For once, she left the orchard and wandered out into the open desert, moved by an uncanny desire to let the full horror of the desert mystery sweep over her.

How long she sat on a rock, gazing into infinity, she did not know. It seemed to her that her whole shivering, protesting body was being absorbed into the strange radiance of the afterglow. At last she rose. As she did so, a tall figure loomed silently before her. Rhoda was too startled to scream. The figure was that of an Indian, naked save for high moccasins and a magnificently decorated loin-cloth. The man looked down at her with the smile of good fellowship that she knew so well. It was Kut-le, standing like a young bronze god against the faint pink of the afterglow.

"Hello!" he said nonchalantly. "I've been watching for you."

"What do you want!" gasped Rhoda. "What do you mean by coming before me in—in—"

"You mean when I'm dressed as a chief on the war-path? Well, you said you'd be keen about me this way; so here I am. I tried all the white methods I knew to win you and failed. Now the only thing left is the Indian method."

Rhoda moved uneasily.

Kut-le went on:

"As a white man I can no longer pester you. As an Indian I can steal you and marry you."

Rhoda struggled to make him and his words seem real to her.

"You aren't going to be so absurd as to try to steal me, I hope!" she tried to laugh.

"That's just what I'm going to do!" answered Kut-le. "If I steal as a white would steal, I would be caught at once. If I use Apache methods, no white on earth can catch me."

Rhoda gasped as the Indian's evident sincerity sank in on her.

"But," she pleaded, fighting for time, "you can't

INDIAN AND CAUCASIAN 51

want to marry me by force! Don't you know that I shall grow to loathe you?"

"No! No!" answered the Indian earnestly. "Not after I've shown you life as I have seen it."

"Nonsense!" cried Rhoda. "Don't you realize that the whole county will be after you by morning?"

Kut-le laughed, deliberately walked up to the girl and lifted her in his arms as he had on the morning of their meeting. Rhoda gave one scream and struggled frantically. He slid a hand over her lips and tightened his hold. For a moment Rhoda lay motionless in abject fear, then, with a muffled cry of utter helplessness, a cry that would have driven a white man mad with pity, she slipped into unconsciousness. Kut-le walked on for a short distance to a horse. He put Rhoda in the saddle and fastened her there with a blanket. He slipped off the twisted bandana that bound his short black hair, fillet wise, and tied it carefully over Rhoda's mouth. Then with one hand steadying the quiet shoulders, he started the horse on through the dusk.

CHAPTER IV

THE INDIAN WAY

IT was some time before the call of a coyote close beside her penetrated Rhoda's senses. At its third or fourth repetition, she sighed and opened her eyes. Night had come, the luminous lavender night of the desert. Her first discovery was that she was seated on a horse, held firmly by a strong arm across her shoulders. Next she found that her uneasy breathing was due to the cloth tied round her mouth. With this came realization of her predicament and she tossed her arms in a wild attempt to free herself.

The arm about her tightened, the horse stopped, and the voice went on repeating the coyote call, clearly, mournfully. Rhoda ceased her struggling for a moment and looked at the face so close to her own. In the starlight only the eyes and the dim outline of the features were visible, and the eyes were as dark and menacing to her as the desert night that shut her in.

Mad with fear, Rhoda strained at the rigid arm. Kut-le dropped the reins and held her struggling hands, ceased his calling and waited. Off to the left came an answering call and Kut-le started the pony rapidly toward the sound. In a few moments Rhoda saw a pair of horsemen. Utterly exhausted, she sat in terror awaiting her fate. Kut-le gave a low-voiced order. One of the riders immediately rode forward, leading another horse. Kut-le slipped another blanket from this and finished binding Rhoda to her saddle so securely that she scarcely could move a finger. Then he mounted his horse, and he and one of the Indians started off, leading Rhoda's horse between them and leaving the third Indian standing silently behind them.

Rhoda was astride of the pony, half sitting, half lying along his neck. The Indians put the horses to a trot and immediately the discomfort of her position was made agony by the rough motion. But the pain cleared her mind.

Her first thought was that she never would recover from the disgrace of this episode. Following this thought came fury at the man who was so outraging her. If only he would free her hands for a moment she would choke him! Her anger would give her strength for that! Then she fought against her fastenings. They held her all but motionless and the sense of her helplessness brought back the fear panic. Utterly helpless, she thought! Flying through darkness to an end worse than death! In the power of a naked savage! Her fear almost robbed her of her reason.

THE INDIAN WAY

After what seemed to her endless hours, the horses were stopped suddenly. She felt her fastenings removed. Then Kut-le lifted her to the ground where she tumbled, helpless, at his feet. He stooped and took the gag from her mouth. Immediately with what fragment of strength remained to her, she screamed again and again. The two Indians stood stolidly watching her for a time, then Kut-le knelt in the sand beside her huddled form and laid his hand on her arm.

"There, Rhoda," he said, "no one can hear you. You will only make yourself sick."

Rhoda struck his hand feebly.

"Don't touch me!" she cried hoarsely. "Don't touch me, you beast! I loathe you! I am afraid of you! Don't you dare to touch me!"

At this Kut-le imprisoned both her cold hands in one of his warm palms and held them despite her struggles, while with the other hand he smoothed her tumbled hair from her eyes.

"Poor frightened little girl!" he said, in his rich voice. "I wish I might have done otherwise. But there was no other way. I don't know that I believe much in your God but I guess you do. So I tell you, Rhoda, that by your faith in Him, you are absolutely safe in my hands!"

Rhoda caught her breath in a childlike sob while she still struggled to recover her hands.

"I loathe you!" she panted. "I loathe you! I loathe you!"

But Kut-le would not free the cold little hands.

"But do you fear me, too? Answer me! Do you fear me?"

The moon had risen and Rhoda looked into the face that bent above hers. This was a naked savage with hawk-like face. Yet the eyes were the ones that she had come to know so well, half tragic, somber, but clear and, toward her, tender, very, very tender. With a shuddering sigh, Rhoda looked away. But against her own volition she found herself saying:

"I'm not afraid now! But I loathe you, you Apache Indian!"

Something very like a smile touched the grim mouth of the Apache.

"I don't hate you, you Caucasian!" he answered quietly.

He chafed the cold hands for a moment, in silence. Then he lifted her to her saddle. But Rhoda was beyond struggle, beyond even clinging to the saddle. Kut-le caught her as she reeled.

"Don't tie me!" she panted. "Don't tie me! I won't fight! I won't even scream, if you won't tie me!"

"But you can't sit your saddle alone," replied Kut-le. "I'll have to tie you."

THE INDIAN WAY 57

Once more he lifted her to the horse. Once more with the help of his silent companion he fastened her with blankets. Once more the journey was begun. For a little while, distraught and uncertain what course to pursue, Rhoda endured the misery of position and motion in silence. Then the pain was too much and she cried out in protest. Kut-le brought the horses to a walk.

"You certainly have about as much spunk as a chicken with the pip!" he said contemptuously. "I should think your loathing would brace you up a little!"

Stung by the insult to a sudden access of strength, as the Indian had intended her to be, Rhoda answered, "You beast!" but as the horses swung into the trot she made no protest for a long hour. Then once more her strength failed her and she fell to crying with deep-drawn sobs that shook her entire body. After a few moments of this, Kut-le drew close to her.

"Don't!" he said huskily. "Don't!" And again he laid his hand on her shoulder.

Rhoda shuddered but could not cease her sobs. Kut-le seemed to hesitate for a few moments. Then he reached over, undid Rhoda's fastenings and lifted her limp body to the saddle before him, holding her against his broad chest as if he were coddling a child. Then he started the horses on. Too exhausted to struggle, Rhoda lay sobbing while the young Indian sat with his tragic eyes fastened steadily on the mysterious distances of the trail. Finally Rhoda sank into a stupor and, seeing this, Kut-le doubled the speed of the horses.

It was daylight when Rhoda opened her eyes. For a time she lay at ease listening to the trill of birds and the trickle of water. Then, with a start, she raised her head. She was lying on a heap of blankets on a stone ledge. Above her was the boundless sapphire of the sky. Close beside her a little spring bubbled from the blank wall of the mountain. Rhoda lay in helpless silence, looking about her, while the appalling nature of her predicament sank into her consciousness.

Against the wall squatted two Indian women. They were dressed in rough short skirts, tight-fitting calico waists and high leather moccasins. Their black hair was parted in the middle and hung free. Their swarthy features were well cut but both of the women were dirty and ill kept. The younger, heavier squaw had a kindly face, with good eyes, but her hair was matted with clay and her fingers showed traces of recent tortilla making. The older woman was lean and wiry, with a strange gleam of maliciousness and ferocity in her eyes. Her forehead was elaborately tattooed with symbols and her toothless old jaws were covered with blue tribal lines.

Kut-le and his friend of the night lounged on a heap

THE INDIAN WAY 59

of rock at the edge of the ledge. The strange Indian was well past middle age, tall and dignified. He was darker than Kut-le. His face was thin and aquiline. His long hair hung in elf locks over his shoulders. His toilet was elaborate compared with that of Kut-le, for he wore a pair of overalls and a dilapidated flannel shirt, unbelted and fluttering its ends in the morning breeze. As if conscious of her gaze, Kut-le turned and looked at Rhoda. His magnificent height and proportions dwarfed the tall Indian beside him.

"Good-morning, Rhoda!" he said gravely.

The girl looked at the beautiful naked body and reddened.

"You beast!" she said clearly.

Kut-le looked at her with slightly contracted eyes. Then he spoke to the fat squaw. She rose hastily and lifted a pot from the little fire beside the spring. She dipped a steaming cup of broth from this and brought it to Rhoda's side. The girl struck it away. Kut-le walked slowly over, picked up the empty cup at which the squaw stood staring stupidly and filled it once more at the kettle. Then he held it out to Rhoda. His nearness roused the girl to frenzy. With difficulty she brought her stiffened body to a sitting position. Her beautiful gray eyes were black with her sense of outrage.

"Take it away, beast!" she panted.

Kut-le held her gaze.

"Drink it, Rhoda!" he said quietly.

The girl returned his look for a moment then, hating herself for her weakness, she took the cup and drained it. Kut-le tossed the cup to the squaw, pushed Rhoda back to her blankets and covered her very gently. Then he went back to his boulder. The girl lay staring up at the sky. Utterly merciless it gleamed above her. But before she could more than groan she was asleep.

She slept as she had not slept for months. The slanting rays of the westering sun wakened her. She sat up stiffly. The squaws were unpacking a burlap bag. They were greasy and dirty but they were women and their nearness gave Rhoda a vague sense of protection. They in turn gazed at the tangled glory of her hair, at the hopeless beauty of her eyes, at the pathos of the drooping mouth, with unfeigned curiosity.

Kut-le still was watching the desert. The madness of the night before had lifted a little, leaving Rhoda with some of her old poise. After several attempts she rose and made her staggering way to Kut-le's side.

"Kut-le," she said, "perhaps you will tell me what you mean by this outrage?"

The young Indian turned to her. White and exhausted, heavy hair in confusion, Rhoda still was lovely.

THE INDIAN WAY

"You seem to have more interest in life," he said, "than you have had since I have known you. I thought the experiment would have that effect!"

"You brute!" cried Rhoda. "Can't you see how silly you are? You will be caught and lynched before the day is passed."

Kut-le smiled.

"Pshaw! Three Apaches can outwit a hundred white men on the trail!"

Rhoda caught her breath.

"Oh, Kut-le, how could you do this thing! How could you! I am disgraced forever! Let me go, Kut-le! Let me go! I'll not even ask you for a horse. Just let me go by myself!"

"You are better off with me. You will acknowledge that, yourself, before I am through with you."

"Better off!" Rhoda's appalled eyes cut the Indian deeper than words. "Better off! Why, Kut-le, I am a dying woman! You will just have to leave me dead beside the trail somewhere. Look at me! Look at my hands! See how emaciated I am! See how I tremble! I am a sick wreck, Kut-le. You cannot want me! Let me go! Try, try to remember all that you learned of pity from the whites! O Kut-le, let me go!"

"I haven't forgotten what I learned from the whites," replied the young man. He looked off at the desert with a quiet smile. "Now I want the whites to learn from me."

"But can't you see what a futile game you are playing? John DeWitt and Jack must be on your trail now!"

There was a cruel gleam in the Apache's eyes.

"Don't be too sure! They are going to spend a few days looking for the foolish Eastern girl who took a stroll and lost her way in the desert. How can they dream that you are stolen?"

Rhoda wrung her hands.

"What shall I do! What shall I do! What an awful, awful thing to come to me! As if life had not been hard enough! This catastrophe! This disgrace!"

Kut-le eyed her speculatively.

"It's all race prejudice, you know. I have the education of the white with the intelligence and physical perfection of the Indian; DeWitt is nowhere near my equal."

Rhoda's eyes blazed.

"Don't *speak* of DeWitt! You're not fit to!"

"Yet," very quietly, "you said the other night that I had as good a brain and was as attractive as any man of your acquaintance!"

"I was a fool!" exclaimed Rhoda.

Kut-le rose and took a stride or two up and down the ledge. Then he folded his arms across his chest and

THE INDIAN WAY

stopped before Rhoda, who leaned weakly against the boulder.

"I am going to tell you what my ideas are," he said. "You are intelligent and will understand me no matter how bitter my words may make you at first. Now look here. Lots of white men are in love with you. Even Billy Porter went off his head. But I guess DeWitt is a pretty fair sample of the type of men you draw, well educated, strong, well-bred and Eastern to the backbone. And they love you as you are, delicate, helpless, appealing, thoroughbred, but utterly useless!

"Except that they hate to see you suffer, they wouldn't want you to change. Now I love you for the possibilities that I see in you. I wouldn't think of marrying you as you are. It would be an insult to my good blood. Your beauty is marred by your illness. You have absolutely no sense of responsibility toward life. You think that life owes everything to you, that you pay your way with your beauty. If you didn't die, but married DeWitt, you would go on through life petted and babied, bridge-playing and going out to lectures, childless, incompetent, self-satisfied—and an utter failure!

"Now I think that humans owe everything to life and that women owe the most of all because they make the race. The more nature has done for them, the more they owe. I believe that you are a thousand times worth saving. I am going to keep you out here in the desert until you wake to your responsibility to yourself and to life. I am going to strip your veneering of culture from you and make you see yourself as you are and life as it is — life, big and clean and glorious, with its one big tenet: keep body and soul right and reproduce your kind. I am going to make you see bigger things in this big country than you ever dreamed of."

He stopped and Rhoda sat appalled, the Indian watching her. To relieve herself from his eyes Rhoda turned toward the desert. The sun had all but touched the far horizon. Crimson and gold, purple and black, desert and sky merged in one unspeakable glory. But Rhoda saw only emptiness, only life's cruelty and futility and loneliness. And once more she wrung her feeble hands.

Kut-le spoke to Molly, the fat squaw. She again brought Rhoda a cup of broth. This time Rhoda drank it mechanically, then sat in abject wretchedness awaiting the next move of her tormentor. She had not long to wait. Kut-le took a bundle from his saddle and began to unfasten it before Rhoda.

"You must get into some suitable clothes," he said. "Put these on."

Rhoda stared at the clothing Kut-le was shaking out. Then she gave him a look of disgust. There was a pair of little buckskin breeches, exquisitely tanned, a little blue flannel shirt, a pair of high-laced hunting boots and a sombrero. She made no motion toward taking the clothes.

"Can't you see," Kut-le went on, "that, at the least, you will be in my power for a day or two, that you must ride and that the clothes you have on are simply silly? Why not be as comfortable as possible, under the circumstances?"

The girl, with the conventions of ages speaking in her disgusted face, the savage with his perfect physique bespeaking ages of undistorted nature, eyed each other narrowly.

"I shall keep on my own clothes," said Rhoda distinctly. "Believe me, you alone give the party the primitive air you admire!"

Kut-le's jaw hardened.

"Rhoda Tuttle, unless you put these clothes on at once I shall call the squaws and have them put on you by force."

Into Rhoda's face came a look of despair. Slowly she put out a shaking hand and took the clothes.

"I can't argue against a brute," she said. "The men I have known have been gentlemen. Tell one of your filthy squaws to come and help me."

"Molly! *Pronto!*" Like a brown lizard the fat squaw scuttled to Rhoda's side.

In a little dressing-room formed by fallen rock, Rhoda

put on the boy's clothing. Molly helped the girl very gently. When she was done she smoothed the blue-shirted shoulder complacently.

"Heap nice!" she said. "Make 'em sick squaw heap warm. You no 'fraid! Kut-le say cut off nose, kill 'em with cactus torture, if Injuns not good to white squaw."

The touch was the touch of a woman and Molly, though a squaw, had a woman's understanding. Rhoda gave a little sob.

"Kut-le, he good!" Molly went on. "He a big chief's son. He strong, rich. You no be afraid. You look heap pretty."

Involuntarily Rhoda glanced at herself. The new clothes were very comfortable. With the loveliness and breeding that neither clothing nor circumstance could mar, Rhoda was a fascinating figure. She was tall for a woman, but now she looked a mere lad. The buckskin clung like velvet. The high-laced boots came to her knees. The sombrero concealed all of the golden hair save for short curling locks in front. She would have charmed a painter, Kut-le thought, as she stepped from her dressing-room; but he kept his voice coolly impersonal.

"All right, you're in shape to travel, now. Where are your other clothes? Molly, bring them all here!"

Rhoda followed the squaw and together they folded the

cast-off clothing. Rhoda saw that her scarf had blown near the cañon edge. A quick thought came to her. Molly was fully occupied with muttering adoration of the dainty underwear. Rhoda tied a pebble into the scarf and dropped it far out into the depths below. Then she returned to Molly.

CHAPTER V

THE PURSUIT

AS twilight deepened, Katherine lay in the hammock thankful for the soothing effect of the darkness on her aching eyes. She felt a little troubled about Kut-le. She was very fond of the young Indian. She understood him as did no one else, perhaps, and had the utmost faith in his honor and loyalty. She suspected that Rhoda had had much to do with the young Indian's sudden departure and she felt irritated with the girl, though at the same time she acknowledged that Rhoda had done only what she, Katherine, had advised—had treated Kut-le as if he had been a white man!

She watched the trail for Rhoda's return but darkness came and there was no sign of the frail figure. A little disturbed, she walked to the corral bars and looked down to the lights of the cowboys' quarters. If only John DeWitt and Jack would return! But she did not expect them before midnight. She returned to the house and telephoned to the ranch foreman.

"Don't you worry, ma'am," he answered cheerily. "No harm could come to her! She just walked till it got dark and is just starting for home now, I bet! She can't have got out of sight of the ranch lights."

"But she may have! You can't tell what she's done, she's such a tenderfoot," insisted Katherine nervously. "She may have been hurt!"

It was well that Katherine could not see the foreman's face during the conversation. It had a decided scowl of apprehension, but he managed a cheerful laugh.

"Well, you *have* got nervous, Mrs. Newman! I'll just send three or four of the boys out to meet her. Eh?"

"Oh, yes, do!" cried Katherine. "I shall feel easier. Good-by!"

Dick Freeman dropped the receiver and hurried into the neighboring bunk-house.

"Boys," he said quietly, "Mrs. Newman just 'phoned me that Miss Tuttle went to walk at sunset, to be gone half an hour. She ain't got back yet. She is alone. Will some of you come with me?"

Every hand of cards was dropped before Dick was half through his statement. In less than twenty minutes twenty cowboys were circling slowly out into the desert. For two hours Katherine paced from the living-room to the veranda, from the veranda to the corral. She changed her light evening gown to her khaki riding habit. Her nervousness grew to panic. She sent Li Chung to bed, then she paced the lawn, listening, listening.

THE PURSUIT

At last she heard the thud of hoofs and Dick Freeman dismounted in the light that streamed from the open door.

"We haven't found her, Mrs. Newman. Has Mr. Newman got back? I think we must get up an organized search."

Katherine could feel her heart thump heavily.

"No, he hasn't. Have you found her trail?"

"No; it's awful hard to trail in the dark, and the desert for miles around the ranch is all cut up with footprints and hoof-marks, you know."

Katherine wrung her hands.

"Oh, poor little Rhoda!" she cried. "What shall we do!"

"No harm can come to her," insisted Dick. "She will know enough to sit tight till daylight, then we will have her before the heat gets up."

"Oh, if she only will!" moaned Katherine. "Do whatever you think best, Dick, and I'll send Jack and John DeWitt to you as soon as they return."

Dick swung himself to the saddle again.

"Better go in and read something, Mrs. Newman. You mustn't worry yourself sick until you are sure you have something to worry about."

How she passed the rest of the night, Katherine never knew. A little after midnight, Jack came in, his face tense and anxious. Katherine paled as she saw his expression. She knew he had met some of the searchers. When Jack saw the color leave his wife's pretty cheeks, he kissed her very tenderly and for a moment they clung to each other silently, thinking of the delicate girl adrift on the desert.

"Where is John DeWitt?" asked Katherine after a moment.

"He's almost crazy. He's with Dick Freeman. Only stopped for a fresh horse."

"They have no trace?" questioned Katherine.

Jack shook his head.

"You know what a proposition it is to hunt for as small an object as a human, in the desert. Give me your smelling salts and the little Navajo blanket. One—one can't tell whether she's hurt or not."

Katherine began to sob as she obeyed.

"You are all angel good not to blame me, but I know it's my fault. I shouldn't have let her go. But she is so sensible, usually."

"Dear heart!" said Jack, rolling up the Navajo. "Any one that knows dear old Rhoda knows that what she will, she will, and you are not to blame. Go to bed and sleep if you can."

"Oh, Jack, I can't! Let me go with you, do!"

But Jack shook his head.

THE PURSUIT

"You aren't strong enough to do any good and some one must stay here to run things."

So again Katherine was left to pace the veranda. All night the search went on. Jack sent messages to the neighboring ranches and the following morning fifty men were in the saddle seeking Rhoda's trail. Jack also sent into the Pueblo country for Kut-le, feeling that his aid would be invaluable. It would take some time to get a reply from the Indians and in the meantime the search went on rigorously, with no trace of the trail to be found.

John DeWitt did not return to the ranch until the afternoon after Rhoda's disappearance. Then, disheveled, with bloodshot eyes, cracked lips and blistered face, he dropped exhausted on the veranda steps. Katherine and Jack greeted him with quiet sympathy.

"I came in to get fixed up for a long cruise," said John. "My pony went lame, and I want a flannel shirt instead of this silk thing I had on last night. I wish to God Kut-le would come! I suppose he could read what we are blind to."

"You bet!" cried Jack. "I expect an answer from his friends this afternoon. I just had a telegram from Porter, in answer to one I sent him this morning. I caught him at Brown's and he will be here this afternoon. He knows almost as much as an Indian about following a trail."

They all spoke in the hushed tones one employs in the sick-room. Jack tried to persuade DeWitt to eat and sleep but he refused, his forced calm giving way to a hoarse, "For heaven's sake, can I rest when she is dying out there!"

John had not finished his feverish preparations when Billy Porter stalked into the living-room. As he entered, the telephone rang and Jack answered it. Then he returned to the eager group.

"Kut-le has gone on a long hunt with some of his people. They don't know where he went and refuse to look for him."

Billy Porter gave a hard, mirthless laugh.

"Why certainly! Jack, you ought to have a hole bored into your head to let in a little light. Kut-le gone. Can't find Rhoda's trail. Kut-le in love with Rhoda. Kut-le an Indian. Rhoda refuses him—he goes off— gets some of his chums and when he catches Rhoda alone he steals her. He will keep a man behind, covering his trail. Oh, you easy Easterners make me sick!"

The Newmans and DeWitt stood staring at Porter with horror in their eyes. The clock ticked for an instant then DeWitt gave a groan and bowed his head against the mantelpiece. Katherine ran to him and tried to pull his head to her little shoulder.

THE PURSUIT

"O John, don't! Don't! Maybe Billy is right. I'm afraid he is! But one thing I do know. Rhoda is as safe in Kut-le's hands as she would be in Jack's. I *know* it, John!"

John did not move, but at Katherine's words the color came back into Jack Newman's face.

"That's right!" he said stoutly. "It's a devilish thing for Kut-le to do. But she's safe, John, old boy, I'm sure she is."

Billy Porter, conscience-stricken at the effect of his words, clapped John on the shoulder.

"Aw shucks! I let my Injun hate get the best of my tongue. Of course she's safe enough; only the darn devil's got to be caught before he gets to Mexico and makes some padre marry 'em. So it's us to the saddle a whole heap."

"We'd better get an Indian to help trail," said Jack.

"You'll have a sweet time getting an Injun to trail Kut-le!" said Porter. "The Injuns half worship him. They think he's got some kind of strong medicine; you know that. You get one and he'll keep you off the trail instead of on. I can follow the trail as soon as he quits covering it. Get the canteens and come on. We don't need a million cowboys running round promiscuous over the sand. Numbers don't help in trailing an Injun. It's experience and patience. It may take us two weeks and we'll outfit for that. But we'll get him in the end. Crook always did."

There was that in Billy Porter's voice which put heart into his listeners. John DeWitt lifted his head, and while his blue eyes returned the gaze of the others miserably, he squared his shoulders doggedly.

"I'm ready," he said briefly.

"Oh, let me come!" cried Katherine. "I can't bear this waiting!"

Billy smiled.

"Why, Mrs. Jack, you'd be dried up and blowed away before the first day was over."

"But Rhoda is enduring it!" protested Katherine, with quivering lips.

"God!" John DeWitt muttered and flung himself from the house to the corral. The other two followed him at once.

It was mid-afternoon when the three rode into the quivering yellow haze of the desert followed by a little string of pack horses. It was now nearing twenty-four hours since Rhoda had disappeared and in that time there had been little sand blowing. This meant that the trail could be easily followed were it found. The men rode single file, Billy Porter leading. All wore blue flannel shirts and khaki trousers. John DeWitt rode Eastern park fashion, with short stirrup, rising from the

THE PURSUIT 77

saddle with the trot. Jack and Billy rode Western fashion, long stirrup, an inseparable part of their horses, a fashion that John DeWitt was to be forced to learn in the fearful days to come.

Billy Porter declaimed in a loud voice from the head of the procession.

"Of course, Kut-le has taken to the mountains. He'll steer clear of ranches and cowboys for a while. Our chance lies in his giving up covering his trail after he gets well into the ranges. We will get his trail and hang on till we can outwit him. If he was alone, we'd never get him, barring accident. But he will be a lot hampered by Miss Rhoda and I trust to her to hamper him a whole lot after she gets her hand in."

All the rest of the burning afternoon they moved toward the mountains. It was quite dusk when they entered the foothills. The way, not good at best, grew difficult and dangerous to follow. Billy led on, however, until darkness closed down on them in a little cactus-grown cañon. Here he halted and ordered camp for a few hours.

"Lord!" exclaimed DeWitt. "You're not going to camp! I thought you were really going to do something!"

Billy finished lighting the fire and by its light he gave an impatient glance at the tenderfoot. But the look of the burned, sand-grimed face, the bloodshot eyes, blazing with anxiety, caused him to speak patiently.

"Can't kill the horses, DeWitt. You must make up your mind that this is going to be a hard hunt. You got to call out all the strength you've been storing up all your life, and then some. We've got to use common sense. Lord, I want to get ahead, don't I! I seen Miss Rhoda. I know what she's like. This ain't any joy ride for me, either. I got a lot of feeling in it."

John DeWitt extended his sun-blistered right hand and Billy Porter clasped it with his brown paw.

Jack Newman cleared his throat.

"Did you give your horse enough rope, John? There is a good lot of grass close to the cañon wall. Quick as you finish your coffee, old man, roll in your blanket. We will rest till midnight when the moon comes up, eh, Billy?"

DeWitt, finally convinced of the good sense and earnestness of his friends, obeyed. The cañon was still in darkness when Jack shook him into wakefulness but the mountain peak above was a glorious silver. Camp was broken quickly and in a short time Billy was leading the way up the wretched trail. DeWitt's four hours of sleep had helped him. He could, to some degree, control the feverish anxiety that was consuming him and he tried to turn his mind from picturing Rhoda's agonies

THE PURSUIT 79

to castigating himself for leaving her unguarded even though Kut-le had left the ranch. Before leaving the ranch that afternoon he had telegraphed and written Rhoda's only living relative, her Aunt Mary. He had been thankful as he wrote that Rhoda had no mother. He had so liked the young Indian; there had been such good feeling between them that he could not yet believe that Porter's surmise was wholly correct.

"Supposing," he said aloud, "that you are wrong, Porter? Supposing that she's—she's dying of thirst down there in the desert? You have no proof of Kut-le's doing it. It's only founded on your Indian hate, you say yourself."

"That's right," said Newman. "Are you sure we aren't wasting time, Billy?"

Billy turned in the saddle to face them.

"Well, boys," he said, "you've got half the county scratching the desert with a fine-tooth comb. I don't see how we three can help very much there. On the other hand we might do some good up here. Now I'll make a bargain with you. If by midnight tonight we ain't struck any trace of her, you folks can quit."

"And what will you do?" asked Jack.

"Me?" Billy shrugged his shoulders. "Why, I'll keep on this trail till my legs is wore off above my boots!" and he turned to guide his pony up a little branch trail at the top of which stood a tent with the telltale windlass and forge close by.

Before the tent they drew rein. In response to Billy's call a rough-bearded fellow lifted the tent flap and stood suppressing a yawn, as if visitors to his lonely claim were of daily occurrence.

"Say, friend," said Billy, "do you know Newman's ranch?"

"Sure," returned the prospector.

"Well, this is Mr. Newman. A young lady has been visiting him and his wife. She disappeared night before last. We suspicion that Cartwell, that educated Injun, has stole her. We're trying to find his trail. Can you give us a hunch?"

The sleepy look left the prospector's eyes. He crossed the rocks to put a hand on Billy's pommel.

"Gee! Ain't that ungodly!" he exclaimed. "I ain't seen a soul. But night before last I heard a screaming in my sleep. It woke me up but when I got out here I couldn't hear a thing. It was faint and far away and I decided it was a wildcat. Do you suppose it was *her?*"

DeWitt ground his teeth together and his hands shook but he made no sound. Jack breathed heavily.

"You think it was a woman?" asked Billy hoarsely.

The prospector spoke hesitatingly.

"If I'd been shore, I'd a gone on a hunt. But it was

THE PURSUIT

all kind of in my sleep. It was from way back in the mountain there."

"Thanks," said Billy, "we'll be on our way."

"It's four o'clock. Better stop and have some grub with me, then I'll join in and help you."

"No!" cried DeWitt, breaking his silence. "No!"

"That's the young lady's financier," said Billy, nodding toward John.

"Sho!" said the prospector sympathetically.

Billy lifted his reins.

"Thanks, we'll be getting along, I guess. Just as much obliged to you. We'll water here in your spring."

They moved on in the direction whither the prospector had pointed. They rode in silence. Dawn came slowly, clearly. The peaks lifted magnificently, range after range against the rosy sky. There was no trail. They followed the possible way. The patient little cow ponies clambered over rocks and slid down inclines of a frightful angle as cleverly as mountain goats. At ten o'clock, they stopped for breakfast and a three hours' sleep. It was some time before DeWitt could be persuaded to lie down but at last, perceiving that he was keeping the others from their rest, he took his blanket to the edge of the ledge and lay down.

His sleepless eyes roved up and down the adjoining cañon. Far to the south, near the desert floor, he saw a fluttering bit of white. Now a fluttering bit of white, far from human byways, means something! Tenderfoot though he was, DeWitt realized this and sleep left his eyes. He sat erect. For a moment he was tempted to call the others but he restrained himself. He would let them rest while he kept watch over the little white beacon, for so, unaccountably, it seemed to him. He eyed it hungrily, and then a vague comfort and hopefulness came to him and he fell asleep.

Jack's lusty call to coffee woke him. DeWitt jumped to his feet and with a new light in his eyes he pointed out his discovery. The meal was disposed of very hurriedly and, leaving Jack to watch the camp, John and Billy crossed the cañon southward. After heavy scrambling they reached the foot of the cañon wall. Twenty feet above them dangled a white cloth. Catching any sort of hand and foot hold, John clambered upward. Then he gave a great shout of joy. Rhoda's neck scarf with the pebble pinned in one end was in his hands! DeWitt slid to the ground and he and Billy examined the scarf tenderly, eagerly.

"I told you! I told you!" exulted Billy hoarsely. "See that weight fastened to it? Wasn't that smart of her? Bless her heart! Now we got to get above, somehow, and find where she dropped it from!"

CHAPTER VI

ENTERING THE DESERT KINDERGARTEN

"WE'LL start now," said Kut-le.

Alchise led out the horses. The squaws each threw an emancipated, sinewy leg across a pony's back and followed Alchise's fluttering shirt up the mountain. Kut-le stood holding the bridle of a sedate little horse on which he had fastened a comfortable high-backed saddle.

"Come, Rhoda," he said. "I'll shorten the stirrups after you are mounted."

Rhoda stood with her back to the wall, her blue-veined hands clutching the rough out-croppings on either side, horror and fear in her eyes.

"I can't ride cross-saddle!" she exclaimed. "I used to be a good horsewoman in the side-saddle. But I'm so weak that even keeping in the side-saddle is out of the question."

"Anything except cross-saddle is utterly out of the question," replied the Indian, "on the sort of trails we have to take. You might as well begin to control your nerves now as later. I'm going to have an expert rider in you by the time you have regained your strength. Come, Rhoda."

The girl turned her face to the afterglow. Remote and pitiless lay the distant crimson ranges. She shuddered and turned back to the young Indian who stood watching her. For the moment all the agony of her situation was concentrated in horror of another night in the saddle.

"Kut-le, I *can't!*"

"Shall I pick you up and carry you over here?" asked Kut-le patiently.

In her weakness and misery, Rhoda's cleft chin quivered. There was only merciless determination in the Indian's face. Slowly the girl walked to his side. He swung her to the saddle, adjusted the stirrups carefully, then fastened her securely to the saddle with a strap about her waist. Rhoda watched him in the silence of utter fear. Having settled the girl to his satisfaction, he mounted his own horse, and Rhoda's pony followed him tractably up the trail.

The trail rose steeply. After the first few dizzy moments, Rhoda, clinging to the saddle with hands and knees, was thankful for the security of her new seat. The scenery was uncanny to her terrorized eyes. To the left were great overhanging walls with cactus growing from every crevice; to the right, depth of cañon toward which she dared not look but only trusted herself prayerfully to her steady little horse.

As the trail led higher and darkness settled, the cold grew intense and Rhoda cowered and shivered. Yet through her fear and discomfort was creeping surprise that her strength had endured even this long. In a spot where the trail widened Kut-le dropped back beside her and she felt the warm folds of a Navajo blanket about her shoulders. Neither she nor the Indian spoke. The madness of the night before, the fear and disgust of the afternoon gave way, slowly, to a lethargy of exhaustion. All thought of her frightful predicament, of her friends' anxiety, of Kut-le's treachery, was dulled by a weariness so great that she could only cling to the saddle and pray for the trail to end.

Kut-le, riding just ahead, glanced back constantly at the girl's dim figure. But Rhoda was beyond pleading or protesting. The trail twisted and undulated on and on. Each moment Rhoda felt less certain of her seat. Each moment the motion of the horse grew more painful. At last a faint odor of pine-needles roused her sinking senses and she opened her heavy eyes. They had left the sickening edge of the cañon and Alchise was leading them into a beautiful growth of pines where the mournful hooting of owls gave a graveyard sadness to the moon-flecked shadows.

Here, in a long aisle of columnar pines, Kut-le called the first halt. Rhoda reeled in her saddle. Before her horse had stopped, Kut-le was beside her, unfastening her waist strap and lifting her to the ground. He pulled the blanket from his own shoulders and Molly stretched it on the soft pine-needles. Rhoda, half delirious, looked up into the young Indian's face with the pathetic unconsciousness of a sick child. He laid her carefully on the blanket. The two squaws hurriedly knelt at Rhoda's side and with clever hands rubbed and manipulated the slender, exhausted body until the girl opened her languid eyes.

Kut-le, while this was being done, stood quietly by the blanket, his fine face stern and intent. When Rhoda opened her eyes, he put aside the two squaws, knelt and raised the girl's head and held a cup of the rich broth to her lips. It was cold, yet it tasted good, and Rhoda finished the cup without protest, then struggled to a sitting position. After a moment Kut-le raised her gently to her feet. Here, however, she pushed him away and walked unsteadily to her horse. Kut-le's hands dropped to his side and he stood in the moonlight watching the frail boyish figure clamber with infinite travail into the saddle.

From the pine wood, the trail led downward. The rubbing and the broth had put new life into Rhoda, and for a little while she kept a clear brain. For the first time it occurred to her that instead of following the Indians so stupidly she ought to watch her chance and at the first opportunity make a wild dash off into the darkness. Kut-le was so sure of her weakness and cowardice that she felt that he would be taken completely by surprise and she might elude him. With a definite purpose in her mind she was able to fight off again and again the blur of weakness that threatened her.

As the trail widened in the descent, Kut-le rode in beside her.

"Feeling better?" he asked cheerfully.

Rhoda made no reply. Such a passion of hatred for the man shook her that words failed her. She turned a white face toward him, the eyes black, the nostrils quivering with passion.

Kut-le laughed softly.

"Hate me, Rhoda! Hate me as much as you wish! That's a heap more hopeful than indifference. I'll bet you aren't thinking of dying of ennui now!"

What fiend, thought Rhoda, ever had induced her to make a friend of this savage! She clung to the pommel of her saddle, her eyes fastened on him. If only he would drop dead as he sat! If only his Indians would turn on him and kill him!

They were riding through the desert now, desert

thick-grown with cactus and sage-brush. Suddenly a far away roar came to Rhoda's ears. There was a faint whistle repeated with increasing loudness. Off to the north appeared a light that grew till it threw a dazzling beam on the strange little waiting group. The train passed, a half-dozen dimly lighted Pullmans. The roaring decreased, the whistle sounded lower and lower and the night was silent. Rhoda sat following the last dim light with burning eyes. Kut-le led the way from the difficult going of the desert to the road-bed. As Rhoda saw the long line of rails the panic of the previous night overwhelmed her. Like a mad thing, unmindful of the strap about her waist she threw herself from the saddle and hung against the stolid pony. Kut-le dismounted and undid the strap. The girl dropped to the ties and lay crouched with her face against the steel rail.

"O John! O John DeWitt!" she sobbed.

"Alchise, go ahead with the horses," said Kut-le. "Wait for me at the painted rock."

Then as the Indians became indistinguishable along the track he lifted Rhoda to her feet.

"Walk for a while," he said. "It will rest you. Poor little girl! I wish I could have managed differently but this was best for you. Come, don't be afraid of me!"

Some savage instinct stirred in Rhoda. For the first time in her life she felt an insane joy in anger.

ENTERING THE DESERT KINDERGARTEN 89

"I'm not afraid of you, you Apache Indian!" she said clearly. "I loathe you! Your touch poisons me! But I'm not afraid of you! I shall choke myself with my bare hands before you shall harm me! And if you keep me long enough I shall try to kill you!"

Kut-le gave a short laugh.

"Listen, Rhoda. Your protests show that you are afraid of me. But you need not be. Your protection lies in the fact that I love you—love you with all the passion of a savage, all the restraint of a Caucasian. I'd rather die than harm you! Why, girl, I'm *saving* you, not destroying you! Rhoda! Dear one!" He paused and Rhoda could hear his quickened breath. Then he added lightly, "Let's get on with our little stroll!"

Rhoda wrung her hands and groaned. Only to escape —to escape! Suddenly turning, she ran down the track. Kut-le watched her, motionless, until she had run perhaps a hundred yards, then with a few mighty leaps he overtook her and gathered her to his great chest. Moaning, Rhoda lay still.

"Dear," said Kut-le, "don't exert yourself foolishly. If you must escape, lay your plans carefully. Use your brain. Don't act like a child. I love you, Rhoda!"

"I loathe you! I loathe you!" whispered the girl.

"You don't—ah—" He stopped abruptly and set the girl on the ground. They were standing beside a sidetrack near a desert water-tank. "I've caught my foot in a switch-frog," muttered Kut-le, keeping his hold on Rhoda with one hand while with the other he tugged at his moccasined foot.

Rhoda stood rigid.

"I hear a train!" she cried. "O dear God, I hear a train!" Then, "The other Indians are too far away to reach you before the train does," she added calmly.

"But I'll never loose my grip on you," returned the Indian grimly.

He tore at the imprisoned foot, ripping the moccasin and tearing at the road bed. The rails began to sing. Far down the track they saw a star of light. Rhoda's heart stood still. This, then, was to be the end! After all the months of distant menace, death was to be upon her in a moment! This, then, was to be the solution! And with all the horror of what life might mean to her, she cried out with a sob:

"Oh, not this way! Not this way!"

Kut-le gave her a quick push.

"Hurry," he said, "and try to remember good things of me!"

With a cry of joy, Rhoda jumped from the track, then stopped. There flashed across her inner vision the face of young Cartwell, debonair and dark, with unfathomable eyes; young Cartwell who had saved her life when the scor-

ENTERING THE DESERT KINDERGARTEN

pion had stung her, who had spent hours trying to lead her back to health. Instantly she turned and staggered back to the Indian.

"I can't let a human being die like a trapped animal!" she panted, and she threw herself wildly against him.

Kut-le fell at the unexpected impact of her weight and his foot was freed! He lifted Rhoda, leaped from the track, and the second section of the tourist train thundered into the west.

"You are as fine as I thought you were—" he began. But Rhoda was a limp heap at his feet.

The girl came to her senses partially when Kut-le set her in the saddle and fastened her there with strap and blanket. But happily she was practically unconscious for the hour or two that remained till dawn. Just as day was breaking the Indians made their way across an arroyo and up a long slope to a group of cottonwoods. Here Rhoda was put to bed on a heap of blankets.

Sometime in the afternoon she woke with a clear head. It was the first time in months that she had wakened without a headache. She stared from the shade of the cottonwoods to the distant lavender haze of the desert. There was not a sound in all the world. Mysterious, remote, the desert stared back at her, mocking her little grief. More terrible to her than her danger in Kut-le's hands, more appalling than the death threat that had hung over her so long, was this sense of awful space, of barren nothingness with which the desert oppressed her. Instinctively she turned to look for human companionship. Kut-le and Alchise were not to be seen but Molly nodded beside Rhoda's blankets and the thin hag Cesca was curled in the grass near by, asleep.

"You awake? Heap hungry?" asked Molly suddenly.

Rhoda sat up, groaning at the torturing stiffness of her muscles.

"Where is Kut-le?" she asked.

"Gone get 'em supper. Alchise gone too."

"Molly," Rhoda took the rough brown hand between both her soft cold palms, "Molly, will you help me to run away?"

Molly looked from the clasping fingers up to Rhoda's sweet face. Molly was a squaw, dirty and ignorant. Rhoda was the delicate product of a highly cultivated civilization, egoistic, narrow-viewed, self-centered. And yet Rhoda, looking into Molly's deep brown eyes, saw there that limitless patience and fortitude and gentleness which is woman's without regard to class or color. And not knowing why, the white girl bowed her head on the squaw's fat shoulder and sobbed a little. A strange look came into Molly's face. She was childless and had worked fearfully to justify her existence to her tribe. Few hands had touched hers in tenderness. Few voices had appealed to her for sympathy. Suddenly Molly clasped Rhoda in her strong arms and swayed back and forth with her gently.

"You no cry!" she said. "You no cry, little Sunhead, you no cry!"

"Molly, dear kind Molly, won't you help me to get back to my own people? Suppose it was your daughter that a white man had stolen! O Molly, I want to go home!"

Molly still rocked and spoke in the singsong voice one uses to a sobbing child.

"You no run 'way! Kut-le catch right off! Make it all harder for you!"

Rhoda shivered a little.

"If I once get away, Kut-le never will catch me alive!"

Molly chuckled indulgently.

"How you run? No *sabe* how eat, how drink, how find the trail! Better stay with Molly."

"I would wait till I thought we were near a town. Won't you help me? Dear, kind Molly, won't you help me?"

"Kut-le kill Molly with cactus torture!"

"But you go with me!" The sobs ceased and Rhoda

sat back on her blankets as the idea developed. "You go with me and I'll make you—"

Neither noticed the soft thud of moccasined feet. Suddenly Alchise seized Molly's black hair and with a violent jerk pulled the woman backward. Rhoda forgot her stiffened muscles, forgot her gentle ancestry. She sprang at Alchise with catlike fury and struck his fingers from Molly's hair.

"You fiend! I wish I could shoot you!" she panted, her fingers twitching.

Alchise retreated a step.

"She try help 'em run!" he said sullenly.

"She was not! And no matter if she was! Don't you touch a woman before me!"

A swift shadow crossed the camp and Alchise was hurled six feet away.

"What's the matter!" cried Kut-le. "Has he laid finger on you, Rhoda?" He strode to her side and looked down at her with eyes in which struggled anger and anxiety.

"No!" blazed Rhoda. "But he pulled Molly over backward by her hair!"

"Oh!" in evident relief. "And what was Molly doing?"

"She maybe help 'em run," said Alchise, coming forward.

The relief in Kut-le's voice increased Rhoda's anger.

ENTERING THE DESERT KINDERGARTEN 95

"No such thing! She was persuading me not to go! Kut-le, you give Alchise orders not to touch Molly again. I won't have it!"

"Oh, that's not necessary," said Kut-le serenely. "Indians are pretty good to their women as a general thing. They average up with the whites, I guess. Molly, get up and help Cesca with these!" He flung some newly killed rabbits at the gaping squaw, who still lay where she had fallen.

Rhoda, trembling and glowering, walked unsteadily up and down beneath the cottonwoods. The details of her new existence, the dirt, the roughness, were beginning to sink in on her. She paced back and forth, lips compressed, eyes black. Kut-le stood with his back against a cottonwood eying the slender figure with frank delight. Now and again he chuckled as he rolled a cigarette with his facile finger. His hands were fine as only an Indians can be: strong and sinewy yet supple with slender fingers and almond-shaped nails.

He smoked contentedly with his eyes on the girl. Inscrutable as was his face at a casual glance, had Rhoda observed keenly she might have read much in the changing light of his eyes. There was appreciation of her and love of her and a merciless determination to hold her at all costs. And still as he gazed there was that tragedy in his look which is part and portion of the Indian's face.

Silence in the camp had continued for some time when a strange young Indian strode up the slope, nodded to the group in the camp, and deliberately rolled himself in a blanket and dropped to sleep. Rhoda stared at him questioningly.

"Alchise's and Cesca's son," said Kut-le. "His job is to follow us at a distance and remove all trace of our trail. Not an overturned pebble misses his eye. I'll need him only for a day or two."

"Kut-le," said Rhoda suddenly, "when are you going to end the farce and let me go?"

The young man smiled.

"You know the way the farce usually ends! The man always gets the girl and they live happily forever after!"

"What do you suppose Jack and Katherine think of you? They have loved and trusted you so!"

For the first time the Indian's face showed pain.

"My hope is," he said, "that after they see how happy I am going to make you they will forgive me."

Rhoda controlled her voice with difficulty.

"Can't you see what you have done? No matter what the outcome, can you believe that I or any one that loves me can forgive the outrage to me?"

"After we have married and lived abroad for a year or two people will remember only the romance of it!"

ENTERING THE DESERT KINDERGARTEN 97

"Heavens!" ejaculated Rhoda. She returned to her angry walking.

Molly was preparing supper. She worked always with one eye on Rhoda, as if she could not see enough of the girl's fragile loveliness. With her attention thus divided, she stumbled constantly, dropping the pots and spilling the food. She herself was not at all disturbed by her mishaps but, with a grimace and a chuckle, picked up the food. But Cesca was annoyed. She was tending the fire which by a marvel of skill she kept always clear and all but smokeless. At each of Molly's mishaps, Cesca hurled a stone at her friend's back with a savage "Me-yah!" that disturbed Molly not at all.

Mercifully night was on the camp by the time the rabbits were cooked and Rhoda ate unconscious of the dirt the food had acquired in the cooking. When the silent meal was finished, Kut-le pointed to Rhoda's blankets.

"We will start in half an hour. You must rest during that time."

Too weary to resent the peremptory tone, Rhoda obeyed. The fire long since had been extinguished and the camp was dark. The Indians were to be located only by faint whispers under the trees. The opportunity seemed providential! Rhoda slipped from her blankets and crept through the darkness away from the camp.

CHAPTER VII

THE FIRST LESSON

AFTER crawling on her hands and knees for several yards, Rhoda rose and started on a run down the long slope to the open desert. But after a few steps she found running impossible, for the slope was a wilderness of rock, thickly grown with cholla and yucca with here and there a thicker growth of cat's-claw.

Almost at once her hands were torn and bleeding and she thought gratefully for the first time of her buckskin trousers which valiantly resisted all detaining thorns. The way dropped rapidly and after her first wild spurt Rhoda leaned exhausted and panting against a boulder. She had not the vaguest idea of where she was going or of what she was going to do, except that she was going to lose herself so thoroughly that not even Kut-le could find her. After that she was quite willing to trust to fate.

After a short rest she started on, every sense keen for the sound of pursuit, but none came. As the silent minutes passed Rhoda became elated. How easy it was! What a pity that she had not tried before! At the foot of the slope, she turned up the arroyo. Here her course grew heavier. The arroyo was cut by deep ruts and gullies down which the girl slid and tumbled in mad haste only to find rock masses over which she crawled with utmost difficulty. Now and again the stout vamps of her hunting boots were pierced by chollas and, half frantic in her haste, she was forced to stop and struggle to pull out the thorns.

It was not long before the girl's scant strength was gone, and when after a mad scramble she fell from a boulder to the ground, she was too done up to rise. She lay face to the stars, half sobbing with excitement and disappointment. After a time, however, the sobs ceased and she lay thinking. She knew now that until she was inured to the desert and had a working knowledge of its ways, escape was impossible. She must bide her time and wait for her friends to rescue her. She had no idea how far she had come from the Indian camp. Whether or not Kut-le could find her again she could not guess. If he did not, then unless a white stumbled on her she must die in the desert. Well then, let it be so! The old lethargy closed in on her and she lay motionless and hopeless.

From all sides she heard the night howls of the coyote packs circling nearer and nearer. Nothing could more perfectly interpret the horrible desolation of the desert, Rhoda thought, than the demoniacal, long-drawn laughter of the coyote. How long she lay she neither knew nor cared. But just as she fancied that the coyotes had drawn so near that she could hear their footsteps, a hand was laid on her arm.

"Have you had enough, Rhoda?" asked Kut-le.

"No!" shuddered Rhoda. "I'd rather die here!"

The Indian laughed softly as he lifted her from the ground.

"A good hater makes a good lover, Rhoda," he said. "I wish I'd had time to let you learn your lesson more thoroughly. I haven't been twenty-five feet away from you since you left the camp. I wanted you to try your hand at it just so you'd realize what you are up against. But you've tired yourself badly."

Rhoda lay mute in the young man's arms. She was not thinking of his words but of the first time that the Indian had carried her. She saw John DeWitt's protesting face, and tears of weakness and despair ran silently down her cheeks. Kut-le strode rapidly and unhesitatingly over the course she had followed so painfully and in a few moments they were among the waiting Indians.

Kut-le put Rhoda in her saddle, fastened her securely and put a Navajo about her shoulders. The night's misery was begun. Whether they went up and down mountains, whether they crossed deserts, Rhoda neither knew nor cared. The blind purpose of clinging to the saddle was the one aim of the dreadful night. She was a little light-headed at times and with her head against the horse's neck, she murmured John DeWitt's name, or sitting erect she called to him wildly. At such times Kut-le's fingers tightened and he clinched his teeth, but he did not go to her. When, however, the frail figure drooped silently and inertly against the waist strap he seemed to know even in the darkness. Then and then only he lifted her down, the squaws massaged her wracked body, and she was put in the saddle again. Over and over during the night this was repeated until at dawn Rhoda was barely conscious that after being lifted to the ground she was not remounted but was covered carefully and left in peace.

It was late in the afternoon again when Rhoda woke. She pushed aside her blankets and tried to get up but fell back with a groan. The stiffness of the previous days was nothing whatever to the misery that now held every muscle rigid. The overexertion of three nights in the saddle which the massaging had so far mitigated had asserted itself and every muscle in the girl's body seemed acutely painful. To lift her hand to her hair, to draw a long breath, to turn her head, was almost impossible.

Rhoda looked dismally about her. The camp this

THE FIRST LESSON

time was on the side of a mountain that lay in a series of mighty ranges, each separated from the other by a narrow strip of desert. White and gold gleamed the snow-capped peaks. Purple and lavender melted the shimmering desert into the lifting mesas. Rhoda threw her arm across her eyes to hide the hateful sight, and moaned in pain at the movement.

Molly ran to her side.

"Your bones heap sick? Molly rub 'em?" she asked eagerly.

"O Molly, if you would!" replied Rhoda gratefully, and she wondered at the skill and gentleness of the Indian woman who manipulated the aching muscles with such rapidity and firmness that in a little while Rhoda staggered stiffly to her feet.

"Molly," she said, "I want to wash my face."

Molly puckered up her own face in her effort to understand, and scratched her head.

"Don't *sabe* that," she said.

"Wash my face!" repeated Rhoda in atonishment. "Of course you understand."

Molly laughed.

"No! You no wash! No use! You just get cold—heap cold!"

"Molly!" called Kut-le's authoritative voice.

Molly went flying toward the packs, from which she

returned with a canteen and a tiny pitch-smeared basket. Kut-le followed with a towel. He grinned at Rhoda.

"Molly is possessed with the idea that anything as frail as you would be snuffed out like a candle by a drop of water. You and I each possess a lone lorn towel which we must wash out ourselves till the end of the trip. The squaws don't know when a thing is clean."

Rhoda took the towel silently, and the young Indian, after waiting a minute as if in hope of a word from her, left the girl to her difficult toilet. When Rhoda had finished she picked up the field-glasses that Kut-le had left on her blankets and with her back to the Indians sat down on a rock to watch the desert.

The sordid discomforts of the camp seemed to her unbearable. She hated the blue haze of the desert below and beyond her. She hated the very ponies that Alchise was leading up from water. It was the fourth day since her abduction. Rhoda could not understand why John and the Newmans were so slow to overtake her. She knew nothing as yet of the skill of her abductors. She was like an ignorant child placed in a new world whose very A B C was closed to her. After always having been cared for and protected, after never having known a hardship, the girl suddenly was thrust into an existence whose savage simplicity was sufficient to try the hardiest man.

THE FIRST LESSON

Supper was eaten in silence, Kut-le finally giving up his attempts to make conversation. It was dusk when they mounted and rode up the mountain. Near the crest a whirling cloud of mist enveloped them. It became desperately cold and Rhoda shivered beneath her Navajo but Kut-le gave no heed to her. He led on and on, the horses slipping, the cold growing every minute more intense. At last there appeared before them a dim figure silhouetted against a flickering light. Kut-le halted his party and rode forward; Rhoda saw the dim figure rise hastily and after a short time Kut-le called back.

"Come ahead!"

The little camp was only an open space at the cañon edge, with a sheepskin shelter over a tiny fire. Beside the fire stood a sheep-herder, a swarthy figure wrapped from head to foot in sheepskins. Over in the darkness by the mountain wall were the many nameless sounds that tell of animals herding for the night. The shepherd greeted them with the perfect courtesy of the Mexican.

"Señors, the camp is yours!"

Kut-le lifted the shivering Rhoda from her horse. The rain was lessening but the cold was still so great that Rhoda huddled gratefully by the little fire under the sheepskin shelter. Kut-le refused the Mexican's offer of tortillas and the man sat down to enjoy their society. He eyed Rhoda keenly.

"Ah! It is a señorita!" Then he gasped. 'It is perhaps the Señorita Rhoda Tuttle!"

Rhoda jumped to her feet.

"Yes! Yes! How did you know?"

Kut-le glared at the herder menacingly, but the little fellow did not see. He spoke up bravely, as if he had a message for Rhoda.

"Some people told me yesterday. They look for her everywhere!"

Rhoda's eyes lighted joyfully.

"Who? Where?" she cried.

Kut-le spoke concisely:

"You know nothing!" he said.

The Mexican looked into the Apache's eyes and shivered slightly.

"Nothing, of course, Señor," he replied.

But Rhoda was not daunted.

"Who were they?" she repeated. "What did they say? Where did they go?"

The herder glanced at Rhoda and shook his head.

"*Quién sabe?*"

Rhoda turned to Kut-le in anger.

"Don't be more brutal than you have to be!" she cried. "What harm can it do for this man to give me word of my friends?"

Kut-le's eyes softened.

THE FIRST LESSON

"Answer the señorita's questions, *amigo*," he said.

The Mexican began eagerly.

"There were three. They rode up the trail one day ago. They called the dark man Porter, the big blue-eyed one DeWitt, and the yellow-haired one Newman."

Rhoda clasped her hands with a little murmur of relief.

"The blue-eyed one acted as if locoed. They cursed much at a name, Kut-le. But otherwise they talked little. They went that way," pointing back over the trail. They had found a scarf with a stone tied in it—"

"What's that?" interrupted Kut-le sharply.

Rhoda's eyes shone in the firelight.

"'Not an overturned pebble escapes his eye,'" she said serenely.

"Bully for you!" exclaimed Kut-le, smiling at Rhoda in understanding. "However, I guess we will move on, having gleaned this interesting news!"

He remounted his little party. Rhoda reeled a little but she made no protest. As they took to the trail again the sheep-herder stood by the fire, watching, and Rhoda called to him:

"If you see them again tell them that I'm all right but that they must hurry!"

Rhoda felt new life in her veins after the meeting with the sheep-herder and finished the night's trail in better shape than she had done before. Yet not the next day nor for many days did they sight pursuers. With ingenuity that seemed diabolical, Kut-le laid his course. He seldom moved hurriedly. Indeed, except for the fact that the traveling was done by night, the expedition had every aspect of unlimited leisure.

As the days passed, Rhoda forced herself to the calm of desperation. Slowly she realized that she was in the hands of the masters of the art of flight, an art that the very cruelty of the country abetted. But to her utter astonishment her delirium of physical misery began to lift. Saddle stiffness after the first two weeks left her. Though Kut-le still fastened her to the saddle by the waist strap and rested her for a short time every hour or so during the night's ride, the hours in the saddle ceased to tax her strength. She was surprised to find that she could eat—eat the wretched cooking of the squaws!

At last she laid out a definite course for herself. Every night on the trail and at every camp she tried to leave some mark for the whites—a scratch on pebble or stone, a bit of marked yucca or a twisted cat's-claw. She ceased entirely to speak to Kut-le, treating him with a contemptuous silence that was torture to the Indian though he gave no outward sign.

Molly was her devoted friend and Rhoda derived great comfort from this faithful servitor. Rhoda sat in the camp one afternoon with the two squaws while

THE FIRST LESSON

Kut-le and Alchise were off on a turkey hunt. Some of the girl's pallor had given way to a delicate tan. The dark circles about her eyes had lightened a little. Molly was busily pounding grass-seeds between two stones. Rhoda watched her idly. Suddenly a new idea sent the blood to her thin cheeks.

Why shouldn't she learn to make seed meal, to catch and cook rabbits, to distinguish edible cactus from inedible? Then indeed she would be able to care for herself on the trail! To Rhoda, who never had worked with her hands, who indeed had come to look on manual labor as belonging to inferiors, the idea was revolutionary. For a long time she turned it over in her mind, watching Molly the while. The most violent housewifely task that Rhoda ever had undertaken had been the concocting of chafing-dish messes at school.

"Molly," she said suddenly, "teach me how to do that!"

Molly paused and grinned delightedly.

"All right! You come help poor Molly!"

With Cesca looking on sardonically, Molly poured fresh seeds on her rude metate and showed Rhoda the grinding roll that flattened and broke the little grains. Despite her weak fingers Rhoda took to the work easily. As she emptied out the first handful of meal, a curious sense of pleasure came to her. Squatting before the metate, she looked at the little pile of bruised seeds with the utmost satisfaction. Molly poured more seeds on the metate and Rhoda began again. She was hard at her task, her cheeks flushed with interest, when Kut-le returned. Rhoda did not see the sudden look of pleasure in his eyes.

"You will tire yourself," he said.

Rhoda did not answer, but poured another handful of seed on the metate.

"You'll begin to like the life," he went on, "by the time you are educated enough to leave us." He turned teasingly to Cesca. "You think the white squaw can cross the desert soon by herself?"

Cesca spat disdainfully.

"No! White squaw no good! All time sit, sit, no work! Kut-le heap fool!"

"Oh, Cesca," cried Rhoda, "I'm too sick to work! And see this meal I've made! Isn't it good?"

Cesca glanced disdainfully at the little heap of meal Rhoda had bruised out so painfully.

"Huh!" she grunted. "Feed 'em to the horses. Injuns no eat 'em!"

Rhoda looked from the meal to her slender, tired fingers. Cesca's contempt hurt her unaccountably. In her weakness her cleft chin quivered. She turned to Molly.

THE FIRST LESSON 111

"Do you think it's so bad, Molly?"

That faithful friend grunted with rage and aimed a vicious kick at Cesca. Then she put a protecting arm about Rhoda.

"It's heap fine! Cesca just old fool. You love Molly. Let Cesca go to hell!"

Kut-le had been watching the little scene with tender eyes. Now he stooped and lifted Rhoda to her feet, then he raised one of the delicate hands and touched it softly with his lips.

"Leave such work to the squaws, dear! You aren't built for it. Cesca, you old lobster, you make me tired! Go fix the turkeys!"

Cesca rose with dignity, flipped away her cigarette and walked with a sniff over to the cooking-pot. Rhoda drew her hands from the young Indian's clasp and walked to the edge of the camp. The hot pulse that the touch of Kut-le's lips sent through her body startled her.

"I hate him!" she said to herself. "I hate him! I hate him!"

The trail that night was unusually difficult and Rhoda had to be rested frequently. At each stop, Kut-le tried to talk to her but she maintained her silence. They paused at dawn in a pocket formed by the meeting of three divergent cañons. Far, far above the desert as they were, still farther above them stretched the wonderful barren ridges, snow-capped and silent. As Rhoda stood waiting for the squaws to spread her blankets the peaks were lighted suddenly by the rays of the still unseen sun. For one unspeakable instant their snow crowns flashed a translucent scarlet that trembled, shimmered, then melted to a pink, then to a white so pure, so piercing that Rhoda trembled with sudden awe. Then as she looked, the sun rolled into view, blinding her eyes, and she turned to her waiting blankets.

She had slept for several hours when she was wakened by a soft tap on her shoulder. She opened her eyes and would have risen but a voice whispered:

"Hush! Don't move!"

CHAPTER VIII

A BROADENING HORIZON

RHODA lay stiffly, her heart beating wildly. Kut-le and the squaws, each a muffled, blanketed figure, lay sleeping some distance away. Old Alchise stood on solitary guard at the edge of the camp with his back to her.

"Make as if you wanted to shift your blankets toward the cat's-claw bush behind you!" went on the whispered voice.

Obediently, Rhoda sat erect. Alchise turned slowly to light a cigarette out of the wind. Rhoda yawned, rose sleepily, looked under her blanket and shook her head irritably, then dragged her blankets toward the neighboring cat's-claw. Again she settled herself to sleep. Alchise turned back to his view of the desert.

"I'm behind the bush here," whispered the voice. "I'm a prospector. Saw you make camp. I don't know where any of the search parties are but if you can crawl round to me I'll guarantee to get you to 'em somehow. Slip out of your blankets and leave 'em rounded up as if you was still under 'em. Quick now and careful!"

Rhoda, her eyes never leaving Alchise's impassive back, drew herself silently and swiftly from her blankets and with a clever touch or two rounded them. Then she crept around the cat's-claw, where a man squatted, his eyes blazing with excitement. He put up a sinewy hand to pull her from sight when, without warning, Rhoda sneezed.

Instantly there was the click of a rifle and Alchise shouted:

"Stop!"

"Confound it!" growled the man, rising to full view, "why didn't you swallow it!"

"I couldn't!" replied Rhoda indignantly. "You don't suppose I wanted to!"

She turned toward the camp. Alchise was standing stolidly covering them with his rifle. Kut-le was walking coolly toward them, while the squaws sat gaping.

"Well!" exclaimed Kut-le. "What can we do for you, Jim?"

The stranger, a rough tramp-like fellow in tattered overalls, wiped his face, on which was a week's stubble.

"I'd always thought you was about white, Cartwell," he said, "but I see you're no better than the rest of them. What are you going to do with me?"

Kut-le eyed his unbidden guest speculatively.

"Well, we'll have something to eat first. I don't

A BROADENING HORIZON

like to think on an empty stomach. Come over to my blanket and sit down, Jim."

Ignoring Rhoda, who was watching him closely, Kut-le seated himself on his blanket beside Jim and offered him a cigarette, which was refused.

"I don't want no favors from you, Cartwell." His voice was surly. There was something more than his rough appearance that Rhoda disliked about the man but she didn't know just what it was. Kut-le's eyes narrowed, but he lighted his own cigarette without replying. "You're up to a rotten trick and you know it, Cartwell," went on Jim. "You take my advice and let me take the girl back to her friends and you make tracks down into Mexico as fast as the Lord'll let you."

Kut-le shifted the Navajo that hung over his naked shoulders. He gave a short laugh that Rhoda had never heard from him before.

"Let her go with you, Jim Provenso! You know as well as I do that she is safer with an Apache! Anything else?"

"Yes, this else!" Jim's voice rose angrily. "If ever we get a chance at you, we'll hang you sky high, see? This may go with Injuns but not with whites, you dirty pup!"

Suddenly Kut-le rose and, dropping his blanket, stood before the white man in his bronze perfection.

"Provenso, you aren't fit to look at a decent woman! Don't put on dog just because you belong to the white race. You're disreputable, and you know it. Don't speak to Miss Tuttle again; you are too rotten!"

The prospector had risen and stood glaring at Kut-le.

"I'll kill you for that yet, you dirty Injun!" he shouted.

"Shucks!" sniffed the Indian. "You haven't the nerve to injure anything but a woman!"

Jim's face went purple.

"For two bits I'd knock your block off, right now."

"There isn't a cent in the camp." Kut-le turned to Rhoda. "You get the point of the conversation, I hope?"

Rhoda's eyes were blazing. She had gotten the point, and yet—Jim was a white man! Anything white was better than an Indian.

"I'd take my chances with Mr. Provenso," she said, joyfully conscious that nothing could have hurt Kut-le more than this reply.

Kut-le's lips stiffened.

"Lunch is ready," he said.

"None of *your* grub for mine," remarked Jim. "What are you going to do with me?"

"Alchise!" called Kut-le. "Eat something, then take this fellow out and lose him. Take the rest of the day to it. You know the next camp!"

Then he folded his arms across his chest and waited

A BROADENING HORIZON

for Alchise to finish his meal. Jim stood in sullen silence for a minute. Then he seated himself on a nearby rock.

"No, you don't," he said. "If you get me out of here, you'll have to use force."

Kut-le shrugged his shoulders.

"A gun at your back will move you!"

Rhoda was looking at the white man's face with a great longing. He was rough and ugly, but he was of her own breed. Suddenly the longing for her own that she was beginning to control surged to her lips.

"I can't bear this!" she cried. "I'm going mad! I'm going mad!"

All the camp turned startled faces toward the girl, and Rhoda recovered her self-possession. She ran to Kut-le and laid her hand on his arm, lifting a lovely, pleading face to his.

"O Kut-le! Kut-le!" in the tone that she had used to Cartwell. "Can't you see that it's no use? He is white, Kut-le! Let me go with him! Let me go back to my own people! O Kut-le, let me go! O let me go!"

Kut-le looked down at the hand on his arm. Rhoda was too excited to notice that his whole body shook at this unwonted touch. His voice was caressing but his face remained inscrutable.

"Dear girl," he answered, "he is not your kind! He

might originally have been of your color, but now he's streaked with yellow. Let him go. You are safer here with me!"

Rhoda turned from him impatiently.

"It's quite useless," she said to Jim; "no pleading or threat will move him. But I do thank you—" her voice breaking a little. "Go back with Alchise and tell them to come for me quickly!"

Some responsive flash of sympathy came to Jim's bleared eyes.

Rhoda stood watching Alchise marshall him out of the camp. She moaned helplessly:

"O my people, my own people!" and Kut-le eyed her with unfathomable gaze.

As soon as lunch was finished, camp was broken. All the rest of the day and until toward midnight they wound up a wretched trail that circled the mountain ranges. For hours, Kut-le did not speak to Rhoda. These days of Rhoda's contempt were very hard on him. The touch of her hand that morning, the old note in her voice, still thrilled him. At midnight as they watched the squaws unroll her blankets, he touched her shoulder.

"Dear," he said, in his rich voice, "it is in you to love me if only I am patient. And—God, but it's worth all the starvation in the meantime! Won't you say good-night to me, Rhoda?"

A BROADENING HORIZON

Rhoda looked at the stalwart figure in the firelight. The young eyes so tragic in their youth, the beautiful mouth, sad in its firm curves, were strangely appealing. Just for an instant the horrors of the past weeks vanished.

"Good-night!" said Rhoda. Then she rolled herself in her blankets and slept. By the next morning, however, the old repulsion had returned and she made no response to Kut-le's overtures.

Day succeeded day now, until Rhoda lost all track of time. Endlessly they crossed desert and mountain ridges. Endlessly they circled through dusky cañon and sun-baked arroyo. Always Rhoda looked forward to each new camping-place with excitement. Here, the rescuers might stumble upon them! Always she started at each unexpected shadow along the trail. Always she thrilled at a wisp of smokelike cloud beyond the cañon edge. Always she felt a quiver of certainty at sudden break of twig or fall of stone. But the days passed and gradually hope changed to desperation.

The difficulties of the camp life would have been unbearable to her had not her natural fortitude and her intense pride come to her rescue. The estimate of her that Kut-le had so mercilessly presented to her the first day of her abduction returned to her more and more clearly as the days wore on. At first she thought of them only with scorn. Then as her loneliness increased and she was forced back upon herself she grew to wonder what in her had given the Indian such an opinion. There was something in the nakedness of the desert, something in its piercing austerity that forced her to truthfulness with herself. Little by little she found herself trying to acquire Kut-le's view of her.

Her liking for Molly grew. She spent long afternoons with the squaw, picking up desert lore.

"Do you like to work, Molly?" she asked the squaw one afternoon, as she sorted seed for Molly to bruise.

"What else to do?" asked Molly. "Sit with hands folded on stomach, so? No! Still hands make crazy head. Now you work with your hands you no so sorry in head, huh?"

Rhoda thought for a moment. There was a joy in the rude camp tasks that she had assumed that she never had found in golf or automobiling. She nodded, then said wistfully:

"You think I'm no good at all, don't you, Molly?"

Molly shrugged her shoulders.

"Me not got papooses. You not got papooses. Molly and you no good! Molly is heap strong. What good is that? When she die she no has given her strength to tribe, no done any good that will last. You are heap beautiful. What good is that? You no give your face to your tribe. What good are you? Molly and you might as well die tomorrow. Work, have papooses, die. That all squaws are for. Great Spirit says so. Squaw's own heart says so."

Rhoda sat silently looking at the squaw's squat figure, the toil-scarred fingers, the good brown eyes out of which looked a woman's soul. Vaguely Rhoda caught a point of view that made her old ideals seem futile. She smoothed the Indian woman's hands.

"I sometimes think you are a bigger woman than I am, Molly," she said humbly.

"You are heap good to look at." Molly spoke wistfully. "Molly heap homely. You think that makes any difference to the Great Spirit?"

Rhoda's eyes widened a little. Did it make any difference? After all, what counted with the Great Spirit? She stared at the barren ranges that lifted mute peaks to the silent heavens. Always, always the questions and so vague the answers! Suddenly Rhoda knew that her beauty had counted greatly with her all her life, had given her her sense of superiority to the rest of the world. Rhoda squirmed. She hated this faculty of the Indians and the desert to make her seem small. She never had felt so with her own kind. Her own kind! Would she never again know the deference, the gentleness, the loving tenderness of her own people? Rhoda forgot Molly's wistful question.

"O Molly!" she cried. "I can't stand this! I want my own people! I want my own people!"

Molly's eyes filled with tears.

"No! No cry, little Sun-streak!" she pleaded, putting an arm around Rhoda and holding her to her tenderly. "Any peoples that loves you is your own peoples. Kut-le loves you. Molly loves you. We your peoples too!"

"No! No! Never!" sobbed Rhoda. "Molly, if you love me, take me back to my own kind! You shall never leave me, Molly! I do love you. You are an Indian but somehow I have a feeling for you I never had for any one else."

A sudden light of passionate adoration burned in Molly's eyes, a light that never was to leave them again when they gazed on Rhoda. But she shook her head.

"You ask Molly to give up her peoples but you don't want to give up yours. You stay with Molly and Kut-le. Learn what desert say 'bout life, 'bout people. When you *sabe* what the desert say 'bout that you *sabe* almost much as Great Spirit!"

Molly, listen! When Kut-le and Alchise go off on one of their hunts and Cesca goes to sleep, you and I will steal off and hide until night, and you will show me how to get home again. O Molly, I'll be very good to you if you will do this for me! Don't you see how foolish

A BROADENING HORIZON 123

Kut-le is? I can never, never marry him! His ways are not my ways. My ways are not his! Always I will be white and he Indian. He will get over this craze for me and want one of his own kind. Molly, listen to your heart! It must tell you white to the white, Indian to the Indian. Dear, dear Molly, I want to go home!"

"No! No! Molly promise Kut-le to keep his white squaw for him. Injuns they always keep promises. And Molly *sabe* some day when you learn more you be heap glad old Molly keep you for Kut-le."

Rhoda turned away with a sigh at the note of finality in Molly's voice. Kut-le was climbing the trail toward the camp with a little pile of provisions. So far he had not failed to procure when needed some sort of rations—bacon, flour and coffee—though since her abduction Rhoda had seen no human habitation. Cesca was preparing supper. She was pounding a piece of meat on a flat stone, muttering to herself when a piece fell to the ground. Sometimes she wiped the sand from the fallen bit on her skirt. More often she flung it into the stew-pot unwiped.

"Cesca!" cried Rhoda, "do keep the burro out of the meat!" The burro that Kut-le recently had acquired was sniffing at the meat.

Cesca gave no heed except to murmur, "Burro heap hungry!"

"I am going to begin to cook my own meals, Molly,"

said Rhoda. "I am strong enough now, and Cesca is so dirty!"

Kut-le entered the camp in time to hear Rhoda's resolution.

"Will you let me eat with you?" he asked courteously. "I don't enjoy dirt, myself!"

Rhoda stared at the young man. The calm effrontery of him, the cleverness of him, to ask a favor of her! She turned from him to the distant ranges. She did not realize how much she turned from the roughness of the camp to the far desert views! Brooding, aloof, how big the ranges were, how free, how calm! For the first time her keeping Kut-le in Coventry seemed foolish to her. Of what avail was her silence, except to increase her own loneliness? Suddenly she smiled grimly. The game was a good one. Perhaps she could play it as well as the Indian.

"If you wish, you may," she said coldly.

Then she ignored the utter joy and astonishment in the young man's face and set about roasting the rabbit that Molly had dressed. She tossed the tortillas as Molly had taught her and baked them over the coals. She set forth the cans and baskets that formed the camp dinner-set and served the primitive meal. Kut-le watched the preparations silently. When the rabbit was cooked the two sat down on either side of the flat rock that served as a table while the other three squatted about Cesca's stewpot near the fire.

It was the first time that Rhoda and Kut-le had eaten tête-à-tête. Hitherto Rhoda had taken her food off to a secluded corner and eaten it alone. There was an intimacy in thus sitting together at the meal Rhoda had prepared, that both felt.

"Are you glad you did this for me, Rhoda?" asked Kut-le.

"I didn't do it for you!" returned Rhoda. "I did it for my own comfort!"

Something in her tone narrowed the Indian's eyes.

"Why should you speak as a queen to a poor devil of a subject? By what particular mark of superiority are you exempt from work? For a time you have had the excuse of illness, but you no longer have that. I should say that making tortillas was better than sitting in sloth while they are made for you! Do you never have any sense of shame that you are forever taking and never giving?"

Rhoda answered angrily.

"I'm not at all interested in your opinions."

But the young Apache went on.

"It makes me tired to hear the white women of your class talk of their equality to men! You don't do a thing to make you equal. You live off some one else. You don't even produce children. Huh! No wonder nature kicks you out with all manner of illness. You are mere cloggers of the machinery. For heaven's sake, wake up, Rhoda! Except for your latent possibilities, you aren't in it with Molly!"

"You have some touchstone, I suppose," replied Rhoda contemptuously, "by which you are made competent to sit in judgment on mankind?"

"I sure have!" said Kut-le. "It is that you so live that you die spiritually richer than you were born. Life is a simple thing, after all. To keep one's body and soul healthy, to bear children, to give more than we take. And I believe that in the end it will seem to have been worth while."

Rhoda made no answer. Kut-le ate on in silence for a time, then he said wistfully:

"Don't you enjoy this meal with me, just a little?"

Rhoda glanced from Kut-le's naked body to her own torn clothing, then at the crude meal.

"I don't enjoy it, no," she answered quietly.

Something in the quiet sincerity of the voice caused Kut-le to rise abruptly and order the Indians to break camp. But on the trail that night he rode close beside her whenever the way permitted and talked to her of the beauty of the desert. At last, lashed to desperation by her indifference, he cried:

A BROADENING HORIZON

"Can't you see that your silence leads to nothing—that it maddens me!"

"That is what I want it to do," returned Rhoda calmly. "I shall be so glad if I can make you suffer a touch of what I am enduring!"

Kut-le did not reply for a moment, then he began slowly:

"You imagine that I am not suffering? Try to put yourself in my place for a moment! Can't you see how I love you? Can't you see that my stealing was the only thing that I could do, loving you so? Wouldn't you have done the same in my place? If I had been a white man I wouldn't have been driven to this. I would have had an equal chance with DeWitt and could have won easily. But I had all the prejudice against my alien race to fight. There was but one thing to do: to take you to the naked desert where you would be forced to see life as I see it, where you would be forced to see me, the man, far from any false standards of civilization."

Rhoda would have replied but Kut-le gave her no chance.

"I know what white conventions demand of me. But, I tell you, my love is above them. I, not suffer! Rhoda! To see you in pain! To see your loathing of me! To have you helpless in my arms and yet to keep you safe! Rhoda! Rhoda! Do you believe I do not suffer?"

Anger died out of Rhoda. She saw tragedy in the

situation, tragedy that was not hers. She saw herself and Kut-le racially, not individually. She saw Kut-le suffering all the helpless grief of race alienation, saw him the victim of passions as great as the desires of the alien races for the white always must be. Rhoda forgot herself. She laid a slender hand on Kut-le's.

"I am sorry," she said softly. "I think I begin to understand. But, Kut-le, it can never, never be! You are fighting a battle that was lost when the white and Indian races were created. It can never, never be, Kut-le."

The strong brown hand had closed over the small white one instantly.

"It must be!" he said hoarsely. "I put my whole life on it! It must be!"

Rhoda pulled her hand away gently.

"It never, never can be!"

"It shall be! Love like this comes but seldom to a human. It is the most potent thing in the world. It shall—"

"Kut-le!" Alchise rode forward, pointing to the right.

Rhoda followed his look. It was nearly dawn. At the right was the sheer wall of a mesa as smooth and impregnable to her eyes as a wall of glass. Moving toward them, silent as ghosts in the veil-like dawn, and cutting them from the mesa, was a group of horsemen.

CHAPTER IX

TOUCH AND GO

THE John DeWitt who helped break camp after finding Rhoda's scarf was a different man from the half-crazed person of the three days previous. He had begun to hope. Somehow that white scarf with Rhoda's perfume clinging to it was a living thing to him, a living, pulsing promise that Rhoda was helping him to find her. Now, while Jack and Billy were feverishly eager, he was cool and clear-headed, leaving the leadership to Billy still, yet doing more than his share of the work in preparing for the hard night ahead of them. The horses were well watered, their own canteens were filled and saturated and food so prepared that it could be eaten from the saddle.

"For," said Porter, "when we do hit the little girl's trail, starvation or thirst or high hell ain't goin' to stop us!"

It was mid-afternoon when they started down the mountainside. There was no trail and going was painful but the men moved with the care of desperation.

Once in the cañon they moved slowly along the wall and some two miles from where the scarf had been found, they discovered a fault where climbing was possible. It was nearing sundown when they reached a wide ledge where the way was easy. Porter led the way back over this to the spot below which fluttered a white paper to mark the place where the scarf had been found. The ledge deepened here to make room for a tiny, bubbling spring. Giant boulders were scattered across the rocky floor.

The three men dismounted. The ledge gave no trace of human occupancy and yet Porter and Jack nodded at each other.

"Here was his camp, all right. Water, and no one could come within a mile of him without his being seen."

"He's still covering his traces carefully," said Jack.

"Not so very," answered Porter. "He's banking a whole lot on our stupidity, but Miss Tuttle beat him to it with her scarf."

The three men treated the ledge to a microscopic examination but they found no trace of previous occupation until Billy knelt and put his nose against a black outcropping of stone in the wall. Then he gave a satisfied grunt.

"Come here, Jack, and take a sniff."

Jack knelt obediently and cried excitedly:

"It smells of smoke, by Jove! Don't it John, old scout!"

"They knew smoke wouldn't show against a black outcrop, but they didn't bank on my nose!" said Billy complacently. "Come ahead, boys."

A short distance from the spring they found a trail which led back up the mountain, and as dusk came on they followed its dizzy turns until darkness forced them to halt and wait until the moon rose. By its light they moved up into a piñon forest.

"Let's wait here until daylight," suggested Jack. "It's a good place for a camp."

"No, it's too near the ledge," objected Billy. "Of course we are working on faith mostly. I'm no Sherlock Holmes. We'll keep to the backbone of this range for a while. It's the wildest spot in New Mexico. Kut-le will avoid the railroad over by the next range."

So Billy led his little band steadfastly southward. At dawn they met a Mexican shepherd herding his sheep in a grassy cañon. Jack Newman called to him eagerly and the Mexican as eagerly answered. A visitor was worth a month's pay to the lonely fellow. The red of dawn was painting the fleecy backs of his charges as the tired Americans rode into his little camp.

"Seen anything of an Injun running away with a white girl?" asked Billy without preliminaries.

The Mexican's jaw dropped.

"*Sacra Maria!*" he gasped. "Not I! Who is she?"

"Listen!" broke in Jack. "You be on the watch. An educated Indian has stolen a young lady who was visiting my wife. I own the Newman ranch. That Indian Cartwell it was, three days ago."

John DeWitt interrupted.

"If you can catch that Indian, if you can give us a clue to him, you needn't herd sheep any more. Lord, man, speak up! Don't stand there like a chump!"

"But, señors!" stammered the poor fellow to whom this sudden torrent of conversation was as overwhelming as a cloudburst. "But I have not seen—"

Billy Porter spoke again.

"Hold up, boys! We are scaring the poor devil to death. Friend pastor," he said, "we'll have breakfast here with you, if you don't object, and tell you our troubles."

The shepherd glowed with hospitality.

"Yonder is good water and I have tortillas and frijoles."

Unshaven and dirty, gaunt from lack of sleep, the three men dismounted wearily and gladly turned their coffee and bacon over to the herder to whom the mere odor of either was worth any amount of service. As they ate, Jack and Billy quizzed the Mexican as to the topography of the surrounding country. The little herder was a canny chap.

"He will not try to cover his trail carefully now," he said, swallowing huge slabs of bacon. "He has a good start. You will have to fool him. He sleeps by day and travels by night, you will see. You are working too hard and your horses will be dead. You should have slept last night. Now you will lose today because you must rest your horses."

Porter looked at his two companions. Jack was doing fairly well, but the calm that DeWitt had found with Rhoda's scarf had deserted him. He was eating scarcely anything and stared impatiently at the fire, waiting for the start.

"I'm a blamed double-action jackass, with a peanut for a mind!" exclaimed Porter. "Taking on myself to lead this hunt when I don't *sabe* frijoles! We take a sleep now."

DeWitt jumped to his feet, expostulating, but Jack and Billy laid a hand on either of his shoulders and forced him to lie down on his blanket. There nature claimed her own and in a short time the poor fellow was in the slumber of exhaustion.

"Poor old chap!" said Jack as he spread his own blanket. "I can't help thinking all the time 'What if it were Katherine!' Dear old Rhoda! Why, Billy, we used to play together as kids! She's slapped my face many a time!"

"Probably you deserved it!" answered Billy in an uncertain voice. "By the limping piper! I'm glad I ain't her financier. I'm most crazy, as it is!"

The sheep herder woke the sleepers at noon. After a bath at the spring, and dinner, the trio felt as if reborn. They left the herder with minute directions as to what he was to do in case he heard of Rhoda. Then they rode out of the cañon into the burning desert.

And now for several days they lost all clues. They beat up and down the ranges like tired hunting-dogs, all their efforts fruitless. Little by little, panic and excitement left them. Even DeWitt realized that the hunt was to be a long and serious one as Porter told of the fearful chases the Apaches had led the whites, time and again. He began to realize that to keep alive in the terrible region through which the hunt was set he must help the others to conserve their own and his energies. To this end they ate and slept as regularly as they could.

Occasionally they met other parties of searchers, but this was only when they beat to the eastward toward the ranch, for most of the searchers were now convinced that Kut-le had made toward Mexico and they were patrolling the border. But Billy insisted that Kut-le was making for some eerie that he knew and would ensconce himself there for months, if need be, till the search was given up. Then and then only would he make for Mexico. And John DeWitt and Jack had come to agree with Billy.

"He'll keep her up in some haunt of his," said Jack, again and again, "until he's worn her into consenting to marry him. And before that happens, if I know old Rhoda, we'll find them."

"He's mine when we do find him, remember that," John DeWitt always said through his teeth at this point in the discussion.

It was on the twelfth day of the hunt that the sheep-herder found them. They were cinching up the packs after the noon rest when he rode up on a burro. He was dust-coated and both he and the burro were panting.

"I've seen her! I've seen the señorita!" he shouted as he clambered stiffly from the burro.

The three Americans stood rigid.

"Where? How? When?" came from three heat-cracked mouths.

The Mexican started to answer, but his throat was raw with alkali dust and his voice was scarcely audible. DeWitt impatiently thrust a canteen into the little fellow's hands.

"Hurry, for heaven's sake!" he urged.

The Mexican took a deep draught.

"The night after you left I moved up into the peaks, intending to cross the range to lower pastures next day.

A big storm came up and I made camp. Then an Indian in a blanket rode up to me and asked me if I was alone. I *sabed* him at once. 'But yes, señor,' I answered, 'except for the sheep!'"

"But Miss Tuttle! The señorita!" shouted DeWitt.

The Mexican glanced at the tired blue eyes, the strained face, pityingly.

"She was well," he answered. "Be patient, señor. Then there rode up another Indian, two squaws and what looked to be a young boy. The Indian lifted the boy from the saddle so tenderly, señors. And it was your señorita! She did not look strong, yet I think the Indian is taking good care of her. They sat by the fire till the storm was over. The señorita ignored Kut-le as if he had been a dog."

Porter clinched his teeth at this, while Jack murmured with a gleam of savage satisfaction in his eyes, "Old Rhoda!" But DeWitt only gnawed his lip, with his blue eyes on the Mexican.

"The Indian said I was to say nothing, but the señorita made him let me tell about you after I said I had seen you. She—she cried with happiness. They rode away in a little while but I followed as long as I dared to leave my sheep. They were going north. I think they were in the railroad range the night you were with me, then doubled back. I left my sheep the next day with the salt-boy who came up. I tramped twenty miles to the rancho and got a burro and left word about the señorita. Then I started on your trail. Everyone I met I told. I thought that my news was not worth much except that the señor there would be glad to know that the Indian is tender to his señorita."

DeWitt turned to Porter and Newman.

"Friends, perhaps she is being taken care of!" he said. "Perhaps that devil is trying to keep her health, at least. God! If nothing worse has befallen her!"

He stopped and drew his wrist across his forehead. Something like tears shone in Jack's eyes, and Porter coughed. John turned to the Mexican and grasped the little fellow's hand.

"My boy," he said, "you'll never regret this day's work. If you have a señorita you know what you have done for me!"

The Mexican looked up into DeWitt's face seriously.

"I have one. She has a dimple in her chin."

John turned abruptly and stood staring into the desert while tears seared his eyes. Billy hastily unpacked and gave Carlos and his burro the best that the outfit afforded.

"Can the salt-boy stay on with the sheep while you come with us?" asked John DeWitt. "I'll pay your boss for the whole flock if anything goes wrong." He wanted the keen wit of the herder on the hunt.

The Mexican nodded eagerly.

"I'll stay!"

Shortly the four were riding northward across the desert. They were in fairly good shape for a hard ride. Two days before, they had stopped at Squaw Spring ranch and re-outfitted. With proper care of the horses they were good for three weeks away from supplies. And for two weeks now they scoured the desert, meeting scarcely a human, finding none of the traces that Rhoda was so painfully dropping along her course. The hugeness, the cruelty of the region drove the hopelessness of their mission more and more deeply into DeWitt's brain. It seemed impossible except by the merest chance to find trace of another human in a waste so vast. It seemed to him that it was not skill but the gambler's instinct for luck that guided Carlos and Billy.

They rode through open desert country one afternoon, the only mountains discernible being a far purple haze along the horizon. For hours the little cavalcade had moved without speech. Then to the north, Porter discerned a dot moving toward them. Gradually under their eager eyes the dot grew into a man who staggered as he walked. When he observed the horsemen coming toward him he sat down and waited.

"Jim Provenso! By the limping Piper!" cried Billy. "Thought you was in Silver City."

Jim was beyond useless speech. He caught the canteen which Jack swung to him and drank deeply. Then he said hoarsely:

"I almost got away with the Tuttle girl last week!"

Every man left his saddle as if at a word of command. Jim took another drink.

"If I catch that Injun alone I'll cut his throat!"

"Was Miss Tuttle bad off?" gasped Porter.

"She? Naw; she looked fine. He sassed me, though, as I won't take it from any man!"

"Tell us what happened, for heaven's sake," cried DeWitt, eying Provenso disgustedly.

Jim told his story in detail.

"That Injun Alkus," he ended, "he tied a rag over my eyes, tied my hands up and, say, he lost me for fair! He took all day to it. At night he tied me up to a tree and I stood there all night before I got my hands loose. I was sure lost, now, I can tell you! I struck a cowman up on the range the next night. He give me some grub and a canteen and I made out pretty good till yesterday, working south all the time. Then I got crazy with thirst and threw my canteen away. Found a spring last night again, but I'm about all in."

"How did Miss Tuttle seem?" asked John with curious quietness. It seemed to him the strangest thing of all that first the Mexican, then this coarse, tramp-like fellow, should have talked to Rhoda while he could only wander wildly through the Hades of the desert without a trace of her camp to solace him.

"Say, she was looking good! She thanked me and told me to tell you all to hurry."

They gave to Provenso a burro whose pack was nearly empty, what food and water they could spare, and he left them. They started on dejectedly. Provenso had told them where Kut-le had camped ten days before. They could only find that spot and attempt to pick up the trail from there.

"Just the same," said Billy, "it's just as well he didn't get away with Miss Rhoda. He's a tough pill, that Provenso. She'd better be with the Injun than him!"

"Provenso must be a bad lot," said Jack.

"He is!" replied Billy grimly.

The camp was made that night near a smooth-faced mesa. Before dawn they had eaten breakfast and were mounting, when Carlos gave a low whistle. Every ear was strained. On the exquisite stillness of the dawn sounded a woman's voice which a man's voice answered.

CHAPTER X

A LONG TRAIL

RHODA gave a cry of joy. From the horsemen rose a sudden shout.

"Spread! Spread! There they are!"

"Don't shoot!" It was Porter's voice, shrill and high with excitement. "That's her, the boy there! Rhoda! Rhoda! We're coming!"

With a quick responsive cry, Rhoda struck her horse. With the blow, Kut-le leaned from his own horse and seized her bridle, turning her horse with his own away from the mesa and to the left. The other Indians followed and with hoarse cries of exultation the rescuers took up the pursuit.

Rhoda looked back.

"Shoot!" she screamed. "Shoot!"

Before the second scream had left her lips she was lifted bodily from the saddle to Kut-le's arms where, understanding his device, she struggled like a mad woman. But she only wasted her strength. Without a glance at her, Kut-le turned his pony almost in its tracks and made for the mesa.

"Cut him off! He'll get away from us!" It was

DeWitt's voice, and "John! John DeWitt!" Rhoda cried.

But the young Indian had gaged his distance well. He brought his horse to its haunches and with Rhoda in his arms was running into a fissure seemingly too narrow for human to enter, while the pursuers were still a hundred yards away.

"Hold 'em, Alchise!" he said briefly as he ran.

Alchise, with rifle cocked, stopped by the opening. The fissure widened immediately into a narrow passageway. High, high above them rolled a strip of pink and blue morning sky. Before them was a seemingly interminable crevice along which the squaws scuttled. As Rhoda watched them they disappeared around a sudden curve. When Kut-le reached this point with his burden, the squaws were climbing like monkeys up the wall which here gave back, roughly, ending the fissure in a rude chimney which it seemed to Rhoda only a bear or an Apache could have climbed. Kut-le set Rhoda on her feet. She looked up into his face mockingly. To her mind she was as good as rescued. But the young Apache seemed in no wise hurried or excited.

"Our old friends seem to want something!" he commented with his boyish grin.

"What are you going to do now?" asked Rhoda, with calm equal to the Apache's.

A LONG TRAIL

"I can't carry you up this wall," suggested Kut-le.

"Very well!" returned Rhoda pleasantly. "I am quite willing that you should leave me here."

Kut-le's eyes glittered.

"Rhoda, you must climb this wall with me!"

"I won't!" replied Rhoda laconically.

"Then I shall force you to," said the Indian, shifting his rifle and prodding Rhoda ever so gently with the barrel.

Rhoda gave Kut-le a look of scorn that he was not soon to forget and slowly mounted the first broken ledge. The wall was composed of a series of jutting rocks and of ledges that barely offered hand or foot hold. Up and up and up! Kut-le was now beside her, now above her, now lifting, now pulling. Half-way to the top, Rhoda stopped, dizzy and afraid. Kneeling on the ledge above, with one hand thrust down to lift her, Kut-le looked into her eyes almost pleadingly. That handsome face so close to hers affected Rhoda strangely.

"Don't be afraid," whispered Kut-le. "Nothing can happen to you while I am taking care of you."

Rhoda looked into his eyes proudly.

"I am not afraid," she said, reaching for a fresh handhold with trembling fingers.

The jutting rocks were sharp. Kut-le from his ledge saw Rhoda look at her hold then turn white. Her nails were torn to the quick and bleeding. She swayed with only an atom of gravity lacking to send her to death below. Instantly Kut-le was back beside her, his sinewy hand between her shoulders, supporting and lifting her to the ledge above. As they neared the top the broken surface became prickly with cactus and Rhoda winced with misery as the thorns pierced and tore her flesh. But finally, in what actually had been an incredibly short time, they emerged on the plateau, where the two squaws huddled high above the pursuers.

"They think they have you now!" said Kut-le, as Rhoda dropped panting to the ground. "We must move out of here before they investigate the mesa top."

He allowed, however, a few minutes' breathing spell for Rhoda. She sat quietly, though her gray eyes were brilliant with excitement. It seemed to her but a matter of a few hours now when she would be with her own. Yet she could not but notice with that curious observance of detail which comes at moments of intensest excitement the varied colors of the distances that opened before her. The great mesa on which she sat was a mighty peninsula of chalcedony that stretched into the desert. It was patched by rocks of lavender, of yellow, and of green, and belled over by the intensity of the morning blue above.

"Come!" said Kut-le. "There will be little rest for us today."

A LONG TRAIL

Rhoda rose, took a few staggering steps, then sat down.

"I can't start yet," she said. "I'm too worn out."

Kut-le's expression was amused while it was impatient.

"I suppose you may be sleepy, but I think you can walk a little way. Hurry, Rhoda! Hurry!"

Rhoda sat staring calmly into the palpitating blue above.

"I hate to have you carry me," she said after a moment, "but I don't feel at all like walking!"

Her tired face was irresistibly lovely as she looked up at the Apache, but by an effort he remained obdurate.

"You must walk as long as you can," he insisted. "We have got to hustle today!"

"I really don't feel like hustling!" sighed Rhoda.

"Rhoda!" cried Kut-le impatiently, "get up and walk after me! Cesca, see that the white squaw keeps moving!" and he handed his rifle to the brown hag who took it with evident pleasure. Molly ran forward as if to protest but at a look from Kut-le she dropped back.

Rhoda rose slowly, with her lower lip caught between her teeth. She followed silently after Kut-le, Cesca and the rifle at her shoulder and Molly in the rear. It seemed to the girl that of all the strange scenes through which the past weeks had carried her this was of all the most unreal. All about her was a world of vivid rock heaps so intensely colored that she doubted her vision.

Away to the south lay the boundless floor of the desert, a purple and gold infinity that rolled into the horizon. Far to the north mountains were faintly blue in the yellow sunlight.

Kut-le headed straight for the mountains. His pace was swift and unrelenting. Almost immediately Rhoda felt the debilitating effects of overheat. The sun, now sailing high, burned through her flannel shirt until her flesh was blistered beneath it. The light on the brilliantly colored rocks made her eyes blink with pain. Before long she was parched with thirst and faint with hunger. This was her first experience in tramping for any distance under the desert sun. But Kut-le kept the pace long after the two squaws were half leading, half carrying the girl.

Rhoda had long since learned the uselessness of protesting. She kept on until the way danced in reeling colors before her eyes. Then without a sound she dropped in the scant shadow of a rock. At the cry from Molly, Kut-le turned, and after one glance at Rhoda's white face and limp figure he knelt in the sand and lifted the drooping, yellow head. Molly unslung her canteen and forced a few drops of water between Rhoda's lips. Then she tenderly chafed the small hands and the delicate throat and Rhoda opened her eyes. Immediately Kut-le lifted her in his arms and the flight was resumed.

A LONG TRAIL

At short intervals during the morning, Rhoda walked, but for the most part Kut-le packed her as dispassionately as if she had been a lame puppy. He held her across his broad chest as if her fragile weight were nothing. Lying so, Rhoda watched the merciless landscape or the brown squaws jogging at Kut-le's heels. Surely, she thought, the ancient mesa never had seen a stranger procession or known of a wilder mission. She looked up into Kut-le's face and wondered as she stared at his bare head how his eyes could look so steadily into the sun-drenched landscape.

As she lay, the elation of the early morning left her. More and more surely the conviction came to her that the Apache's boast was true; that no white could catch him on his own ground. Dizzy and ill from the heat, she closed her eyes and lay without hope or coherent thought.

At noon they stopped for a short time that Rhoda might eat. Their resting-place was in the shadow of a beetling, weather-beaten rock that still bore traces of hieroglyphic carvings. There were broken bits of clay pots among the tufts of cactus. Rhoda stared at them languidly and wondered what the forgotten vessels could have contained in a region so barren of life or hope.

Kut-le strolled over to a cat's-claw bush at whose base lay a tangle of dead leaves. With a bit of stick, he scattered this litter, struck the ground several good blows and returned with a string of fat desert mice. With infinite care Cesca kindled a fire so tiny, so clear, that scarcely a wisp of smoke escaped into the quivering air. Into this she flung the eviscerated mice and in an instant the tiny things were a delicate brown. The aroma was pleasant but Rhoda turned whiter still when Molly brought her the fattest of the mice.

"Take it away!" she whispered. "Take it away!"

Molly looked at the girl in stupid surprise.

"You must eat, Rhoda girl!" said Kut-le.

Rhoda made no reply but leaned limply against the ancient rock, her golden hair touching the crude drawings of long ago. She was a very different Rhoda from the eager girl of the early morning. She ignored every effort Kut-le made to tempt her to eat. Her tired gaze wandered to her hands, still blood-grimed, and her cleft chin quivered. Kut-le saw the expressive little look.

"I'm sorry," he said simply.

Rhoda looked up at him.

"I don't believe you," she returned calmly.

The Indian's jaw stiffened.

"Come, we'll start now."

The afternoon was like the morning, except that the sun was more burning overhead, the way more scorching underfoot; except that the course became more broken, the clambering heavier, the drops more wracking. All the afternoon, Kut-le carried Rhoda. At last the sun sank below the mesa and the day was ended.

The place of their camping seemed to Rhoda damp and cold. It was close beside a spring that gave out a faint, miasmic odor. The bitter water was grateful, however. Again more mice were seered over before the fire was stamped out hastily. This time Rhoda forced herself to eat. Then she drank deeply of the bitter water and lay down on the cold ground. Despite the fact that she was shivering with the cold, she fell asleep at once. Toward midnight she awoke and moving close to Molly's broad back for warmth, she looked up into the sky. For the first time the great southern stars seemed near and kindly to her and before she fell asleep again she wondered why.

At earliest peep of dawn the squaws were astir waiting for Kut-le, who shortly staggered into camp with a load of meat on his shoulder. Alchise was with him.

"Mule meat!" said Kut-le to Rhoda. "I went to find horses but there was nothing but an old lame mule. I brought him back this way!"

"Heavens!" ejaculated Rhoda.

The squaws worked busily, cutting the meat into strips which they hung over their shoulders to sun dry during the day. Alchise cleansed a length of mule's intestine in the spring, to serve as a canteen. Rhoda gave small heed to these preparations. She was too ill and feverish even to be disgusted by them. She refused to eat but drank constantly from the spring. When at Kut-le's command she took up the march with the others the young man eyed her anxiously. He slung Molly's canteen from his own to Alchise's shoulder and felt Rhoda's pulse.

"This water was bad for you," he said. "But it was the only spring within miles. Perhaps you will throw off the effects of it when we get into the heat of the sun."

Rhoda made no reply but staggered miserably after Molly. The spring lay in a pocket between mountains and mesa. The mountains seemed cruelly high to Rhoda as she looked at them and thought of toiling across them. With head sunk on her breast and feverishly twitching hands she followed for half an hour. Then Kut-le turned.

"I'm going to carry you, Rhoda," he said.

The girl shrank away from him.

"You and Molly and all of them think I'm just a parasite," she muttered. "You don't have to do anything for me! Just let me drop anywhere and die!"

Kut-le looked at her strangely. Without comment, he picked her up. There was a sternly tender look on his face that never had been there before. He did not carry her dispassionately today, but very gently. Something in his manner pierced through Rhoda's half delirium and she looked up at him with a faint replica of her old lovely smile that Kut-le had not seen since he had stolen her. He trembled at its beauty and started forward at a tremendous pace.

"I'll get you to good water by noon," he said.

At noon they were well up in the mountains by a clear spring fringed with aspens. Watercress grew below it, and high above it were pines and junipers. It was a spot of surpassing loveliness, but Rhoda, tossing and panting, could not know it. Kut-le laid his burden on the ground and Molly drew off her tattered petticoat to lay beneath the feverish head. The young Apache stood looking down at the little figure, so graceful in its boyish abandonment of gesture, so pitiful in its broken unconsciousness. Molly bathed the burning face and hands in the pure cold water, muttering tender Apache phrases. Kut-le constantly interrupted her to change the girl's position. For an hour or so he waited for the fever to turn. By three o'clock there was no change for the better and he left Rhoda's side to pace back and forth by the spring in anxious thought.

At last he came to a conclusion and with stern set face he issued a few short orders to his companions. The canteens were refilled. Kut-le lifted Rhoda and the trail was taken to the west. Alchise would have relieved him of his burden, willingly, but Kut-le would not listen to it.

Molly trotted anxiously by the young Apache's side, constantly moistening the girl's lips with water.

Rhoda was quite delirious now. She murmured and sometimes sobbed, trying to free herself from Kut-le's arms.

"I'm not sick!" she said, looking up into the Indian's face with unseeing eyes. "Don't let him see that I am sick!"

"No! No! Dear one!" answered Kut-le.

"Don't let him see I'm sick!" she sobbed. "He hurts me so!"

"No! No!" exclaimed Kut-le huskily. "Molly, give her a little more water!"

"Molly!" panted Rhoda, "you tell him how hard I worked—how I earned my way a little! And don't let him do anything for me!"

CHAPTER XI

THE TURN IN THE TRAIL

THE little group, trudging the long difficult trail along the mountain was a rich study in degrees: Rhoda, the fragile Caucasian, a product of centuries of civilization; and Kut-le, the Indian, with the keenness, the ferocious courage, the cunning of the Indian leavened inextricably with the thousand softening influences of a score of years' contact with civilization; then Cesca, the lean and stoical product of an ancient and terrible savagery; and Alchise, her mate. Finally Molly—squat, dirty Molly—the stupid, squalid aborigine, as distinct from Cesca's type as is the brown snail from the stinging wasp.

Alchise, striding after his chief, was smitten with a sudden idea. After ruminating on it for some time, he communicated it to his squaw. Cesca shook her head with a grunt of disapproval. Alchise insisted and the squaw looked at Kut-le cunningly.

"*Quién sabe?*" she said at last.

At this Alchise hurried forward and touched Kut-le on the shoulder.

"Take 'em squaw to Reservation. Medicine dance. Squaw heap sick. *Sabe?*"

"Reservation's too far away," replied Kut-le, shifting Rhoda's head to lie more easily on his arm. "I'm making for Chira."

Alchise shook his head vigorously.

"Too many mens! We go Reservation. Alchise help carry sick squaw."

"Nope! You're way off, Alchise. I'm going where I can get some white man's medicine the quickest. I'm not so afraid of getting caught as I am of her getting a bad run of fever. I have friends at Chira."

Alchise fell back, muttering disappointment. White man's medicine was no good. He cared little about Rhoda but he adored Kut-le. It was necessary therefore that the white squaw be saved, since his chief evidently was quite mad about her. All the rest of the day Alchise was very thoughtful. Late at night the next halt was made. High up in the mountain on a sheltered ledge Kut-le laid down his burden.

"Keep her quiet till I get back," he said, and disappeared.

Rhoda was in a stupor and lay quietly unconscious with the stars blinking down on her, a limp dark heap against the mountain wall. The three Indians munched mule meat, then Molly curled herself on the ground and in three minutes was snoring. Alchise stood erect and still on the ledge for perhaps ten minutes after Kut-le's

THE TURN IN THE TRAIL

departure. Then he touched Cesca on the shoulder, lifted Rhoda in his arms and, followed by Cesca, left the sleeping Molly alone on the ledge.

Swiftly, silently, Alchise strode up the mountainside, Rhoda making neither sound nor motion. For hours, with wonderful endurance the two Indians held the pace. They moved up the mountain to the summit, which they crossed, then dropped rapidly downward. Just at dawn Alchise stopped at a gray *campos* under some pines and called. A voice from the hut answered him. The canvas flap was put back and an old Indian buck appeared, followed by several squaws and young bucks, yawning and staring.

Alchise laid Rhoda on the ground while he spoke rapidly to the Indian. The old man protested at first but on the repeated use of Kut-le's name he finally nodded and Alchise carried Rhoda into the *campos*. A squaw kindled a fire which, blazing up brightly, showed a huge, dark room, canvas-roofed and dirt-floored, quite bare except for the soiled blankets on the floor.

Rhoda was laid in the center of the hut. The old buck knelt beside her. He was very old indeed. His time-ravaged features were lean and ascetic. His clay-matted hair was streaked with white; his black eyes were deep-sunk and his temples were hollow. But there was a fine sort of dignity about the old medicine-man, despite his squalor. He gazed on Rhoda in silence for some time. Alchise and Cesca sat on the floor, and little by little they were joined by a dozen other Indians who formed a circle about the girl. The firelight flickered on the dark, intent faces and on Rhoda's delicate beauty as she lay passing rapidly from stupor to delirium.

Suddenly the old man raised his lean hand, shaking a gourd filled with pebbles, and began softly to chant. Instantly the other Indians joined him and the *campos* was filled with the rhythm of a weird song. Rhoda tossed her arms and began to cough a little from the smoke. The chant quickened. It was but the mechanical repetition of two notes falling always from high to low. Yet it had an indescribable effect of melancholy, this aboriginal song. It was as hopeless and melancholy as all of nature's chants: the wail of the wind, the sob of the rain, the beat of the waves.

Rhoda sat erect, her eyes wild and wide. The old buck, without ceasing his song, attempted to thrust her back with one lean brown claw, but Rhoda struck him feebly.

"Go away!" she cried. "Be quiet! You hurt my head! Don't make that dreadful noise!"

The chant quickened. The medicine-man now rocked back and forth on his knees, accenting the throb of the song by beating his bare feet on the earth. He seemed by some strange suppleness to flatten his instep paddle-wise and to bring the entire leg from toe to knee at one blow against the ground. Never did his glowing old eyes leave Rhoda's face.

The girl, thrown into misery and excitement by the insistence of the chant, began to wring her hands. The words said nothing to her but the rhythmic repetition of the notes told her a story as old as life itself: that life passes swifter than a weaver's shuttle, and without hope; that our days are as grass and as the clouds that are consumed and are no more; that the soul sinks to the land of darkness and of the shadow of death. Rhoda struggled, with horror in her eyes, to rise; but the old man with a hand on her shoulder forced her back on the blanket.

"Oh, what is it!" wailed Rhoda, clutching at the mass of yellow-brown hair about her face. "Where am I? What are you doing? Have I died? Where is Kut-le? Kut-le!" she screamed. "Kut-le!"

The medicine-man held her to the blanket and for a time she sat quiescent. Then as the Indian lifted his hand from her shoulder the bewilderment of her gray eyes changed to the wildness of delirium. She looked toward the doorway where the dawn light made but little headway against the dark interior. With one blue-veined hand on her panting breast she slowly, stealthily gathered herself together, and with unbelievable swiftness she sprang for the square of dawn light. She leaped almost into the arms of a young buck who sat near the door. He bore her back to her place while the chant continued without interruption.

Exhausted, Rhoda lay listening to the song. Gradually it began to exert its hypnotic influence over her. Its sense of melancholy enveloped her drug-like. She lay prone, the tears coursing down her cheeks, her twitching hands turned upward beside her. Slowly she floated outward upon a dark sea whose waves beat a ceaseless requiem of anguish on her ears. It seemed to her that she was enduring all the sorrows of the ages; that she was brain-tortured by the death agonies of all humanity; that all the uselessness, all the meaninglessness, all the utter weariness of the death-ridden world pressed upon her, suffocating her, forcing her to stillness, slowing the beating of her heart, the intake of her breath. Slowly her white lids closed, yet with one last conscious cry for life:

"Kut-le!" she wailed. "Kut-le!"

A quick shadow filled the doorway.

"Here, Rhoda! Here!"

Kut-le bounded into the room, upsetting the medicine-man, and lifted Rhoda in his arms. She clung to him wildly.

THE TURN IN THE TRAIL

"Take me away, Kut-le! Take me away!"

He soothed her with great tenderness.

"Dear one!" he murmured. "Dear one!" and she closed her eyes quietly.

During this time the Indians sat silent and watchful. Kut-le turned to Alchise.

"You cursed fool!" he said.

"She get well now," replied Alchise anxiously. "Alchise save her for you. Molly tell you where come."

For a moment Kut-le stared at Alchise; then, as if realizing the futility of speech, "Come!" he said, and ignoring the other Indians, he strode from the *campos*. Alchise and Cesca followed him, and outside the anxious Molly seized Rhoda's limp hand with a little cry of joy. Kut-le led the way to a quiet spot among the pines. Here he laid Rhoda on a sheepskin and covered her with a tattered blanket, the spoils of his previous night's trip.

About the middle of the morning Rhoda opened her eyes. As she stirred, Kut-le came to her.

"I've had such horrible dreams, Kut-le. You won't go and leave me to the Indians again?"

This appeal from Rhoda in her weakness almost overcame Kut-le but he only smoothed her tangled hair and answered:

"No, dear one!"

"Where are we now?" she asked feebly.

Kut-le smiled.

"In the Rockies."

"I think I am very sick," continued Rhoda. "Do you think we can stay quiet in one place today?"

Kut-le shook his head.

"I am going to get you to some quinine as quick as I can. There is some about twenty-four hours from here."

Rhoda's eyes widened.

"Shall I be with white people?"

"Don't bother. You'll have good care."

The light faded from Rhoda's eyes.

"It's hard for me, isn't it?" she said, as if appealing to the college man of the ranch.

"Rhoda! Rhoda!" whispered Kut-le, "your suffering kills me! But I must have you, I must!"

Rhoda moved her head impatiently, as if the Indian's tense, handsome face annoyed her. She refused food but drank deeply of the tepid water and shortly they were again on the trail.

For several hours Rhoda lay in Kut-le's arms, weak and ill but with lucid mind. They were making their way up a long cañon. It was very narrow. Rhoda could see the individual leaves of the aspens on the opposite wall as they moved close in the shadow of the other. The floor, watered by a clear brook, was level

THE TURN IN THE TRAIL

and green. On either side the walls were murmurous with delicately quivering aspens and sighing pines.

Suddenly Cesca gave a grunt of warning. Far down the valley a sheep-herder was approaching with his flocks. Kut-le turned to the right and Alchise sprang to his aid. In the shelter of the trees, Kut-le twisted a handkerchief across Rhoda's mouth; and in reply to her outraged eyes, he said:

"I don't mind single visitors as a rule but I haven't time to fuss with one now."

Together the two men carried Rhoda up the cañon side. They lifted her from trunk to trunk, now a roothold, now a jutting bit of rock, till far up the sheer wall Rhoda lay at last on a little ledge heaped with pine-needles. By the time the Indians were settled on the rock Rhoda was delirious again. The fever had returned twofold and Molly's entire efforts were toward keeping the tossing form on the ledge.

Slowly, very slowly, the herder, a sturdy ragged Mexican, moved up the cañon, pausing now and again to scratch his head. He was whistling *La Paloma*. The Indians' black eyes did not leave him and after his flute-like notes had melted into the distance they still crouched in cramped stillness on the ledge.

But shortly Kut-le freed Rhoda's mouth, gave Alchise a swift look, and with infinite care the descent was begun.

Kut-le did not like traveling in the daylight, for many reasons. Carefully, swiftly they moved up the cañon, always hugging the wall. Late in the afternoon they emerged on an open mesa. All the wretched day Rhoda had traveled in a fearsome world of her own, peopled with uncanny figures, alight with a glare that seared her eyes, held in a vice that gripped her until she screamed with restless pain. The song that the shepherd had whistled tortured her tired brain.

> "The day that I left my home for the rolling sea,
> I said, 'Mother dear, O pray to thy God for me!'
> But e'er we set sail I went a fond leave to take—"

Over and over she sang the three lines, ending each time with a frightened stare up into Kut-le's face.

"Whom did I say good-by to? Whom? But they don't care!"

Then again the tired voice:

> "The day that I left my home for the rolling sea—"

Night came and the weary, weary crossing of a craggy, heavily wooded mountain. Kut-le did not relinquish his burden. He seemed not to tire of the weight of the slender body that lay now in helpless stupor. If the squaws or Alchise felt fatigue or impatience as Kut-le held them to a pace on the tortuous trail that would early have exhausted a Caucasian athlete, they gave

THE TURN IN THE TRAIL 163

no sign. All the endless night Kut-le led the way under the midnight blackness of the piñon or the violet light of the stars, until the lifting light of the dawn found them across the ranges and standing at the edge of a little river.

In the dim light there lifted a terraced adobe building with ladders faintly outlined on the terraces. There was no sound save the barking of a dog and the ripple of the river. With a muttered admonition, Kut-le left Rhoda to the others and climbed one of the ladders. He returned with a blanketed figure that gazed on Rhoda non-committally. At a sign, Kut-le lifted Rhoda, and the little group moved noiselessly toward the dwelling, clambered up a ladder, and disappeared.

Rhoda opened her eyes with a sense of physical comfort that confused her. She was lying on the floor of a long, gray-walled room. In one corner was a tiny adobe fireplace from which a tinier fire threw a jet of flame color on the Navajo that lay before the hearth. Along the walls were benches with splendid Navajos rolled cushion-wise upon them. Above the benches hung several rifles with cougarskin quivers beneath them. A couple of cheap framed mirrors were hung with silver necklaces of beautiful workmanship. In a corner a table was set with heavy but shining china dishes.

Rhoda stared with increasing wonder. She was very

weak and spent but her head was clear. She lifted her arms and looked at them. She was wearing a loose-fitting gray garment of a strange weave. She fingered it, more and more puzzled.

"You wake now?" asked a low voice.

Coming softly down the room was an Indian woman of comely face and strange garb. Over a soft shirt of cut and weave such as Rhoda had on, she wore a dark overdress caught at one shoulder and reaching only to the knees. A many-colored girdle confined the dress at the waist. Her legs and feet were covered with high, loose moccasins. Her black hair hung free on her shoulders.

"You been much sick," the woman went on, "much sick," stooping to straighten Rhoda's blanket.

"Where am I?" asked Rhoda.

"At Chira. You eat breakfast?"

Rhoda caught the woman's hand.

"Who are you?" she asked. "You have been very good to me."

"Me Marie," replied the woman.

"Where are Kut-le and the others?"

"Kut-le here. Others in mountain. You much sick, three days."

Rhoda sighed. Would this kaleidoscope of misery never end!

"I am very tired of it all," she said. "I think it would have been kinder if you had let me die. Will you help me to get back to my white friends?"

Marie shook her head.

"Kut-le friend. We take care Kut-le's squaw."

Rhoda turned wearily on her side.

"Go away and let me sleep," she said.

CHAPTER XII

THE CROSSING TRAILS

AS Kut-le, with Rhoda in his arms, disappeared into the mesa fissure, John DeWitt threw himself from his horse and was at the opening before the others had more than brought their horses to their haunches.

He was met by Alchise's rifle, with Alchise entirely hidden from view. For a moment the four men stood panting and speechless. The encounter had been so sudden, so swift that they could not believe their senses. Then Billy Porter uttered an oath that reverberated from the rocky wall.

"They will get to the top!" he cried. "Jack, you and DeWitt get up there! Carlos and I will hold this!"

The two men mounted immediately and galloped along the mesa wall, looking for an ascent. Neither of them spoke but both were breathing hard, and through his blistered skin DeWitt's cheeks glowed feverishly. For a mile up and down from the fissure the wall was a blank, except for a single wide split which did not come within fifty feet of the ground. After over half an hour of frantic search, DeWitt found, nearly three miles from the fissure, a rough spot where the wall gave back in a few narrow crumbling ledges.

"We'll have to leave the horses," he said, "and try that."

Jack nodded tensely. They dismounted, pulled the reins over the horses' heads and started up the wall, John leading, carefully. One bitter lesson the desert was teaching him: haste in the hot country spells ruin! So, though Rhoda's voice still rang in his ears, though the sight of the slender boyish figure struggling in Kut-le's arms still ravished his eyes, he worked carefully.

The ascent was all but impossible. The few jutting ledges were so narrow that foothold was precarious, so far apart that only the slight backward slant of the wall made it possible for them to flatten their bodies against the crumbling brown rock and thus keep from falling. They toiled desperately, silently. After an hour of utmost effort, they reached the top, and with an exclamation of exultation started in the direction of the fissure. But their exultation was short-lived. The great split that stopped fifty feet from the desert floor cut them off from the main mesa. They ran hastily along its edge but at no point was it to be crossed. Shortly DeWitt left Jack to follow it back and he hastened to the mesa front where he made a perilous descent and returned with the horses to Porter.

That gentleman forced John to eat some breakfast while Carlos rode hastily to scour the mesa front to the

THE CROSSING TRAILS 169

west. Porter and the Mexican had captured two of the horses and the burro that the Indians had left. The other horses had run out into the desert back to the last spring they had camped at, Porter said. To DeWitt's great disappointment, the horses carried only blankets, and the burro was loaded with bacon and flour. There were none of Rhoda's personal belongings. The animals were in good condition, however, and the men annexed them to their outfit gladly.

John was torn betwixt hope and bitter disappointment.

"Do you think they could climb out of the fissure?" he asked half a dozen times, then without waiting for an answer, "Did you see her face, Billy? I had just a glimpse! Didn't she look well! Just that one glance has put new life in me! I know we will get her! Even this cursed desert isn't wide enough to keep me from her! God help that Indian when I get him!"

Porter kept his eyes on Alchise's rifle which had never wavered in the past three hours.

"I've a notion to shoot the barrel off that thing just for luck!" he growled. "John, sit down! You will need all the strength you've got and then some before you catch that Injun!"

"What are you going to do?" asked John, seating himself in the sand some few feet from the fissure.

"The big probability is," said Billy, "that they are in

the crack. It would be just about impossible for a girl to climb out of one of 'em. If they have got out, though, it's just a matter of finding their trail again. We'll have 'em! It's just this chance crack that saved 'em. If you're rested, ride along the west wall and try for the top again."

For the next five hours, Porter guarded the mesa front alone. It was nearing six o'clock when Jack returned, exhausted and disappointed. He had followed the great split back until the mesa top became so cut and striated with mighty fissures that progress was impossible.

"Isn't it the devil's own luck," he growled to Porter as he ate, "that we should have let him get into that one crack! What next! Unless they are still in there, we've lost them and are just losing time squatting here."

As he spoke, there was a sound of voices in the fissure. The two men cocked their rifles as John and Carlos emerged from the opening. John was scowling and breathless.

"Lost 'em as usual, by our infernal stupidity," he panted, while Carlos dropped his empty canteen and lifted Porter's to his lips. "I rode round to the south of the mesa. There are a couple of possible ascents there. I found Carlos making one. We followed a dozen fissures before we located this one. We got into it about a mile back from here. Here's a basket we found at the bottom in a burlap bag."

THE CROSSING TRAILS

He tossed one of Cesca's pitch baskets at Billy, then threw himself in the sand.

"They were down off the mesa, I bet," he went on, "before we fools found the way up, and it was easy for the chap they left guarding the entrance to avoid us. The mesa is covered with big rocks."

"He got away within the last half-hour then," said Billy, "for I didn't stir from this spot until the burro started to eat the grub pack, and I naturally had to wrestle with him. And no human being could a got out the front even then."

"God! What a country!" groaned DeWitt. "The Indians outwit us at every step!"

"Well," Jack answered dejectedly, "tell us what we could have done differently."

"I'm not blaming any one," replied John.

Billy Porter rose briskly.

"You boys quit your kicking. The scent is still warm. You fellows get a couple of hours' sleep while I take the horses back to Coyote Hole for water. By daylight we got to be on the south side of the mesa to pick up the trail."

Billy's businesslike manner heartened Jack and John DeWitt. They turned in beside Carlos, who already was sleeping.

Dawn found them examining the ascents on the south

side of the mesa but they found no traces and as the sun came well up they followed the only possible way toward the mountains. At noon they found a low spring in a pocket between mesa and mountain. Kut-le was growing either defiant or careless, for he had left a heap of ashes and a pile of half-eaten desert mice. Very much cheered they allowed the horses a fair rest. They found no further traces of camp or trail that day and made camp that night in the open desert.

At dawn they were crossing a heavily wooded mountain. The sun had not yet risen when they heard a sound of singing.

"What's that?" asked DeWitt sharply, as the four pulled up their horses.

"A medicine cry," answered Jack. "We must be near some medicine-man's *campos*."

"Come on," cried DeWitt, "we'll quiz them!"

"Hold up, you chump!" exclaimed Billy. "If you rush in on a cry that way you are apt not to come back again. You've got to go at 'em careful. Let me do the talking."

They rode toward the sound of the chant and shortly a dingy *campos* came into view. An Indian buck made his way from the doorway toward them.

"Who is sick, friend?" asked Billy.

"Old buck," said the Indian.

"Apache?" said Billy.

The Indian nodded.

"You *sabe* Apache named Kut-le?"

The buck shook his head, but Billy went on patiently.

"Yes, you *sabe* him. He old Ke-say's son. Apache chief's son. He run off with white squaw. We want squaw, we no hurt him. Squaw sick, no good for Injun. You tell, have money." Billy displayed a silver dollar.

The Indian brightened.

"Long time 'go, some Injun say he *sabe* Kut-le. Some Injun say he all same white man. Some Injun say he heap smart." He looked at Billy inquiringly, and Billy nodded approval. DeWitt swallowed nervously. "Come two, three day 'go," the buck went on, his eyes on the silver dollar, "big Injun, carry white squaw, go by here very fast. He go that way all heap fast." The buck pointed south.

"Did he speak to you? What did he say?" cried DeWitt.

But the Indian lapsed into silence and refused to speak more. Porter felt well rewarded for his efforts and tossed the dollar to the Indian.

"Gee!" said Billy, as they started elated down the mountain. "I wish we could overtake him before he outfits again. That poverty-stricken lot couldn't have had any horses here for him to use. I'll bet he makes for the nearest ranch where he could steal a good bunch. That would be at Kelly's, sixty miles south of here. We'll hike for Kelly's!"

This idea did not meet with enthusiastic approval from the other three but as no one had a better suggestion to make, the trail to Kelly's was taken. It seemed to John Dewitt that Billy relied little on science and much on intuition in trailing the Indians. At first, considering Porter's early boasts about his skill, DeWitt was much disappointed by the old-timer's haphazard methods. But after a few weeks' testing of the terrible hardships of the desert, after a few demonstrations of the Apache's cleverness, John had concluded that intuition was the most reliable weapon that the whites could hope to discover with which to offset the Indian's appalling skill and knowledge.

It was an exhausted quartet with its string of horses that drew up at Kelly's dusty corral. Dick Kelly, a stocky Irishman, greeted the strangers pleasantly. When, however, he learned their names he rose to the occasion as only an Irishman can.

"You gentlemen are at the end of your rope, wid the end frayed at that!" he said. "Now come in for a few hours' rest and the Chinaman will cook you the best meal he knows how."

THE CROSSING TRAILS 175

"Lord, no!" cried Billy. "We're so close on the track now that we can hang on to the end. If you've had no trace here we'll just double back and start from the mountains again!"

By this time a dozen cowboys and ranch hands were gathered about the newcomers. Every one knew about Rhoda's disappearance. Every one knew about every man in the little search party. In the flicker of the lanterns the men looked pityingly at DeWitt's haggard face.

"Say," said a tall, lank cowman, "if you'll go in and sleep till daylight, us'nll scour this part of the desert with a fine-tooth comb. So you all won't lose a minute by taking a little rest. An' if we find the Injun we'll string him up and save you the trouble."

DeWitt spoke for the first time.

"If you find the Indian," he said succinctly, "he's mine!"

There was a moment's silence in the crowd. These men were familiar with elemental passion. DeWitt's feeling was perfectly correct in their eyes. The pause came as each pictured himself in DeWitt's place with the image of the delicate Eastern girl suffering who knew what torments constantly before him.

"If Mr. Kelly can arrange for that," said Jack, "I guess it will about save our lives. I'd like a chance to write a letter to my wife."

"You ought to go back to the ditch, Jack," said DeWitt. "Porter and I will manage somehow."

Jack gave DeWitt a strange look.

"Rhoda's a lifelong friend of mine. She was stolen from my home by my friend whom I told her she could trust. Katherine and the foreman can run the ranch."

By the time that the four had washed themselves, Kelly had his men dotted over the surrounding desert. For the first time in weeks, the searchers sat down at a table. DeWitt, Porter and Newman were in astonishing contrast to the three who had dined at the Newman ranch the night of Cartwell's introduction to Porter. Their khaki clothes had gradually been replaced by nondescript garments picked up at various ranches. DeWitt and Porter boasted of corduroy trousers, while Jack wore overalls. On the other hand, Jack wore a good blue flannel shirt, while the other two displayed only faded gingham garments that might have answered to almost any name. All of them were a deep mahogany color, with chapped, split lips and bleached hair, while DeWitt's eyes were badly inflamed from sun-glare and sand-storm.

They ate silently. Dick Kelly, sitting at the head of the table, plied them with food and asked few questions. DeWitt's shaking hands told him that questions were torture to the poor fellow. After the meal Kelly led

THE CROSSING TRAILS

them to bed at once, and they slept without stirring until four o'clock in the morning, when the Chinaman called them. Breakfast was steaming on the table.

"Now," said Kelly, as his guests ate, "the boys didn't get a smell for ye, but we've a suggestion. Have you been through the Pueblo country yet?"

"No," said Porter.

"Well," the host went on, "Chira is the only place round here except my ranch where he could get a new outfit. He's part Pueblo, you know, too. I'd start for there if I was you."

Carlos entered to hear this suggestion.

"I've got a friend at Chira," he said, "who might help us. He's a half-breed."

The tired men took eagerly to this forlorn hope. With all the population of the ranch, including the cook, gathered to wish them Godspeed, the four started off before the sun had more than tinted the east. Kelly had offered them anything on the ranch, from himself, his cook and his cowboys, to the choice of his horses. His guests left as much heartened by his cheerfulness and good will as they were by the actual physical comforts he had given them.

The trail to Chira was long and hard. They reached the little town at dusk and Carlos set out at once in search of his friend, Philip. He found him easily. He was half Mexican, half Pueblo. He and Carlos chatted briskly in hybrid Spanish while the Americans watched the horses wade in the little river. Visitors were so common in Chira that the newcomers attracted little or no attention.

Carlos finally turned from his friend.

"Philip does not know anything about it. He says for us to come to his house while he finds out anything. His wife is a good cook."

The thought of a hot meal was pleasant to the Americans. They followed gladly to Philip's adobe rooms. Here the half-breed left them to his wife and disappeared. He was gone perhaps an hour when he returned with a bit of cloth in his hand, which he handed to Carlos with a few rapid sentences. Carlos gave the scrap of cloth to DeWitt, who looked at it eagerly then gave a cry of joy. It was Rhoda's handkerchief.

"He found a little girl washing her doll with it at the river," said Carlos. "She said she found it blowing along the street this morning."

"Come on!" cried Jack, making for the door.

"Come on where?" said Billy. "If they are in the village, you don't want to get away very far. And if they ain't, which way are you going?"

"Ask Philip where to go, Carlos," said DeWitt.

He held the little moist handkerchief in his hand tightly

THE CROSSING TRAILS 179

while his heart beat heavily. Once more hope was soaring high.

Philip thought deeply, then he and Carlos talked rapidly together.

"Philip says," reported Carlos, "that you must go out and watch along the river front so that if they have not gone you can catch them if they try. He and I will go visit every family as if I wanted to buy an outfit."

Darkness had settled on the little town when the three Americans took up their vigil opposite the open face of the Pueblo along the river. All that night they stood on guard but not a human being crossed their line of patrol.

CHAPTER XIII

AN INTERLUDE

LATE in the afternoon, Rhoda woke. Kut-le stood beside her. His expression was half eager, half tender.

"How do you feel now?" he asked.

"Quite well," answered Rhoda. "Will you call Marie? I want to dress."

"You must rest in bed today," replied the Indian. "Tomorrow will be soon enough for you to get up."

Rhoda looked at the young man with irritation.

"Can't you learn that I am not a squaw? That it maddens me to be ordered about? That every time you do you alienate me more, if possible?"

"You do foolish stunts," said Kut-le calmly, "and I have to put you right."

Rhoda moaned.

"Oh, how long, how long must I endure this! How could they be so stupid as to let you slip through their fingers so!"

Kut-le's mouth became a narrow seam.

"As soon as I can get you into the Sierra Madre, I

shall marry you. You are practically a well woman now. But I am not going to hurry overmuch. You are going to love me first and you are going to love this life first. Then we will go to Paris until the storm has passed."

Rhoda did not seem to hear him. She tossed her arms restlessly.

"Please send Marie to me," she said finally. "You will permit me to eat something perhaps?"

Kut-le left the room at once. In a short time he returned with Marie, who bore a steaming bowl which he himself flanked with a dish of luscious melon. The woman propped Rhoda adroitly to a sitting position and Kut-le gravely balanced the bowl against the girl's knees. The stew which the bowl contained was delicious, and Rhoda ate it to the last drop. She ate in silence, while Kut-le watched her with unspeakable longing in his eyes. The room was almost dark when the simple meal was finished. Marie brightened the fire and smoothed Rhoda's blankets.

"Kut-le go now," said the Pueblo woman. "You rest. In morning, Marie bring white squaw some clothes."

Rhoda was glad to pillow her head on her arm but it was long before she slept. She tried to piece together her faint and distorted recollection of the occurrences since the morning when the mesa had risen through the

AN INTERLUDE

dawn. But her only clear picture was of John DeWitt's wild face as she disappeared into the fissure. She recalled its look of agony and sobbed a little to herself as she realized what torture he and the Newmans must have endured since her disappearance. And yet she was very hopeful. If her friends could come as close to her as they did before the mesa, they must be learning Kut-le's methods. Surely the next time luck would not play so well for the Indian.

Rhoda woke in the morning to the sound of song. Marie knelt on the ground before a sloping slab of stone and patiently kneeded corn with a smaller stone. Her song, a quaint repetition of short mellow syllables pleased Rhoda's sensitive ear and she lay listening. When Marie saw Rhoda's wide eyes she came to the girl's side.

"You feel good now?" she queried.

"Yes, much better. I want to get up."

The Indian woman nodded.

"Marie clean white squaw's clothes. White squaw wear Marie's. Now Marie help you wash."

Rhoda smiled.

"You are not an Apache if you want me to bathe!"

Marie answered indignantly.

"Marie is Pueblo squaw!"

The clothes that Marie brought, Rhoda thought very

attractive. There was a soft wool underdress of creamiest tint. Over this Marie pulled, fastening it at one shoulder, a gay, many-colored overdress which, like the one she herself wore, reached to the knees. Rhoda pulled on her own high laced boots which had been neatly mended. Then the two turned their attention to the neglected braid of hair.

When it was loosened and hung in tangled masses nearly to Rhoda's knees, Marie's delight in its loveliness knew no expression. She fetched a queer battered old comb which she washed and then proceeded with true feminine rapture to comb the wonderful waving locks. In the midst of this Kut-le entered. He gazed on Rhoda's new disguise with delight. Indeed her delicate face, above the many-hued garment, was like a harebell growing in a gaudy nasturtium bed.

"We can only let you on the roof," said Kut-le, who was carrying Rhoda's sombrero.

Rhoda made no reply but when Marie had plaited her hair in a rippling braid she followed Kut-le up the short ladder. Her sense of cleanliness after the weeks of disorder was delightful. As she stepped on the flat-topped roof and the sweet clear air filled her lungs she felt as if reborn. With Navajo blankets, Kut-le had contrived an awning that not only made a bit of shade but precluded view from below. The rich tints of the blankets were startlingly picturesque against the yellow gray of the adobe. Rhoda dropped luxuriantly to the heap of blankets and turned her face toward the mountain, many-colored and bare toward the base, deep-cloaked with piñon, oak and juniper on the uplands. From its base flowed the little river, gurgling over its shallow bed of stone and rich with green along its flat banks. Close beside the river was the Pueblo village, the many-terraced buildings, on one of the roofs of which Rhoda sat.

Kut-le, stretched on the roof near by, smoked cigarette after cigarette as he watched the girl's quiet face, but he did not speak. For three or four hours the two sat thus in silence. Just as the sun sank behind the mountain, a bell clanged and then fell to tolling softly. Then Kut-le broke his silence.

"That's the bell of the old mission. Some one has been buried, I guess. We can look. There are no tourists now."

There was a sound of wailing: a deep mournful sound that caught Rhoda's heart to her throat and blanched her face. It was the sound of the grief of primitive man, the cry of the forlorn and broken-hearted, uncloaked by convention. It touched a primitive chord of response in Rhoda that set her to trembling. Surely, when the world was young she too had wept so. Surely she too had voiced a poignant, unbearable loss in just such a wild outpouring of grief!

They moved to the edge of the terrace and looked below into the street. Down the rocky way a line of Indians was bearing hand-mills and jars and armloads of ornaments.

"They will take those to the 'killing place' and break them that the dead owner may have them afterward," explained Kut-le softly. "It always makes me think of a verse in the Bible. I can't recall the words exactly though."

Rhoda glanced up into the dark face with a look of appreciation.

" 'And the grinders shall cease because they are few!'" she said, "'and those that look out of the windows be darkened. And the doors shall be shut in the street when the sound of the grinding is low, because man goeth to his long home and mourners go about the street.'"

"And there is something else," murmured Kut-le, "about 'the silver cord.'"

" 'Or ever the silver cord be loosed or the golden bowl be broken or the pitcher be broken at the fountain or the wheel broken at the cistern. Then shall the dust return to the earth as it was and the spirit to God who gave it.'"

They stood in silence again. The wailing died into

the distance. The sun touched to molten gold the heavy shadows of the mountain arroyos. Rhoda was deeply moved by the scene below her. She felt as if she had been thrust back through the ages to look upon the sorrow of some little Judean town. The little rocky street, the vivid robes, the weird, dying wail, the broken ornaments and utensils that some folded tired hands would use no more, and, above all, the simple unquestioning faith, roused in her a sudden longing for a life that she never had known. For a long time she stood in thought. As darkness fell she roused herself.

"Let me go back to my room," she said.

As they turned, neither noticed that Rhoda's little handkerchief, which she had carried through all her experiences, fluttered from her sleeve to the street.

Again it was long before Rhoda slept. Through her window there floated the sound of song, the evening singing of Indian lads in the village street. There was a vibrant quality in their voices that Rhoda could liken only to the music of stringed instruments. There was neither the mellow smoothness of the negro voice nor the flute-like sweetness of the white, yet the voices compassed all the mystical appealing quality of violin notes.

The music woke in Rhoda a longing for she knew not what. It seemed to her as if she were peering past a misty veil into the childhood of the world to whose simple beauty and delights civilization had made her alien. The vibrating voices chanted slower and slower. Rhoda stirred uneasily. To be free again as these voices were free! Not to long for the civilization she had left but for open skies and trails! To be free again!

As the voices melted into silence, a guitar was touched softly under Rhoda's window and Kut-le's voice rose in *La Golondrina:*

> "Whither so swiftly flies the timid swallow?
> What distant bourne seeks her untiring wing?
> To reach her nest what needle does she follow
> When darkness wraps the poor wee storm-tossed thing?"

Rhoda stirred restlessly and threw her arms above her head.

> "To build her nest near to my couch I'll call her!
> Why go so far dark and strange skies to seek?
> Safe would she be, no evil should befall her,
> For I'm an exile sad, too sad to weep!"

Mist-like floated across Rhoda's mind a memory of the trail with voice of mating bird at dawn, with stars and the night wind and the open way. And going before, always Kut-le—Kut-le of the unfathomable eyes, of the merry smile, of the gentle touch. The music merged itself into Rhoda's dreams.

She spent the following day on the roof. Curled on her Navajo she watched the changing tones on the mountains and listened to the soft voices of the Pueblo women in

AN INTERLUDE

the street below. Naked brown babies climbed up and down the ladders and paddled in the shallow river. Indian women with scarlet shawls across their shoulders filled their ollas at the river and stood gossiping, the brimming ollas on their heads. In the early morning the men had trudged to the alfalfa and melon fields and returned at sundown to be greeted joyfully by the women and children.

Kut-le spent the day at Rhoda's side. They talked but little, though Rhoda had definitely abandoned her rôle of silence toward the Indian. Her mind during most of the day was absorbed in wondering why she so enjoyed watching the life in this Indian town and why she was not more impatient to be gone.

As the sun dropped behind the mountain Marie appeared on the roof, her black eyes very bright.

"Half-bread Philip find white squaw's handkerchief. Give to white men, maybe! Marie see Philip get handkerchief from little girl."

Kut-le gave Rhoda an inscrutable look, but she did not tell him that she shared his surprise.

"Well," said Kut-le calmly, "maybe we had better mosey along."

They descended to find Marie hastily doing up a bundle of bread and fruit. While Kut-le went for blankets Rhoda, at Marie's request, donned her old clothing of the trail. She had been wearing the squaw's holiday outfit. Very shortly, with a hasty farewell to Marie, they were in the dusky street. "Shall I gag you," asked Kut-le, "or will you give me your word of honor to give neither sign nor sound until we get to the mountain, and to keep your face covered with your Navajo?"

Rhoda sighed.

"Very well, I promise," she said.

In a very short time they had reached the end of the little street and were climbing an arroyo up into the mountain. When they reached the piñons Kut-le gave the coyote call. It thrilled Rhoda with the misery of the night of her capture. Almost immediately there was an answering call and close in the shadow of the piñon they found Alchise and the two squaws. Molly ran to Rhoda with a squeal of joy and patted the girl's hand but Alchise and Cesca gave no heed to her greeting.

The ponies were ready and Rhoda swung herself to her saddle, with a thrill at the touch of the muscular little horse. And once more she rode after Kut-le with the mystery of the night trail before her.

The sound of water falling, the cheep of wakening birds, the subtle odor of moisture-drenched soil roused Rhoda from her half sleep on the horse's back at the end of the night's journey. The trail had not been hard, through an endless pine forest for the most part. Kut-le drew rein beside a little waterfall deep in the mountain fastness. Rhoda saw a chaos of rock masses huge and distorted, as if an inconceivably cruel and gigantic hand had juggled with weights seemingly immovable; about these the loveliness of vine and shrub; above them the towering junipers dwarfed by the rocks they shaded; and falling softly over the harsh brown rifts of rock, the liquid green and white of a mountain brook which, as it reached the level, rushed away in a roar of foam.

Rhoda's horse drank thirstily and she stood beside him watching the mystical gray of the dawn lift to the riotous rose of the sunrise. She wondered at the quick throb of her pulse. It was very different from its wonted soft beat. Then she threw herself on her blanket to sleep.

When Rhoda woke, late in the day, Kut-le had spread Marie's cakes and fruit on leaves which he had washed in the brook.

"They are quite clean, I think," he said a little anxiously. "At least the squaws haven't touched them."

Rhoda and Kut-le sat on a rock and ate hungrily. When she had finished Rhoda clasped her hands about her knees. She looked singularly boyish, with her sombrero pushed back from her face and short locks of damp hair curling from beneath the crown.

"Isn't it queer," she said, "that you elude Jack and John DeWitt so easily?"

"The trouble is," said Kut-le, "that you don't appreciate the prowess of your captors."

"Humph!" sniffed Rhoda.

"Listen!" cried Kut-le with sudden enthusiasm. "Once in my boyhood Geronima and about twenty warriors, with twice as many squaws and children, fled to the mountains. They never drew rein until they were one hundred and twenty miles from the reservation. Then for six months they were pursued by two thousand American soldiers and they never lost a man!"

"How many whites were killed?" asked Rhoda.

"About a hundred!"

"I don't understand yet," Rhoda shook her head, "how savages could outwit whites for so long a time."

"But it's not a contest of brains. Whites must travel like whites, with food and rests. The Apache travels like the coyote, living off the country. Your ancestors have been training your brain for a thousand years. Mine have spent centuries of days, twenty-four hours a day, training the body to endure hardships. You have had a glimpse of what the hardships of this country might mean to a white!"

As Kut-le talked, Rhoda sat with her eyes fastened on the rough face of a distant rock. As she watched she saw a thick, leafy bush move up to the rock. Rhoda caught her breath, glanced at the unconscious Kut-le,

AN INTERLUDE

then back at the bush. It moved slowly back among the trees and after a moment Rhoda saw the undergrowth far beyond move as with a passing breeze. She glanced at the nodding Alchise and the squaws, then smiled and turned to Kut-le.

"Go on with your boasting, Kut-le. It's your one weakness, I think."

Kut-le grinned.

"Well now, honestly, what do you think that a lot of Caucasians can do with an enemy whose existence has always been a fist to fist fight with nature at her cruelest? We have fought with our bare hands and we have won," he continued, half to himself. "No white man or any number of whites can capture me on my own ground!"

"Boaster!" laughed Rhoda.

Just beyond the falls an aspen quivered. John DeWitt stepped into view. Haggard and wild-eyed, he stared at Rhoda. She raised her finger to her lips, but too late. Kut-le too looked up, and raised his gun. Rhoda hurled herself toward him and struck up the barrel. Kut-le dropped the gun and caught Rhoda in his arms.

"The woods are full of them!" he grunted. With one hand across Rhoda's mouth, he ran around the falls and dropped six feet to a narrow back trail.

"My own ground!" Rhoda heard him chuckle.

CHAPTER XIV

THE BEAUTY OF THE WORLD

FOR many hurrying minutes, Rhoda saw only the passing tree branches black against the evening sky as she lay across Kut-le's breast. The pursuers had made no sound nor had Kut-le broken a single twig. The entire incident might have been a pantomime, with every actor tragically intent.

Having long learned the futility of struggling, Rhoda lay quietly enough, her ears keen to catch the sound of pursuit. Kut-le did not remove his hand from her mouth. But as he dropped rapidly and skilfully down the mountainside he whispered:

"My own ground, you see! It will take them a good while in the dusk to find that back trail. Only a few Indians know it."

But Rhoda's heart was beating high. Let Kut-le boast as he would, she was sure that Jack and John DeWitt were learning to follow the trail. The most vivid picture in her mind was of the utter weariness of John's face. In the past weeks Rhoda had learned how fearful had been the hardships that would bring such weariness to a human face. Tears came to her eyes. No one so weak, so useless as herself, she felt, could be worth such travail.

Silently they moved through the dusk. Rhoda knew that the other Indians must be close behind them, yet no sound betrayed their presence. After a half-hour or so she struggled to be set down. But Kut-le only tightened his hold and it was fully two hours later that he set her on her feet.

"Don't move," he said. "We are on a cañon edge."

Rhoda swung her blanket to her shoulders, for the night was stinging sharp. She was not afraid. She had grown so accustomed to the night trail that she moved unhesitatingly along black rims that had at first paralyzed her with fear.

"Now," said Kut-le, "I'm not going to travel on foot. The only horses within easy distance are some that a bunch of Navajos have in the cañon below here. So we will go down and get them. We will go together because I can't risk coming back for you. We will have to hike *pronto* after we get 'em. Just remember that you are contaminated by the company you are keeping and that if you make any noise, the Navajos will shoot you up, with the rest of us! Keep right behind me."

The little group moved carefully down the cañon trail. In a short time they reached a growth of trees. They

THE BEAUTY OF THE WORLD

stole through these, the only sound Rhoda's panting breaths. Suddenly Kut-le stopped.

"Wait here!" he breathed in Rhoda's ear, and he and Alchise disappeared.

A hand was laid on her arm and Rhoda knew that Molly and Cesca were guarding her. Almost immediately the soft thud of hoofs was upon them. Kut-le seized Rhoda and tossed her to a pony's back.

"It was dead easy!" he whispered. "They were all asleep! I even took a saddle for you! Now hike!"

Rhoda gripped her pony with her knees as the little fellow cantered unerringly through the darkness after Kut-le. She felt a sudden pride and exultation in the security she had developed in the saddle during the travail of her night rides. She knew that no man of her acquaintance could ride a horse as she could now. And with the exultation she was trembling with excitement. She knew that none of them could expect mercy if the Navajos discovered their loss in time to take up the chase. All the eagerness of the gambler who stakes his life on a throw of the dice; all the wild thrill of the chase; all the trembling of the panting, woodland things that hunt and are hunted, were Rhoda's as the night wind rushed past her face. The apathy of illness was gone. Tonight she was as wild a thing as the night's birds that brushed across their trail on sweeping wing.

When they made camp at dawn Rhoda tumbled into her blanket and was asleep before Alchise finished covering their trail. When she woke she found that they were camped in a strange eerie. They were high up on a mountain on a shelf that gave back into a shallow cave. In front, facing the desert, was a heap of rock that formed a natural rampart. A tiny spring bubbled from the cave floor. Here the little party would seem as secure in their dizzy seclusion as eagles of the Andes.

It was barely noon and the mountain air was sweet and exhilarating. Kut-le sat against the rampart, smoking a cigarette, while Molly and Cesca worked over the fire. Rhoda lunched on the tortillas to which Molly had clung through all the vicissitudes of flight.

"Where are the horses?" she asked Kut-le.

"Oh, Alchise took them back. We must stay here a while till your mob of friends disperses. I couldn't feed them and I wanted to pacify the Navajos and get some supplies from them. Alchise will fix it up with them."

And here on this dizzy brink of the desert Kut-le did pause as if for a long, long holiday. The wisdom of the proceeding did not trouble him at all. The call of the desert was an allurement to which he yielded unresistingly, trusting to elude capture through his skill and unfailing good fortune.

To Rhoda the pause was welcome. She still had

THE BEAUTY OF THE WORLD 199

faith that the longer they camped in one spot the surer would be the pursuers to stumble upon them. Kut-le began to devote himself entirely to Rhoda's amusement. He knew all the plant and animal life of the desert, not only as an Indian but as a college man who had loved biology. By degrees Rhoda's good brain began to respond to his vivid interest and the girl in her stay on the mountain shelf learned the desert as has been given to few whites to learn it. Besides what she learned from the men Rhoda became expert in camp work under Molly's patient teaching. She could kindle the tiny, smokeless fire. She could concoct appetizing messes from the crude food. She could detect good water from bad and could find forage for horses. The crowning pride of her achievements was learning to weave the dish basketry.

They had lived in the mountain niche some three weeks when Alchise and Kut-le left the camp one afternoon, Alchise on a turkey hunt, Kut-le on one of his mysterious trips for supplies. Alchise returned at dusk with a beautiful bird which Rhoda and Molly roasted with enthusiasm. But Kut-le did not appear at supper time as he had promised. When the meal was almost spoiled from waiting, Rhoda and the Indians ate. As the evening wore on, Alchise grew uneasy, but he dared not disobey Kut-le's orders and leave the camp unguarded at night.

Rhoda speculated, torn between hope and fear. Perhaps the searchers had captured Kut-le at last. Perhaps he had given up hope of winning her love and had gone for good. Perhaps, somewhere or other, he was lying badly hurt! The little group sat up much later than usual, Cesca silently smoking her endless cigarettes, Alchise and Molly talking now in Apache, now in English. Rhoda was convinced that they were puzzled and worried.

Even after she had lain down on her blankets Rhoda could not sleep. With Kut-le gone her sense of the camp's security was gone. She rose finally and sat beside Alchise who, rifle in hand, guarded the ledge. There was no moon but the stars were very large and near. Rhoda was growing to know the stars. They were remote in the East; in the desert they become a part of one's existence. The sense of stupendous distance was greater at night than in the daytime. The infinite heavens, stretching depth beyond depth, the faint far spaces of the desert, were as if one looked on the Great Mystery itself.

When dawn came, Alchise wakened Cesca, put the rifle into her hands, and hurried back up over the mountain. The purple shadows had lightened to gray when Rhoda saw Kut-le staggering up the trail from the desert. Rhoda gave a little cry and ran down to meet him.

"Kut-le! What happened to you? We were so worried!"

There was a bloody rag tied just below the young Indian's knee. He paused, supporting himself against a rock. Across his eyes, drawn and haggard with pain, flashed a look of joy that Rhoda, eying the bandage, did not see.

"I was late starting back," he said briefly. "In the darkness a bit of the trail gave way, dropped me into a cañon and laid my leg open. I was unconscious a long time and lost a lot of blood, so it has taken me the rest of the night to get here. Would you mind getting Alchise to help me up the trail?"

"Alchise has gone to look for you. Lean on me," said Rhoda simply.

Despite his weakness, the dark blood flushed the young man's face, while Rhoda's utter unconsciousness of her changed manner brought a smile to his set lips. Not if the torture of dragging himself up the trail were to be ten times greater would he now have availed himself of help from Alchise.

"If you will let me put my arm across your shoulder we can make it," he said as quietly as though his heart were not leaping.

Rhoda's squaring of her slender shoulders was distractingly boyish. Utterly heedless of the pain which each step cost him, Kut-le made his way slowly to the ledge, ordering back the flustered squaws and leaning on Rhoda only enough to feel the tender girlish shoulders beneath the worn blue blouse.

In the camp, Rhoda assumed command while Kut-le lay on his blanket watching her in silent content. She put one of Alchise's two calico shirts on to boil over the breakfast fire. She washed out the nasty cut and bandaged it with strips from the sterilized shirt. She brought Kut-le's breakfast and her own to his blanket side and coaxed the young man to eat, he assuming great indifference merely for the happiness of being urged. Rhoda was so energetic and efficient that the sun was just climbing from behind the far peaks when Kut-le finished his bacon and coffee. The girl stood looking at him, hands on hips, head on one side, with that look in her eyes of superiority, maternity and complacent tenderness which a woman can assume only when she has ministered to the needs of a helpless masculine thing.

"There!" she said with a sigh of satisfaction.

"Rhoda," said Kut-le, hoping that the heavy thumping of his heart did not shake his whole broad chest, "how long ago was it that you were a helpless, dying little girl without strength to cut up your own food? How long since you have served any one but yourself?"

Rhoda drew a quick breath. She stood staring from

the Indian to the desert, to her slender body, and back again. She held out her hands and looked at them. They were scratched and brown and did not tremble. Then she looked at the young Indian and he never was to forget the light in her eyes.

"Kut-le!" she cried. "Kut-le! I am well again! I am well again!"

She paced back and forth along the ledge. Through the creamy tan her cheeks flushed richly crimson. Finally she stopped before the Apache.

"You have outraged all my civilized instincts," she said slowly, "yet you have saved my life and given me health. Whatever comes, Kut-le, I never shall forget that!"

"I have changed more than that," said Kut-le quietly. "Where is your old hatred of the desert?"

Rhoda turned to look. At the edge of the distant ranges showed a rim of red. Crimson spokes of fire flashed to the zenith. The sky grew brighter, more translucent, the ranges melted into molten gold. The sun, hot and scarlet, rolled into view. Into Rhoda's heart flooded a sense of infinite splendor, infinite beauty, infinite peace.

"Why!" she gasped to Kut-le, "it is beautiful! It's not terrible! It's unadorned beauty!"

The Indian nodded but did not speak. Rhoda never

was to forget that day. Long years after she was to catch the afterglow of that day of her rebirth. Suddenly she realized that never could a human have found health in a setting more marvelous. The realization was almost too much. Kut-le, with sympathy for which she was grateful, did not talk to her much. Once, however, as she brought him a drink and mechanically smoothed his blanket he said softly:

"You who have been served and demanded service all your life, why do you do this?"

Rhoda answered slowly.

"I'm not serving you. I'm trying to pay up some of the debt of my life."

Kut-le was about in a day or so and by the end of the week he was quite himself. He resumed the daily expeditions with Rhoda and Alchise which provided text for the girl's desert learning. Rhoda's old despondency, her old agony of prayer for immediate rescue had given way to a strange conflict of desires. She was eager for rescue, was conscious of a constant aching desire for her own people, and yet the old sense of outrage, of grief, of hopelessness was gone.

Of a sudden she found herself pausing, thrusting back the problems that confronted her while she drank to the full this strange mad joy of life which she felt must leave her when she left the desert. She knew only that the fear of death was gone. That hours of fever and pain were no more. That her mind had found its old poise but with an utterly new view-point of life. Her blood ran red. Her lungs breathed deep. Her eyes saw distances too big for their conception, beauties so deep that her spirit had to expand to absorb them.

The silent nights of stars, the laborious crests that tossed sudden and unspeakable views before the eyes, the eternal cañons that led beneath ranges of surpassing majesty, roused in her a passion of delight that could find expression only in her growing physical prowess. She lived and ate like a splendid boy. Day after day she scaled the ranges with Kut-le and Alchise; tenderly reared creature of an ultracivilization as she was, she learned the intricate lore of the aborigines, learned what students of the dying people would give their hearts to know.

Kut-le wakened Rhoda at dawn one day. She prepared the breakfast of coffee, bacon and tortilla. Alchise shared this eagerly with Rhoda and Kut-le, though already he had eaten with the squaws. The day was still gray when the three set out on a long day's trip in search of game. The way this morning led up a cañon deep and quiet, with the night shadows still dark and cool within it. The air was that of a northern day of June.

Rhoda tramped bravely, up and up, from cactus to

bear grass, from bear grass to stunted cedar, from cedar to pines that at last rose triumphant at the crest of a great ridge. Here Rhoda and Kut-le flung themselves to the ground to rest while Alchise prowled about restlessly. Across a hundred miles of desert rose faint snow-capped peaks.

Kut-le watched Rhoda's rapt face for a time. Then, as if unable to keep back the words, he said softly:

"Rhoda! Stay here, always! Marry me and stay here always!"

Rhoda looked at the beautiful pleading eyes. She stirred restlessly; but before she could frame an answer Alchise appeared, followed by a lean old Indian all but toothless who wore a pair of tattered overalls and a gauze shirt. The two Indians stopped before Kut-le, and Alchise jerked a thumb at the stranger.

"*Sabe* no white talk," he said.

Kut-le passed the stranger a cigarette, which he accepted without comment. A rapid conversation followed between the three Indians.

"He is an Apache," explained Kut-le, finally, to Rhoda. "His name is Injun Tom. He says that Newman and Porter hired him to trail us but he is tired of the job. They foolishly advanced him five dollars. He says they are camping in the valley right below here."

Rhoda sprang to her feet.

"Where are you going?" smiled Kut-le. "He says they are going to shoot me on sight!"

Under her tan Rhoda's face whitened.

"Would they shoot you, Kut-le, even if I told them not to?"

At the sight of the paling face the young man murmured, "You dear!" under his breath. Then aloud, "Not if I were your husband."

"How can I marry a savage?" cried Rhoda.

Kut-le put his hand under the cleft chin and lifted the sweet face till it looked directly into his. His gaze was very deep and clear.

"Am I nothing but a naked savage, Rhoda?" he said. "Am I?"

Rhoda's eyes did not leave his.

"No!" she said softly, under her breath.

Kut-le's eyes deepened. He turned and picked up his rifle.

"Bring your friend back to dinner, Alchise," he said. "Our little holiday must end right here."

They reached the camp at noon and while the squaws made ready for breaking camp, Rhoda sat deep in thought. Before her were the burning sky and desert, with hawk and buzzard circling in the clear blue. Where had the old hatred of Kut-le gone? Whence came this new trust and understanding, this thrill at his touch? Kut-le, who had been watching her adoringly, rose and came to her side. The rampart hid the two from the others. Kut-le took one of Rhoda's hands in his firm fingers and laid his lips against her palm. Rhoda flushed and drew her hand away. But Kut-le again put his hand beneath her cleft chin and lifted her face to his.

Just as the brown face all but touched hers a voice sounded from behind the rampart:

"Hello, you! Where's Kut-le?"

CHAPTER XV

AN ESCAPE

RHODA sprang away from Kut-le and they both ran to the other side of the rampart. Billy Porter, worn and tattered but still looking very well able to hold his own, stood staring into the cave where the squaws eyed him open-mouthed and Alchise, his hand on his rifle, scowled at him aggressively. Porter's eye fell on Injun Tom.

"U-huh! You pison Piute, you! I just nacherally snagged your little game, didn't I?"

"Billy!" cried Rhoda. "O Billy Porter!"

Porter jumped as if at a blow. Rhoda stood against the rock in her boyish clothes, her beautiful braid sweeping her shoulder, her face vivid.

"My God! Miss Rhoda!" cried Billy hoarsely, as he ran toward her with outstretched hands. "Why, you are well! What's happened to you!"

Here Kut-le stepped between the two.

"Hello, Mr. Porter," he said.

Billy stepped back and a look of loathing and anger took the place of the joy that had been in his eyes before.

"You Apache devil!" he growled. "You ain't as smart as you thought you were!"

Rhoda ran forward and would have taken Porter's hand but Kut-le restrained her with his hand on her shoulder.

"Where did you come from, Billy?" cried Rhoda. "Where are the others?"

Billy's face cleared a little at the sound of the girl's voice.

"They are right handy, Miss Rhoda."

"I'll give you a few details, Rhoda," said Kut-le coolly. "You see he is without water and his mouth is black with thirst. He started to trail Injun Tom but got lost and stumbled on us."

Rhoda gave a little cry of pity and running into the cave she brought Billy a brimming cup of water.

"Is that true, Billy?" she asked. "Are the others near here?"

Billy nodded then drained the cup and held it out for more.

"They are just around the corner!" with a glance at Kut-le, who smiled skeptically.

"Oh!" exclaimed Rhoda. "What terrible trouble I have made you all!"

"*You* made!" said Porter. "Well that's good! Still, that Apache devil doesn't seem to have harmed you.

AN ESCAPE

Just the same, he'll get his! If I shot him now, the other Injuns would get me and God knows what would happen to you!"

"Whom do you call an Apache devil?" asked Kut-le. Rhoda never had seen him show such evident anger.

"You, by Judas!" replied Porter, looking into the young Indian's face.

For a strained moment the two eyed each other, hatred glaring at hatred, until Rhoda put a hand on Kut-le's arm. His face cleared at once.

"So that's my reputation now, is it?" he said lightly.

"*That's* your reputation!" sneered Billy. "Do you think that's *all*? Why, don't you realize that you can't live in your own country again? Don't you know that the whites will hunt you out like you was a rat? Don't you realize that the folks that believed in you and was fond of you has had to give up their faith in you? Don't you understand that you've lost all your white friends? But I suppose that don't mean anything to an Injun!"

A look of sadness passed over Kut-le's face.

"Porter," he said very gently, "I counted on all of that before I did this thing. I thought that the sacrifice was worth while, and I still think so. I'm sorry, for your sake, that you stumbled on us here. We are going to start on the trail shortly and I must send you out to be lost again. I'll let Alchise help you in the job. As you say, I have sacrificed everything else in life; I can't afford to let anything spoil this now. You can rest for an hour. Eat and drink and fill your canteen. Take a good pack of meat and tortillas. You are welcome to it all."

The Indian spoke with such dignity, with such tragic sincerity, that Porter gave him a look of surprise and Rhoda felt hot tears in her eyes. Kut-le turned to the girl.

"You can see that I can't let you talk alone with Porter, but go ahead and say anything you want to in my hearing. Molly, you bring the white man some dinner and fix him some trail grub. Hurry up, now!"

He seated himself on the rampart and lighted a cigarette. Porter sat down meditatively, with his back against the mountain wall. He was discomfited. Kut-le had guessed correctly as to the circumstances of his finding the camp. He had no idea where his friends might have gone in the twenty-four hours since he had left them. When he stumbled on to Kut-le he had had a sudden hope that the Indian might take him captive. The Indian's quiet reception of him nonplussed him and roused his unwilling admiration.

Rhoda sat down beside Porter.

"How is John?" she asked.

"He is pretty good. He has lasted better than I thought he would."

"And Katherine and Jack?" Rhoda's voice trembled as she uttered the names. It was only with the utmost difficulty that she spoke coherently. All her nerves were on the alert for some unexpected action on the part of either Billy or the Indians.

"Jack's all right," said Billy. "We ain't seen Mrs. Jack since the day after you was took, but she's all to the good, of course, except she's been about crazy about you, like the rest of us."

"Oh, you poor, poor people!" moaned Rhoda.

Porter essayed a smile with his cracked lips.

"But, say, you do look elegant, Miss Rhoda. You ain't the same girl!"

Rhoda blushed through her tan.

"I forgot these," she said; "I've worn them so long."

"It ain't the clothes," said Billy, "and it ain't altogether your fine health. It's more—I don't know what it is! It's like the desert!"

"That's what I tell her," said Kut-le.

"Say," said Billy, scowling, "you've got a nerve, cutting in as if this was a parlor conversation you had cut in on casual. Just keep out of this, will you!"

Rhoda flushed.

"Well, as long as he can hear everything, it's a good deal of a farce not to let him talk," she said.

"Farce!" exclaimed Billy. "Say, Miss Rhoda, you ain't sticking up for this ornery Piute, are you?"

Rhoda looked at the calm eyes of the Indian, at the clean-cut intelligence of his face, and she resented Porter's words. She answered him softly but clearly.

"Kut-le did an awful and unforgivable thing in stealing me. No one knows that better than I do. But he has treated me with respect and he has given me back my health. I thank him for that and—and I do respect him!"

Kut-le's eyes flashed with a deep light but he said nothing. Porter stared at the girl with jaw dropped.

"Good Lord!" he cried. "Respect him! Wouldn't that come and get you! Do you mean that you want to stay with that Injun?"

A slow flush covered Rhoda's tanned cheeks. Her cleft chin lifted a little.

"At the very first chance," she replied, "I shall escape."

Porter sighed in great relief.

"That's all right, Miss Rhoda," he said leniently. "Respect him all you want to. I don't see how you can, but women is queer, if you don't mind my saying so. I don't blame you for feeling thankful about your health. You've stood this business better than any of us. Say, that squaw seems to be puttin' all her time on making up

AN ESCAPE

my pack. Can't I negotiate for something to eat right now? Tell her not to put pison into it."

Kut-le grinned.

"Maybe Miss Tuttle will fix up something for you, so you can eat without worrying."

"Well, she won't, you know!" growled Porter. "*Her* wait on me! She ain't no squaw!"

"Oh, but," cried Rhoda, "you don't know how proud I am of my skill! I can run the camp just as well as the squaws." Then, as Porter scowled at Kut-le, "He didn't make me! I wanted to, so as to be able to take care of myself when I escaped. When you and I get away from him," she looked at the silent Indian with an expression of daring that brought a glint of amusement to his eyes, "I'll be able to live off the trail better than you!"

"Gee!" exclaimed Porter admiringly.

"Of course, in one way it's no credit to me at all," Rhoda went on, stirring the rabbit stew she was warming up. "Kut-le—" she paused. Of what use was it to try to explain what Kut-le had done for her!

She toasted fresh tortillas and poured the stew over them and brought the steaming dish to Porter. He tasted of the mess tentatively.

"By Hen!" he exclaimed, and he set upon the stew as if half starved, while Rhoda watched him complacently.

Seeing him apparently thus engrossed, Kut-le turned to speak to Alchise. Instantly Porter dropped the stew, drew a revolver and fired two rapid shots, one catching Alchise in the leg, the other Injun Tom. Before he could get Kut-le the young Indian was upon him.

"Run, Rhoda, run!" yelled Porter, as he went down, under Kut-le.

Rhoda gave one glance at Injun Tom and Alchise writhing with their wounds, at Porter's fingers tightening at Kut-le's throat, then she seized the canteen she had filled for Porter and started madly down the trail. The screaming squaws gave no heed to her.

She ran swiftly, surely, down the rocky way, watching the trail with secondary sense, for every other was strained to catch the sounds from above. But she heard nothing but the screams of the squaws. The trail twisted violently near the desert floor. She sped about one last jutting buttress, then stopped abruptly, one hand on her heaving breast.

A man was running toward the foot of the trail. He, too, stopped abruptly. The girl seemed a marvel of beauty to him. With the curly hair beneath the drooping sombrero, the tanned, flushed face, the parted scarlet lips, the throat and tiny triangle of chest disclosed by the rough blue shirt with one button missing from the top, and the beautiful lithe legs in the clinging buckskins,

Rhoda was a wonderful thing to come upon unexpectedly. As John DeWitt took off his hat, his haggard face went white, his stalwart shoulders heaved.

"O John! Dear John DeWitt!" cried Rhoda. "Turn back with me quick! I am running away while Mr. Porter holds Kut-le!"

DeWitt held out his shaking hands to her, unbelieving rapture growing in his eyes.

CHAPTER XVI

ADRIFT IN THE DESERT

RHODA put her hands into the outstretched, shaking palms.

"Rhoda! Sweetheart! Sweetheart!" DeWitt gasped. Then his voice failed him.

For an instant Rhoda leaned against his heaving chest. She felt as if after long wandering in a dream she suddenly had stepped back into life. But it was only for the instant that she paused. Her face was blazing with excitement.

"Come!" she cried. "Come!"

"Take my arm! Or had I better carry you?" exclaimed DeWitt.

"Huh!" sniffed Rhoda. "Just try to keep up with me, that's all!"

DeWitt, despite the need for haste, stopped and stared at the girl, open-mouthed. Then as he realized what superb health she showed in every line of face and body, he cried:

"You are well! You are well! O Rhoda, I never thought to see you this way!"

Rhoda squeezed his fingers joyfully.

"I am so strong! Hurry, John! Hurry!"

"Where are the Indians?" panted DeWitt, running along beside her. "What were those shots?"

"Billy Porter found our camp. He shot Alchise and Injun Tom and he and Kut-le were wrestling as I ran." Then Rhoda hesitated. "Perhaps you ought to go back and help Billy!"

But John pulled her ahead.

"Leave you until I get you to safety? Why, Billy himself would half murder me if I thought of it! Our camp is over there, a three hours' trip." DeWitt pointed to a distant peak. "If we swing around to the left, the Indians won't see us!"

Hand in hand the two settled to a swinging trot. The dreadful fear of pursuit was on them both. It submerged their first joy of meeting, and left them panic-stricken. For many minutes they ran without speaking. At last, when well out into the burning heat of the desert, they could keep up the pace no longer and dropped to a rapid walk. Still there came no sound of pursuit.

"Was Porter hurt?" panted John.

"Not when I left," answered Rhoda.

"I wonder what his plan is?" said john. "He left the camp yesterday to trail Injun Tom. We'll go back for him as quick as I can get you to camp."

Rhoda looked up at DeWitt anxiously.

"You are very tired and worn, John," she said.

"And you!" cried the man, looking down at the girl with the swinging, tireless stride. "What miracle has come to you?"

"I never dreamed that there could be health like this! I—" She stopped, with head to one side. "Do you hear anything? What do you suppose they are doing to each other? Oh, I hope neither of them will get killed!"

"I hope— They have all promised to let me deal with Kut-le!" said DeWitt grimly, pausing to listen intently. But no sound came across the burning sands.

Rhoda started at DeWitt's words. Suddenly her early sense of the appalling nature of her experience returned to her. She looked with new eyes at DeWitt's face. It was not the same face that she had last seen at the Newman ranch. John had the look of a man who has passed through the fire of tragedy. She gripped his burned fingers with both her slender hands.

"O John!" she cried, "I wasn't worth it! I wasn't worth it! Let's get to the camp quickly, so that you can rest! It would take a lifetime of devotion to make up for that look in your face!"

John's quiet manner left him.

"It was a devilish thing for him to do!" he said fiercely.

"Heaven help him when I get him!" Then before Rhoda could speak he smiled grimly. "This pace is fearful. If you keep it up you will have sunstroke, Rhoda. And at that, you're standing it better than I!"

They slowed their pace. DeWitt was breathing hard as the burning lava dust bit into his throat.

"I haven't minded the physical discomfort," he went on. "It's the mental torture that's been killing me. We've pushed hot on your trail hour after hour, day in and day out. When they made me rest, I could only lie and listen to you sob for help until—O my love! My love!—"

His voice broke and Rhoda laid her cheek against his arm for a moment.

"I know! O John dear, I know!" she whispered.

They trudged on in silence for a time, both listening for the sound of pursuit. Then DeWitt spoke, as if he forced himself to ask for an answer that he dreaded.

"Rhoda, did they torture you much?"

"No! There was no torture except that of fearful hardships. At first—you know how weak and sick I was, John—at first I just lived in an agony of fear and anger—sort of a nightmare of exhaustion and frenzy. Then at Chira I began to get strong and as my health came, the wonder of it, the—oh, I can't put it into words! Kut-le was—" Rhoda paused, wondering at the reluctance with which she spoke the young Indian's name. "You missed us so narrowly so many times!"

"The Indian had the devil's own luck and we always blundered," said DeWitt. "I have had the feeling lately that my bones would be bleaching on this stretch of Hades before you ever were heard of. Rhoda, if I can get you safely to New York again I'll shoot the first man who says desert to me!"

Rhoda became strangely silent, though she clung to John's hand and now and again lifted it against her cheek. The yellow of the desert reeled in heat waves about them. The deep, intensely deep blue of the sky glowed silently down on them. Never to see them again! Never to waken with the desert stars above her face or to make camp with the crimson dawn blinding her vision! Never to know again the wild thrill of the chase! Finally Rhoda gave herself a mental shake and looked up into John's tired face.

"How did you come to leave the camp, John?" she asked gently.

"It's all been luck," said John. "With the exception of a little trail wisdom that Billy or Carlos raked up once in a while it's just been hit-or-miss luck with us. We suspected that Billy had gone on Injun Tom's trail, so we made camp on the spot so he wouldn't lose us. I stood guard this morning while Jack and Carlos slept and then

I thought that that was fool nonsense, as Kut-le never traveled by day. So I started on a hunt along Billy's trail—and here we are!"

"Are there any other people hunting for me?"

"Lord, yes! At first they were fairly walking over each other. But the ranchers had to go back to their work and the curious got tired. Most of those that are left are down along the Mexican border. They thought of course that Kut-le would get off American territory as soon as he could. Must we keep such a pace, Rhoda girl? You will be half dead before we can reach the camp!"

Rhoda smiled.

"I've followed Kut-le's tremendous pace so many miles that I doubt if I shall ever walk like a perfect lady again!"

"I thought that I would go off my head," DeWitt went on, dropping into a walk, "when I saw you there at Dead Man's Mesa and you escaped into that infernal crevice! Gee, Rhoda, I can't believe that this really is you!"

The sun was setting as they climbed through a wide stretch of greasewood to the first rough rock heaps of the mountains. Then DeWitt paused uncertainly.

"Why, this isn't right! I never was here before!"

Rhoda spoke cheerfully.

"Perhaps you have the right mountain but the wrong trail!"

"No! This is altogether wrong. I remember this peak now, with a sort of saw edge to the top. What a chump I am! I distinctly remember seeing this mountain from the trail this morning."

"How did it lie?" asked Rhoda, sitting down on a convenient stone.

"Gee, I can't remember whether to the right or left!"

Rhoda clasped and unclasped her hands nervously.

"I hate to stop. One can't tell what Kut-le is up to!"

DeWitt squared his broad shoulders.

"Don't you worry, little girl. If he does find us he'll have to take us both! We'll just have to rest here for a moment. There's no use starting till we have our sense of direction again."

Rhoda raised her eyebrows. After all the fearful lessons, DeWitt had not yet come to a full realization of the skill and resourcefulness of Kut-le. The girl said nothing, however, but left the leadership to DeWitt. The sun was setting, turning to clear red and pale lavender a distant peak that then merged with the dusk, one could not tell when nor how. Rhoda and DeWitt sat at the foot of an inhospitable crag whose distant top, baring itself to the heavens, was a fearful climb above them. Rhoda watched the sunset a little wistfully. She must impress on her memory every one that she saw now. She felt that her days in the desert were numbered.

DeWitt shook his empty canteen.

"It was mighty clever of you to bring a canteen. We've got to be careful of the water question. Of course, I'm confident we will reach camp this evening, but you can't be too careful of water anyhow. Lord! Think of Jack Newman's face when we come strolling in! We ought to be back at the ranch in five days."

"Do you know it's going to be strange to talk with Katherine!" exclaimed Rhoda. "She's a white woman, you know!"

DeWitt took both of Rhoda's brown little hands in his.

"I'm not appearing very sympathetic, sweetheart," he said. "But I'm so crazy with joy at having you again and of finding you so well that I don't know what I'm saying."

"John," said Rhoda slowly, "I don't need any sympathy! I tell you that this has been the most wonderful experience that ever came into my life. I have suffered!" Her voice trembled and John's hold on her hands tightened. "God only knows how I have suffered! But I have learned things that were worth the misery!"

DeWitt looked at her wide-eyed.

"You're a wonder!" he exclaimed.

Rhoda laughed softly.

"You ought to hear the Indians' opinion of me! Do you know what I've thought of lots of times lately? You know that place on the Hudson where men go when they are nervous wrecks and the doctor cures them by grilling them mentally and physically clear beyond endurance? Well, that's the sort of cure I've had, except that I've had two doctors, the Indian and the desert!"

DeWitt answered slowly.

"I don't quite see it! But I know one thing. You are about the gamest little thoroughbred I ever heard of!"

The moon was rising and DeWitt watched Rhoda as she sat with her hands clasping her knee in the boyish attitude that had become a habit.

"You are simply fascinating in those clothes, Rhoda. You are like a beautiful slender boy in them."

"They are very comfortable," said Rhoda, in such a sedate matter-of-fact tone despite her blush that DeWitt chuckled. He threw his arm across her shoulder and hugged her to him ecstatically.

"Rhoda! Rhoda! You are the finest ever! I can't believe that this terrible nightmare is over! And to think that instead of finding you all but dead, you are a thousand times more fit than I am myself. Rhoda, just think! You are going to live! To live! You will not be my wife just for a few months, as we thought, but for years and years!"

They stood in silence for a time, each one busy with the picture DeWitt's words had conjured. Then DeWitt emptied the pipe he had been smoking.

"Yonder is our peak, by Jove! It looked just so in the moonlight last night. I didn't recognize it by daylight. If you're rested, we'll start now. You must be dead hungry! I know I am!"

Refreshed and hopeful, they swung out into the wonder of the moonlit desert. They soon settled to each other's pace and with the full moon glowing in their faces they made for the distant peak.

"Now," said John, "tell me the whole story!"

So Rhoda, beginning with the moment of her abduction, told the story of her wanderings, told it simply though omitting no detail. Nothing could have been more dramatic than the quiet voice that now rose, now fell with intensity of feeling. DeWitt did not interrupt her except with a muttered exclamation now and again.

"And the actual sickness was not the worst," Rhoda continued after describing her experiences up to her sickness at Chira; "it was the delirium of fear and anger. Kut-le forced me beyond the limit of my strength. Night after night I was tied to the saddle and kept there till I fainted. Then I was rested only enough to start again. And it angered and frightened me so! I was so sick! I loathed them all so—except Molly. But after

Chira a change came. I got stronger than I ever dreamed of being. And I began to understand Kut-le's methods. He had realized that physically and mentally I was at the lowest ebb and that only heroic measures could save me. He had the courage to apply the measures."

"God!" muttered John.

Rhoda scarcely heeded him.

"It was then that I began to see things that I could not see before and to think thoughts that I could not have thought before. It was as if I had climbed a mental peak that made my old highest ideals seem like mere foothills!"

The quiet voice led on and on, stopping at last with Porter's advent that afternoon. Then Rhoda looked up into DeWitt's face. It was drawn and tense. His eyes were black with feeling and his close-pressed lips twitched.

"Rhoda," he said at la t, "I thought most of the savage had been civilized out of me. But I tell you now that if ever I get a chance I shall kill that Apache with my bare hands!"

Rhoda laid her hand on DeWitt's arm.

"Kut-le, after all, has done me only a great good, John!"

"But think how he did it! The devil risked killing you! Think what you and we all have suffered! God, Rhoda, think!" And DeWitt threw his arm across his face with a sob that wrenched his shoulders.

Inexpressibly touched, Rhoda stopped and drew John's face down to hers, rubbing it softly with her velvet cheek.

"There, dear, there! I can't bear to see you so! My poor tired boy! You have all but killed yourself for me!"

DeWitt lifted the slender little figure and held it tensely in his arms a moment, then set her gently down.

"A woman's magnanimity is a strange thing," he said.

"Kut-le will suffer," said Rhoda. "He risked everything and has lost. He has neither friends nor country now."

"Much he cares," retorted DeWitt, "except for losing you!"

Rhoda made no answer. She realized that it would take careful pleading on her part to win freedom for Kut-le if ever he were caught. She changed the subject.

"Have you found living off the desert hard? I mean as far as food was concerned?"

"Food hasn't bothered us," answered John. "We've kept well supplied."

Rhoda chuckled.

"Then I can't tempt you to stop and have some roast mice with me?"

"Thank you," answered DeWitt. "Try and control your yearning for them, honey girl. We shall be at camp shortly and have some white man's grub."

"How long since you have eaten, John?" asked Rhoda.

She had been watching the tall fellow's difficult and slacking steps for some time.

"Well, not since last night, to tell the truth. You see I was so excited when I struck Porter's trail that I didn't go back to the camp. I just hiked."

"So you are faint with hunger," said Rhoda, "and your feet are blistered, for you have done little tramping in the hot sand before this. John, look at that peak! Are you sure it is the right one?"

DeWitt stared long and perplexedly.

"Rhoda girl," he said, "I don't believe it is, after all. I am the blamedest tenderfoot! But don't you worry. We will find the camp. It's right in this neighborhood."

CHAPTER XVII

THE HEART'S OWN BITTERNESS

"I'M not worrying," answered Rhoda stoutly, "except about you. You are shaking with exhaustion while I am as fit as can be."

"Oh, don't bother about me!" exclaimed John. "I'm just a little tired."

But Rhoda was not to be put off.

"How much did you sleep last night?"

"Not much," admitted DeWitt. "I haven't been a heavy sleeper at times ever since you disappeared, strange as that may seem!" Then he grinned. It was pleasant to have Rhoda bully him.

Yet the big fellow actually was sinking with weariness. The fearful hardships that he had undergone had worked havoc with him. Now that the agonizing nerve-strain was lifted he was going to pieces. He stood wavering for a minute, then he slowly sat down in the sand.

Rhoda stood beside him uncertainly and looked from the man to the immovably distant mountain peak. She realized that, in stopping, the risk of recapture was great, yet her desert experiences told her that John must regain some of his strength before the sun caught them. She had little faith that they would tumble upon the camp as easily as John thought, and wanted to prepare for a day of desert heat.

"If we were sure just where the camp lay," she said, "I would go on for help. But as we aren't certain, I'm afraid to be separated from you, John."

John looked up fiercely with his haggard eyes.

"Don't you dare to move six inches from me, Rhoda. It will kill me to lose you now."

"Of course I won't," said Rhoda. "I've had my lesson about losing myself in the desert. But you must have some sleep before we go any farther."

Rhoda spoke with a cheerfulness she did not feel. She looked about for a comfortable resting-place but the desert was barren.

"There's no use trying to find a comfortable bed," she said. "You had better lie down right where you are."

"Honey," said John, "I've no idea of sleeping. It will be time enough for that when we reach camp. But if you think you could stand guard for just ten minutes I will lie flat in the sand and rest. You take my watch and time me."

"That's splendid!" said Rhoda, helping him to clear of rocks and cactus a space long enough to lie in.

"Just ten minutes," said DeWitt, and as he spoke he sank to sleep.

Rhoda stood in the moonlight looking into the man's unconscious face. His new-grown beard gave him a haggard look that was enhanced by the dark circles under his eyes. That wan face touched Rhoda much more than the healthy face of former days. The lines of weariness and pain that never could be fully erased were all for her, she thought with a little catch of her breath. Then with a pitying, affectionate look at the sleeping man came a whimsical smile. Once she had thought no one could equal John in physical vigor. Now she pictured Kut-le's panther strength and endurance, and smiled.

She looked at the watch. Five hours till dawn. She would let John have the whole of that time in which to sleep. His ten minutes would be worse than useless, while to find the camp after the moon had set would be quite out of the question. Her own eyes were wide and sleepless. She sat in the sand beside DeWitt until driven by the cold to pace back and forth. John slept without stirring; the sleep of complete exhaustion. Rhoda was not afraid, nor did she feel lonely. The desert was hers now. There was no wind, but now and again the cactus rustled as if unseen wings had brushed it. The dried heaps of cholla stirred as if unseen paws had pressed them. From afar came the demoniacal laughter of coyotes on their night hunts. But still Rhoda was not afraid.

At first, in the confusion of thoughts that the day's events had crowded on her, her clearest sense was of thankfulness. Then she fell to wondering what had happened to Porter and Kut-le. Suddenly she caught her breath with a shiver. If Porter won there could be but one answer as to Kut-le's fate. John's attitude of mind told that. Rhoda twisted her hands together.

"I will not have him killed!" she whispered. "No! No! I will not have him killed!"

For many minutes she paced back and forth, battling with her fears. Then she suddenly recalled the fact that vengeance was to be saved for John. This uncanny thought comforted her. She had little fear but that she could manage John.

And then in the utter silence of the desert night, staring at the sinking moon, Rhoda asked herself why, when she should have been mad with joy over her own rescue, she was giving all her thoughts to Kut-le's plight! For a moment the question brought a flood of confusion. Then, standing alone in the night beauty of the desert, the girl acknowledged the truth that she had denied even to herself so long. The young Indian's image returned to her endowed with all the dignity of his remarkable

THE HEART'S OWN BITTERNESS

physical perfection. She knew now that from the first this physical beauty of his had had a strong appeal to her. She knew now that all his unusual characteristics that at first had seemed so strange to her were the ones that had drawn her to him. His strange mental honesty, his courage, his brutal incisiveness, all had fascinated her. All her days with him returned to her, days of weakness, of anger, then the weeks on the ledge, and the day when she had found the desert, and finally the day just past, to the very moment when Billy Porter had come upon them on the ledge.

Rhoda stood with unseeing eyes while before her inward vision passed a magnificent panorama of the glories through which Kut-le had led her. Chaos of mountain and desert, resplendent with color; cool, sweet depth of cañon; burning height of tortured peak; slope of pungent piñon forest—all wrapped in the haze which is the desert's own.

Rhoda knew the truth; knew that she loved Kut-le! She knew that she loved him with all the passionate devotion for which her rebirth had given her the capacity.

With this acknowledgment, all her calm was swept away. With fingers clasped against her breast, with wide eyes on the brooding night, she wished that she might tell him this that had come to her. If only once more the inscrutable tenderness of his black eyes were upon her!

If the deep imperative voice were but sounding in her ears again! If only she could feel now the touch of his powerful arms as he carried her the long sick miles to Chira. Trembling with longing, her gaze fell upon the man sleeping at her feet. She drew a sudden troubled breath. Must she renounce this new rapture of living? Must she?

"Have I found new life in the desert only to lose it?" she whispered. "O Kut-le! Kut-le!"

DeWitt slept on, unmoving, and Rhoda watched him with tragedy-stricken eyes.

"What shall I do!" she whispered, lips quivering, shaking hands twisting together. "Oh, what shall I do!"

She tried to picture a future with Kut-le. She saw his tenderness, his purposefulness, the bigness of his mind and spirit. Then with a cold clutch at her throat came the thought of race barrier, and in a moment Rhoda was plunged into the oldest, the most hopeless, the least solvable of all love's problems. Minute after minute went by and the girl, standing by the sleeping man, fought a fight that shook her slender body and racked her soul. At last she raised her face to the sky.

"I want to do what is right!" she said piteously. "It doesn't matter about me, if only I can decide what is right!" Then after a pause, "I will marry John! I

THE HEART'S OWN BITTERNESS 239

will!" like a child that has been punished and promises to be good. Still another pause, then, "So that part of me is dead!" and she put her fingers before her eyes and fell to crying, not with the easy tears of a woman but with the deep, agonizing sobs of a man over his dead.

"Kut-le, I wanted you! I wanted you for my mate! If I could have heard you, seen you, felt you once more! Nothing else would have mattered. I wanted you!"

A long hour passed in which Rhoda sat in the sand, limp and quiescent, as though all but wrecked by the storm through which she had passed. Dawn came at last. The air was pregnant with new hope, with a vague uplifting of sense and being that told of the coming of a new day. The east quivered with prismatic colors and suddenly the sun appeared.

Rhoda rose and stooped over DeWitt to smooth the hair back from his forehead.

"Come," she said softly. "It's breakfast time!"

DeWitt sat up bewildered. Then his senses returned.

"Rhoda," he exclaimed, "what do you mean by this!"

Rhoda's smile was a little wan.

"You needed the rest and I didn't!"

DeWitt rose and shook himself like a great dog, then looked at Rhoda wonderingly.

"And you don't look much done up! But you had no right to do such a thing! I told you to give me ten minutes. I feel like a brute. Lie down now and get a little sleep yourself."

"Lie in the sun? Thank you, I'd rather push on to the camp and have some breakfast. How do you feel?"

"Much better! It was fine of you, dear, but it wasn't a fair deal."

"I'll be good from now on!" said Rhoda meekly. "What would you like for breakfast?"

DeWitt looked about him. Already the desert was assuming its brazen aspect.

"Water will be enough for me," he answered, "and nothing else. I am seriously considering a rigid diet for a time."

They both drank sparingly of the water in Rhoda's canteen.

"I have three shots in my Colt," said DeWitt, "but I want to save them for an emergency. But if we don't strike camp pretty soon, I'll try to pot a jack-rabbit."

"We can eat desert mice," said Rhoda. "I know how to catch and cook them!"

"Heaven forbid!" ejaculated DeWitt. "Let's start on at once, if you're not too tired."

So they began the day cheerfully. As the morning wore on and they found no trace of the camp, they began to watch the canteen carefully. Gradually their thirst became so great that the desire for food was quite secon-

THE HEART'S OWN BITTERNESS

dary to it and they made no attempt to hunt for a rabbit. They agreed toward noon to save the last few drops in the canteen until they could no longer do without it.

Hour after hour they toiled in the blinding heat, the strange deep blue of the sky reflecting the brazen light of the desert. In their careful avoiding of the mountain where they had rested at sunset the night before, they gradually worked out into a wide barren space with dunes and rock heaps interchanging.

"This won't do at all," said Dewitt at last, wearily. "We had better try for any old mountain at all in the hope of finding water."

They stood panting, staring at the distant haze of a peak. Trackless and tortuous, the way underfoot was incredibly difficult. Yet the distances melted in ephemeral slopes as lovely in their tints as they were accursed in their reality of cruelty. Rhoda, unaccustomed to day travel, panted and gasped as they walked. But she held her own fairly well, while DeWitt, sick and overstrained at the start, was failing rapidly.

"It's noon now," said John a little thickly. "You had better lie in the shade of that rock for an hour."

"You sleep too!" pleaded Rhoda.

"I'm too hot to sleep. I'll wake you in an hour."

When Rhoda awoke it was to see DeWitt leaning against the rock heap, his lips swollen, his eyes uncertain.

Weak and dizzy herself, she rose and laid her hand on John's, every maternal instinct in her stirring and speaking in her gray eyes.

"Come, dear boy, we mustn't give up so easily."

John lifted the little hand to his cheek.

"I won't give up," he said uncertainly. "I'll take care of you, honey girl!"

"Come on, then!" said Rhoda. "You see that queer bunch of cholla yonder? Let's get as far as that before we stop again!"

With a great effort, DeWitt gathered himself together and, fixing his eyes on the fantastic cactus growth, he plodded desperately through the sand. At the cholla bunch, Rhoda pointed to a jutting lavender rock.

"At that we'll rest for a minute. Come on, John!"

John's sick eyes did not waver but his trembling legs described many circles in their journey to the jutting rock. Distances were so many times what they seemed that Rhoda's little scheme carried them over a mile of desert before DeWitt sank to his knees.

"I'm a sick man," he said huskily as he fell in a limp heap.

Nothing could have appeared more opportunely than this new hardship to take Rhoda's mind off her misery of the night. Nothing could have brought John so near to her as this utter helplessness brought about through his

THE HEART'S OWN BITTERNESS 243

toiling for her. She looked at him with tears of pity in her eyes, while her heart sank with fright. She knew the terrible danger that menaced them. But she closed her lips firmly and looked thoughtfully at the mite of water that remained to them. Then she held the canteen to DeWitt's lips. He pushed it away from him and in another moment or so he rose.

Rhoda, fastening their hopes to another distant cholla, led the way on again. But she too was growing a little light-headed. The distant cactus danced grotesquely and black spots flitted between her and the molten iron over which her fancy said they traveled. Suddenly she laughed crazily:

> "'Twas brillig, and the slythy toves
> Did gyre and gimble in the wabe;
> All mimsy were the borogoves,
> And the mome raths outgrabe!"

DeWitt laughed hoarsely.

"That's just the way it looks to me, Rhoda. But you're just as crazy as I am."

Rhoda jerked herself together and tried to moisten her lips with her swollen tongue.

"We must take it turn about. When you are crazy I must try to be sane!"

"Good idea!" croaked DeWitt, "only I'm crazy all the time!"

"'O frabjous day! Calloo! Collay!
 He chortled in his joy!'"

Rhoda patted his hand.

"Poor John! Oh, my poor John! I was not worth all this. You may not have an Apache's strength, but your heart is right!" Two great tears rolled down her cheeks.

DeWitt looked at her seriously.

"You aren't as dry as I am. I haven't enough moisture in me to moisten my eyeballs, let alone cry! I am so cracked and dry that you will have to soak me in the first spring we come to before I'll hold water."

Rhoda laughed weakly and John turned away with a hurt look.

"It's not a joke!" he said.

How long they were, in their staggering, circuitous course, in reaching their goal of cholla, Rhoda never knew. She knew that each heavy foot, tingling and scorched, seemed to drag her back a step for every one that she took forward. She knew that she repeatedly offered the last of their water to John and that he repeatedly refused it, urging it on her. She knew that the pulp of the barrel cactus that she tried to chew turned to bitter sawdust in her mouth and sickened her. Then suddenly, as she struggled to refocus her wandering wits on the cholla, it appeared within touch of her hand.

Afraid to pause, she adopted a new goal in a far mesa, and clutching DeWitt's unresponsive fingers she struggled forward.

And so on and on toward a never nearing goal; now falling, now rising, now pausing to strive to hush Dewitt's cracked voice that wandered aimlessly through all the changes of verse that seemed to his delirium appropriate to the occasion. It seemed to Rhoda that her own brain was reeling as she watched the illimitable space through which they moved. John's voice did not cease.

> "Alone! Alone! All, all, alone!
> Alone on a wide, wide sea!
> So lonely 'twas that God himself,
> Scarce seeméd there to be!"

"Hush, John! Hush!" pleaded Rhoda.

> "Alone! Alone! All, all alone!"

repeated the croaking voice.

"But I'm with you, John!" Rhoda pleaded, but DeWitt rambled on unheeding.

The way grew indescribably rough. The desert floor became a series of sand dunes, a rise and fall of sea-like billows over which they climbed like ants over a new-plowed field. In the hollow of each wave they rested, sinking in the sand, where, breathless and scorching, the air scintillated above their motionless forms. At the crest of each they rested again, the desert wind hurtling the hot sand against their parched skins. Frequently

John refused to rise and Rhoda in her half delirium would sink beside him until the mist lifted from her brain and once more the distant mesa forced itself upon her vision.

"Come, John, we will soon be there. We can't keep on this way forever and not reach some place. Please come, dear!"

"'He maketh me to lie down in green pastures. He leadeth me beside still waters. He restoreth my soul—'"

"Perhaps there will be water there! O John, dear John, if you love me, come!"

"I don't love you, little boy! I love Rhoda Tuttle.

> "O for a draught of vintage that hath been
> Cooled a long age in deep delved earth!"

"Please, John! I'm so sick!"

The man, after two or three attempts, staggered to his feet and stood swaying.

"God help me!" he said. "I can do no more!"

"Yes, you can, John! Yes, you can! Perhaps there is a whole fountain of water there on the mesa!"

The glazed look returned to DeWitt's eyes.

"'Or the pitcher be broken at the fountain,'" he muttered, "'or the wheel broken at the cistern—or the pitcher broken at the fountain, or the wheel—'"

Rhoda threw her arm across her eyes.

"Oh, not that, John! I can't bear that one!"

Again she stood upon the roof at Chira, looking up

THE HEART'S OWN BITTERNESS 247

into Kut-le's face. Again the low wailing of the Indian women and the indescribable depth and hunger of those dear black eyes. Again the sense of protection and content in his nearness.

"O Kut-le! Kut-le!" she moaned.

Instantly sanity returned to John's eyes.

"Why did you say Kut-le?" he demanded thickly. "Were you thinking of him?"

"Yes," answered Rhoda simply. "Come on, John!"

DeWitt struggled on bravely to the crest of the next dune.

"I hate that Apache devil!" he muttered. "I am going to kill him!"

Rhoda quickly saw the magic of Kut-le's name.

"Why should you want to kill Kut-le?" she asked as Dewitt paused at the top of the next dune. Instantly he started on.

"Because I hate him! I hate him, the devil!"

"See how near the mesa is, John! Only a little way! Kut-le would say we were poor stuff!"

"No doubt! Well, I'll let a gun give him my opinion of him!"

The sand dunes had indeed beaten themselves out against the wall of a giant mesa. Rhoda followed blindly along the wall and stumbled upon a precipitous trail leading upward.

CHAPTER XVIII

THE FORGOTTEN CITY

Up this tortuous trail Rhoda staggered, closely followed by DeWitt. At a level spot the girl paused.

"Water, John! Water!" she cried.

The two threw themselves down and drank of the bubbling spring until they could hold no more. Then Rhoda lay down on the sun-warmed rocks and sleep overwhelmed her.

She opened her eyes to stare into a yellow moon that floated liquidly above her. Whether she had slept through a night and a day or whether but a few hours had elapsed since she had staggered to the spring beside which she lay, she could not tell. She lay looking up into the sky languidly, but with clear mind. A deep sigh roused her. DeWitt sat on the other side of the spring, rubbing his eyes.

"Hello!" he said in a hoarse croak. "How did we land here?"

"I led us here sometime in past ages. When or how, *quién sabe?*" answered Rhoda. "John, we must find food somehow."

"Drink all the water you can, Rhoda," said DeWitt;

"it helps some, and I'll pot a rabbit. What a fool I am. You poor girl! More hardships for you!"

Rhoda dipped her burning face into the water, then lifted it, dripping.

"If only you won't be delirious, John, I can stand the hardships."

DeWitt looked at the girl curiously.

"Was I delirious? And you were alone, leading me across that Hades out there? Rhoda dear, you make me ashamed of myself!"

"I don't see how you were to blame," answered Rhoda stoutly. "Think what you have been doing for me!"

John rose stiffly.

"Do you feel equal to climbing this trail with me, to find where we are, or had you rather stay here?"

"I don't want to stay here alone," answered Rhoda.

Very slowly and weakly they started up the trail. The spring was on a broad stone terrace. Above it rose another terrace weathered and disrupted until in the moonlight it looked like an impregnable castle wall, embattled and embuttressed. But clinging to the seemingly invulnerable fortress was the trail, a snake-like shadow in the moonlight.

"Perhaps we had better stay at the spring until morning," suggested Rhoda, her weak legs flagging.

"Not with the hope of shelter a hundred feet above us,"

answered John firmly. "This trail is worn six inches into the solid rock. My guess is that there are some inhabitants here. It's queer that they haven't discovered us."

Slowly and without further protest, Rhoda followed DeWitt up the trail. Deep-worn and smooth though it was, they accomplished their task with infinite difficulty. Rhoda, stumbling like a sleep-sodden child, wondered if ever again she was to accomplish physical feats with the magical ease with which Kut-le had endowed her.

"If he were here, I'd know I was to tumble into a comfortable camp," she thought. Then with a remorseful glance at DeWitt's patient back, "What a selfish beast you are, Rhoda Tuttle!"

She reached John's side and together they paused at the top of the trail. Black against the sky, the moon crowning its top with a frost-like radiance, was a huge flat-topped building. Night birds circled about it. From black openings in its front owls hooted. But otherwise there was neither sight nor sound of living thing. The desert far below and beyond lay like a sea of death. Rhoda unconsciously drew nearer to DeWitt.

"Where are the dogs? At Chira the dogs barked all night. Indians always have dogs!"

"It must be very late," whispered DeWitt. "Even the dogs are asleep!"

"And at Chira," went on Rhoda, whispering as did DeWitt, "owls didn't hoot from the windows."

"Let's go closer," suggested John.

Rhoda thrust cold little fingers into his hand.

The doors were empty and forlorn. The terraced walls, built with the patient labor of the long ago, were sagged and decayed. Riot of greasewood crowned great heaps of débris. A loneliness as of the end of the world came upon the two wanderers. Sick and dismayed, they stood in awe before this relic of the past.

"*Whoo! Whoo!*" an owl's cry sounded from the black window openings.

DeWitt spoke softly.

"Rhoda, it's one of the forgotten cities!"

"Let's go back! Let's go back to the spring!" pleaded Rhoda. "It is so uncanny in the dark!"

"No!" DeWitt rubbed his aching head wearily. "I must contrive some sort of shelter for you. Almost anything is better than another night in the open desert. Come on! We will explore a little."

"Let's wait till morning," begged Rhoda. "I'm so cold and shivery."

"Dear sweetheart, that's just the point. You will be sick if you don't have some sort of shelter. You have suffered enough. Will you sit here and let me look about?"

THE FORGOTTEN CITY 253

"No! No! I don't want to be left alone."

Rhoda followed John closely up into the mass of fallen rock.

DeWitt smiled. It appealed to the tenderest part of his nature that the girl who had led him through the terrible experiences of the desert should show fear now that a haven was reached.

"Come on, little girl," he said.

Painfully, for they both were weak and dizzy, they clambered to a gaunt opening in the gray wall. Rhoda clutched John's arm with a little scream as a bat whirred close by them. Within the opening DeWitt scratched one of his carefully hoarded matches. The tiny flare revealed a small adobe-walled room, quite bare save for broken bits of pottery on the floor. John lighted a handful of greasewood and by its brilliant light they examined the floor and walls.

"What a clean, dry little room!" exclaimed Rhoda. "Oh, I am so tired and sleepy!"

"Let's look a little farther before we stop. What's on the other side of this broken wall?"

They picked their way across the litter of pottery and peered into another room, the duplicate of the first.

"How will these do for our respective sleeping-rooms?" asked DeWitt.

Rhoda stared at John with horror in her eyes.

"I'd as soon sleep in a tomb! Let's make a fire outside and sleep under the stars. I'd rather have sleep than food just now."

"It will have to be just a tiny smudge, up behind this débris, where Kut-le can't spot it," answered DeWitt. "I won't mind having a red eye of fire for company. It will help to keep me awake."

"But you must sleep," protested Rhoda.

"But I musn't," answered John grimly. "I've played the baby act on this picnic as much as I propose to. It is my trick at the wheel."

Too weary to protest further, Rhoda threw herself down with her feet toward the fire and pillowed her head on her arm. DeWitt filled his pipe and sat puffing it, with his arms folded across his knees. Rhoda watched him for a moment or two. She found herself admiring the full forehead, the lines of refinement about the lips that the beard could not fully conceal.

"He's not as handsome as Kut-le," she thought wearily, "but he's—he's—" but before her thought was completed she was asleep.

Rhoda woke at dawn and lay waiting for the stir of the squaws about the morning meal. Then with a start she rose and looked soberly about her. Suddenly she smiled.

"Tenderfoot!" she murmured.

DeWitt lay fast asleep by the ashes of the fire.

THE FORGOTTEN CITY 255

"If Kut-le," she thought. Then she stopped abruptly and stamped her foot. "You are not even to think of Kut-le any more!" And with her cleft chin very firm she descended the trail to the spring. When she returned, DeWitt was rising stiffly to his feet.

"Hello!" he cried. "I was good this time. I never closed my eyes till dawn. I'm so hungry I could eat greasewood. How do you feel?"

"Weak with hunger but otherwise very well. Go wash your face, Johnny."

DeWitt grinned and started down the trail obediently. But Rhoda laid a detaining hand on his arm. The sun was but a moment high. All the mesa front lay in purple shadows, though farther out the desert glowed with the yellow light of a new day.

"I think animals come to the spring to drink," said Rhoda. "There were tiny wet footmarks there when I went down to wash my face."

"Bully!" exclaimed John. "Wait now, let's watch."

The two dropped to the ground and peered over the edge of the upper terrace. The spring bubbled forth serenely, followed its shallow trough a short distance, then disappeared into the insatiable floor of the desert. For several moments the two lay watching until at last Rhoda grew restless. DeWitt laid a detaining hand on her arm.

"Hush!" he whispered.

A pair of jack-rabbits loped up the trail, sniffed the air tentatively, then with forelegs in the water drank greedily. DeWitt's right arm stiffened, there were two puffs of smoke and the two kicking rabbits rolled into the spring.

"I'm beginning to have a little self-respect as the man of the party," said DeWitt, as he blew the smoke from his Colt.

Rhoda ran down to the spring and lifted the two wet little bodies. John took them from her.

"If you'll find some place for a table, I'll bring these up in no time."

When DeWitt came up from the spring with the dressed rabbits, he found a little fire glowing between two rocks. Near by on a big flat-topped stone were set forth two earthen bowls, with a brown water-jar in the center. As he stared, Rhoda came out of the building with interested face.

"Look, John! See what I found on a little corner shelf!" She held in her outstretched hand a tiny jar no bigger than a wine-glass. It was of an exquisitely polished black. "Not even an explorer can have been here, or nothing so perfect as this would have been left! What hands do you suppose made this!"

But DeWitt did not answer her question.

"Now, look here, Rhoda, you aren't to do anything like starting a fire and lugging these heavy jars again! You're not with the Indians now. You've got a man to wait on you!"

Rhoda looked at him curiously.

"But I've learned to like to do it!" she protested. "Nobody can roast a rabbit to suit me but myself," and in spite of DeWitt's protests she spitted the rabbits and would not let him tend the fire which she said was too fine an art for his untrained hands. In a short time the rich odor of roasting flesh rose on the air and John watched the pretty cook with admiration mingled with perplexity. Rhoda insisting on cooking a meal! More than that, Rhoda evidently enjoying the job! The idea left him speechless.

An hour after Rhoda had spitted the game, John sighed with contentment as he looked at the pile of bones beside his earthen bowl.

"And they say jacks aren't good eating!" he said. "Why if they had been salted they would have been better than any game I ever ate!"

"You never were so hungry before," said Rhoda. "Still, they were well roasted, now weren't they?"

"Your vanity is colossal, Miss Tuttle," laughed John; "but I will admit that I never saw better roasting." Then he said soberly, "I believe we had better not try the trail again today, Rhoda dear. We don't know where to go and we've no supplies. We'd better get our strength up, resting here today, and tomorrow start in good shape."

Rhoda looked wistfully from the shade of the pueblo out over the desert. She had become very, very tired of this endless fleeing.

"I wish the Newman ranch was just over beyond," she said. "John, what will you do if Kut-le comes on us here?"

DeWitt's forehead burned a painful red.

"I have a shot left in my revolver," he said.

Rhoda walked over to John and put one hand on his shoulder as he sat looking up at her with somber blue eyes.

"John," she said, "I want you to promise me that you will fire at Kut-le only in the last extremity to keep him from carrying me off, and that you will shoot only as Porter did, to lame and not to kill."

John's jaws came together and he returned the girl's scrutiny with a steel-like glance.

"Why do you plead for him?" he asked finally.

"He saved my life," she answered simply.

John rose and walked up and down restlessly.

"Rhoda, if a white man had done this thing I would shoot him as I would a dog. What do I care for a law in a case like this! We were men long before we had laws. Why should this Indian be let go when he has done what a white would be shot for?"

Rhoda looked at him keenly.

"You talk as if in your heart you knew you were going to kill him because he is an Indian and were trying to justify yourself for it!"

He turned on the girl a look so haunted, so miserable, yet so determined, that her heart sank. For a time there was silence, each afraid to speak. At last Rhoda said coolly:

"Will you get fresh water while I bank in the fire?"

DeWitt's face relaxed. He smiled a little grimly.

"I'll do anything for you but that one thing—promise not to kill the Indian."

"The desert has changed us both, John," said Rhoda. "It has taken the veneer off both of us!"

"Maybe so," replied DeWitt. "I only know that that Apache must pay for the hell you and I have lived through."

"Look at me, John!" cried Rhoda. "Can't you realize that the good Kut-le has done me has been far greater than his affront to me? Do you see how well I am, how strong? Oh, if I could only make you see what a different world I live in! You would have been tied to an invalid, John, if Kut-le hadn't stolen me!

Think now of all I can do for you! Of the home I can make, of the work I can do!"

DeWitt answered tersely.

"I'm mighty glad you're well, but only for your own sake and because I can have you longer. I don't want you to work for me. I'll do all the working that's done in our family!"

"But," protested Rhoda, "that's just keeping me lazy and selfish!"

"You couldn't be selfish if you tried. You pay your way with your beauty. When I think of that Apache devil having the joy of you all this time, watching you grow back to health, taking care of you, carrying you, it makes me feel like a cave man. I could kill him with a club! Thank heaven, the lynch law can hold in this forsaken spot! And there isn't a man in the country but will back me up, not a jury that would find me guilty!"

Rhoda sat in utter consternation. The power of the desert to lay bare the human soul appalled her. This was a DeWitt that the East never could have shown her. It sickened her as she realized that no words of hers could sway this man; to realize that she was trying to stay with her feeble feminine hands passions that were as old a world-force as love itself. All her new-found strength seemed inadequate to solve this new problem.

CHAPTER XIX

THE TRAIL AGAIN

FOR a long time Rhoda sat silently considering her problem and John watched her soberly. Finally she turned to speak. As she did so, she caught on the young man's face a look so weary, so puzzled, so altogether wretched that the girl's heart smote her. This was indeed a poor return for what he had endured for her! Rhoda jumped to her feet with resolution in her eyes.

"Are you too tired to explore the ruins?" she asked.

DeWitt rose languidly. Rhoda had responded at once to rest and food but John would need a month of care and quiet in which to regain his strength.

"I'll do anything you want me to—in that line!"

Rhoda carefully ignored the last phrase.

"Even if we're half dead, it's too bad to miss the opportunity to examine such a wonderful thing as this. You couldn't find as glorious a setting for a ruin anywhere in Europe."

"Oh, yes, you could; lots of 'em," answered DeWitt. "You can't compare a ruin like this with anything in Europe. What makes European ruins appeal to us is not only their intrinsic beauty but the association of big ideas with them. We know that big thoughts built them and perhaps destroyed them."

"What do you call big thoughts?" asked Rhoda. "Wasn't it just as great for these Pueblo Indians to perform such terrible labor in building this for their families as it was for some old king to work thousands of slaves to death to build him a monument?"

DeWitt laughed.

"Rhoda, you can love the desert, its Indians and its ruins all you want to, if you won't ask me to! I've had all I want of the three of them! Lord, how I hate it all!"

Rhoda looked at him wistfully. If only he could understand the spiritual change in her that was even greater than the physical! If only he could see the beauty of those far lavender hazes! If only he could understand how even now she was heartsick for the night trail where one looked up into the sky as into a shadowy opal! If only he knew the peace that had dwelt with her on the holiday ledge where there were tints and beauties too deep for words! And yet with the wistfulness came a strange sense of satisfaction that all this new part of her must belong forever to Kut-le.

John led the way into the dwelling. All was emptiness and ruin. All that remained of the old life within its walls were wonderful bits of pottery. Only once did

DeWitt give evidence of pleasure. He was examining the carefully finished walls of one of the rooms when he called:

"I say, Rhoda, just look at this bit of humanness!"

Rhoda came to him quickly and he pointed low down on the adobe wall where was the perfect imprint of a baby's hand.

"The little rascal got spanked, I'll bet, for putting his hand on the 'dobe before it was dry!" commented John.

Rhoda smiled but said nothing. These departed peoples had become very real and very pitiable to her.

As soon as he could drag Rhoda from the ancient pots, John led the way to the top of the ruin. He was anxious to find if there were more than the one trail leading from the desert. To his great satisfaction he found that the mesa was unscalable except at the point that Rhoda had found as she staggered up from the desert.

"I'm going to guard that trail tonight," he said. "It's just possible, you know, that Kut-le escaped from Porter, though I think if he had he would have been upon us long before this. I've been mighty careless. But my brain is so tired it seems to have been off duty. I could hold that trail single-handed from the upper terrace for a week."

"Just remember," said Rhoda quickly, "that I've asked you not to shoot to kill!"

Again the hard light gleamed in DeWitt's eyes.

"I shall have a few words with him first, then I shall shoot to kill. There is that between that Indian and me which a woman evidently can't understand. I just can't see why you take the stand you do!"

"John dear," cried Rhoda, "put yourself in his place. With all the race prejudice against you that he had, wouldn't you have done as he has?"

"Probably," answered Dewitt calmly. "I also would have expected what he is going to get."

A sudden sense of the bizarre nature of their conversation caused Rhoda to say comically:

"I never knew that you could have such *bloody* ideas, John!"

DeWitt was glad to turn the conversation.

"I am so only occasionally," he said. "For instance, instead of shooting the rabbit for supper, I'm going to try a figure-four trap."

They returned to their little camp on the upper terrace and Rhoda sat with wistful gray eyes fastened on the desert while John busied himself with the trap-making. He worked with the skill of his country boyhood and the trap was cleverly finished.

"It's evident that I'm not the leader of the expedition any more," said Rhoda, looking at the trap admiringly.

John shook his head.

"I've lost my faith in myself as a hero. It's one thing to read of the desert and think how well you could have managed there, and another thing to be on the spot!"

The day passed slowly. As night drew on the two on the mesa top grew more and more anxious. There was little doubt but that they could live for a number of days at the old pueblo, yet it was evident that the ruin was far from any traveled trail and that chances of discovery were slight except by Kut-le. On the other hand, they were absolutely unprepared for a walking trip across the desert. Troubled and uncertain what to do, they watched the wonder of the sunset. Deeper, richer, more divine grew the colors of the desert, and in one supreme, flaming glory the sun sank from view.

DeWitt with his arm across Rhoda's shoulders spoke anxiously.

"Don't you still think we'd better start tomorrow?"

"Yes," she answered, "I suppose so. What direction shall we take?"

"East," replied DeWitt. "We're bound to strike help if we can keep going long enough in one direction. We'll cook a good supply of rabbits and I'll fix up one of those bowl-like ollas with my handkerchief, so we can carry water in it as well as in the two canteens. I think you had better sleep in the little room there tonight and I'll lie across the end of the trail here."

Rhoda sighed.

"I've nothing better to suggest. As you say, it's all guesswork!"

They set the rabbit trap by the spring, then Rhoda, quite recovered from her nervousness of the night before, entered her little sleeping-room and made ready for the night. The front of the room had so crumbled away that she could see John's dark form by the trail, and she lay down with a sense of security and fell asleep at once.

John paced the terrace for a long hour after Rhoda was asleep, trying to plan every detail for the morrow. He dared not confess even to himself how utterly disheartened he felt in the face of this terrible adversary, the desert. Finally, realizing that he must have rest if Rhoda was not to repeat her previous experience in leading him across the desert he stretched himself on the ground across the head of the trail. He must trust to his nervousness to make him sleep lightly.

How long she had slept Rhoda did not know when she was wakened by a half-muffled oath from DeWitt. She jumped to her feet and ran out to the terrace. Never while life remained to her was she to forget what she saw there. DeWitt and Kut-le were wrestling in each other's grip! Rhoda stood horrified. As the two men twisted about, DeWitt saw the girl and panted:

THE TRAIL AGAIN

"Don't stir, Rhoda! Don't call or you'll have his whole bunch up here!"

"Don't worry about that!" exclaimed Kut-le. "You've been wanting to get hold of me. Now we'll fight it out bare-handed and the best man wins."

Rhoda looked wildly down the trail, then ran up to the two men.

"Stop!" she screamed. "Stop!" Then as she caught the look in the men's faces as they glared at each other she cried, "I hate you both, you beasts!"

Her screams carried far in the night air, for in a moment Cesca came panting up the trail. She lunged at DeWitt with catlike fury, but at a sharp word from Kut-le she turned to Rhoda and stood guard beside the girl. Rhoda stood helplessly watching the battle as one watches the horrors of a nightmare.

Kut-le and DeWitt now were fighting as two wolves fight. Both the men were trained wrestlers, but in their fury all their scientific training was forgotten, and rolling over and over on the rocky trail each fought for a hold on the other's throat. With Kut-le was the advantage of perfect condition and superior strength. But DeWitt was fighting for his stolen mate. He was fighting like a cave man who has brooded for months on his revenge, and he was a terrible adversary. He had the sudden strength, the fearful recklessness of a madman. Now rolling on the edge of the terrace, now high against the crumbling pueblo, the savage and the civilized creature dragged each other back and forth. And Rhoda, awed by this display of passions, stood like the First Woman and waited!

Of a sudden Kut-le disentangled himself and with knees on DeWitt's shoulders he clutched at the white man's throat. At the same time, DeWitt gathered together his recumbent body and with a mighty heave he flung Kut-le over his head. Rhoda gave a little cry, thinking the fight was ended; but as Kut-le gained his feet, DeWitt sprang to meet him and the struggle was renewed. Rhoda never had dreamed of a sight so sickening as this of the two men she knew so well fighting for each other's throats with the animal's lust for killing. She did not know what would be Kut-le's course if he gained the mastery, but as she caught glimpses of DeWitt's face with its clenched teeth and terrible look of loathing she knew that if his fingers ever reached Kut-le's throat the Indian could hope for no mercy.

And then she saw DeWitt's face go white and his head drop back.

"Oh!" she screamed. "You've killed him! You've killed him!"

The Indian's voice came in jerks as he eased DeWitt to the ground.

THE TRAIL AGAIN

"He's just fainted. He's put up a tremendous fight for a man in his condition!"

As he spoke he was tying DeWitt's hands and ankles with his own and DeWitt's handkerchiefs. Rhoda would have run to DeWitt's aid but Cesca's hand was tight on her arm. Before the girl could plan any action, Kut-le had turned to her and had lifted her in his arms. She fought him wildly.

"I can't leave him so, Kut-le! You will kill all I've learned to feel for you if you leave him so!"

"He'll be all right!" panted Kut-le, running down the trail. "I've got Billy Porter down here to leave with him!"

At the foot of the trail were horses. Gagged and bound to his saddle Billy Porter sat in the moonlight with Molly on guard. Kut-le put Rhoda on a horse, then quickly thrust Porter to the ground, where the man sat helplessly.

"Oh, Billy!" cried Rhoda. "John is on the terrace! Find him! Help him!"

The last words were spoken as Kut-le turned her horse and led at a trot into the desert.

CHAPTER XX

THE RUINED MISSION

RHODA was so confused that for a moment she could only ease herself to the pony's swift canter and wonder if her encounter with DeWitt had been but a dream after all. A short distance from the pueblo Kut-le rode in beside her. It was very dark, with the heavy blackness that just precedes the dawn, but Rhoda felt that the Indian was looking at her exultingly.

"It seemed as if I never would get Alchise and Injun Tom moved to a friend's *campos* so that I could overtake you. I will say that that fellow Porter is game to the finish. It took me an hour to subdue him! Now, don't worry about the two of them. With a little work they can loose themselves and help each other to safety. I saw Newman's trail ten miles or so over beyond the pueblo mesa and I told Porter just how to go to pick him up."

Rhoda laughed hysterically.

"No wonder you have such a hold on your Indians! You seem never to fail! I do believe as much of it **is** luck as ingenuity!"

Kut-le chuckled.

"What a jolt DeWitt will find when he comes to, and finds Porter!"

"You needn't gloat over the situation, Kut-le!" exclaimed Rhoda, half sobbing in her conflict of emotions.

"Oh, you mustn't mind anything I say," returned the young Indian. "I am crazy with joy at just hearing your voice again! Are you really sorry to be with me again? Did DeWitt mean as much to you as ever? Tell me, Rhoda! Say just one kindly thing to me!"

"O Kut-le," cried Rhoda, "I can't! I can't! You must help me to be strong! You—who are the strongest person that I know! Can't you put yourself in my place and realize what a horrible position I am in?"

Kut-le answered slowly.

"I guess I can realize it. But the end is so great, so much worth while that nothing before that matters much, to me! Rhoda, isn't this good—the lift of the horse under your knees—the air rushing past your face—the weave and twist of the trail—don't they speak to you and doesn't your heart answer?"

"Yes," answered Rhoda simply.

The young Indian rode still closer. Dawn was lifting now, and with a gasp Rhoda saw what she had been too agonized to heed on the terrace in the moonlight. Kut-le was clothed again! He wore the khaki suit, the high-laced riding boots of the ranch days; and he wore them with the grace, the debonair ease that had so charmed Rhoda in young Cartwell. That little sense of his difference that his Indian nakedness had kept in Rhoda's subconsciousness disappeared. She stared at his broad, graceful shoulders, at the fine outline of his head which still was bare, and she knew that her decision was going to be indescribably difficult to keep. Kut-le watched the wistful gray eyes tenderly, as if he realized the depth of anguish behind their wistfulness; yet he watched none the less resolutely, as if he had no qualms over the outcome of his plans. And Rhoda, returning his gaze, caught the depth and splendor of his eyes. And that wordless joy of life whose thrill had touched her the first time that she had met young Cartwell rushed through her veins once more. He was the youth, the splendor, the vivid wholesomeness of the desert! He was the heart itself, of the desert.

Kut-le laid his hand on hers.

"Rhoda," softly, "do you remember the moment before Porter interrupted us? Ah, dear one, you will have to prove much to erase the truth of that moment from our hearts! How much longer must I wait for you, Rhoda?"

Rhoda did not speak, but as she returned the young man's gaze there came her rare slow smile of unspeakable beauty and tenderness. Kut-le trembled; but before he could speak Rhoda seemed to see between his face and hers, DeWitt, haggard and exhausted, expending the last remnant of his strength in his fight for her. She put her hands before her face with a little sob.

Kut-le watched her in silence for a moment, then he said in his low rich voice:

"Neither DeWitt nor I want you to suffer over your decision. And DeWitt doesn't want just the shell of you. I have the real you! O Rhoda, the real you will belong to me if you are seven times DeWitt's wife! Can't you realize that forever and ever you are mine, no matter how you fight or what you do?"

But Rhoda scarcely heard him. She was with DeWitt, struggling across the parching sands.

"O Kut-le! Kut-le! What shall I do! What shall I do!"

Kut-le started to answer, then changed his mind.

"You poor, tired little girl," he said. "You have had a fierce time there in the desert. You look exhausted. What did you have to eat and how did you make out crossing to the mesa? By your trail you went miles out of your way."

Rhoda struggled for calm.

"We nearly died the first day," she said. "But we did very well after we reached the mesa."

Kut-le smiled to himself. It was hard even for him to

THE RUINED MISSION 275

realize that this plucky girl who passed so simply over such an ordeal as he knew she must have endured could be the Rhoda of the ranch. But he said only:

"We'll make for the timber line and let you rest for a while."

At mid-morning they left the desert and began to climb a rough mountain slope. At the piñon line, Kut-le called a halt. Never before had shade seemed so good to Rhoda as it did now. She lay on the pine-needles looking up into the soft green. It was unspeakably grateful to her eyes which had been so long tortured by the desert glare. She lay thus for a long time, her mental pain for a while lost in the access of physical comfort. Shortly Molly, who had been working rapidly, brought her a steaming bowl of stew. Rhoda ate this, then with her head pillowed on her arm she fell asleep.

She was wakened by Molly's touch on her arm. It was late afternoon. Rhoda looked up into the squaw's face and drew a quick hard breath as realization came to her.

"Molly! Molly!" she cried. "I'm in terrible, terrible trouble, Molly!"

The squaw looked worried.

"You no go away! Kut-le heap sorry while you gone!"

But Rhoda scarcely heeded the woman's voice. She

rolled over with her hot face in the fragrant needles and groaned.

"O Molly! Molly! I'm in terrible trouble!"

"What trouble? You tell old Molly!"

Rhoda sat up and stared into the deep brown eyes. Just as Kut-le had become to her the splendor of the desert, so had Molly become the brooding wisdom of the desert. With sudden inspiration she grasped the Indian woman's toil-scarred hands.

"Listen, Molly! Before I knew Kut-le, I was going to marry the white man, DeWitt. And after he stole me I hated Kut-le and I hated the desert. And now, O Molly, I love both Kut-le and the desert, and I must marry the white man!"

"Why? You tell Molly why?"

"Because he is white, Molly, like me. Because he loves me so and has done so much for me! But most of all because he is white!"

Molly scowled.

"Because Kut-le is Injun, you no marry him?"

Rhoda nodded miserably.

"Huh! And you think you so big, Kut-le so big that Great Spirit care if you marry white, marry Injun. All Great Spirit care is for every squaw to have papoose. Squaw, she big fool to listen to her head. Squaw, she

THE RUINED MISSION 277

must always listen to her heart, that is Great Spirit talking. Your heart, it say marry Kut-le!"

Molly paused and looked at the girl, who sat with stormy eyes on the sinking sun. And she forgot her hard-earned wisdom and was just a heart-hungry woman.

"You stay! Stay with Kut-le and old Molly! You so sweet! You like little childs! You lie in old Molly's heart like little girl papoose that never came to Molly. You stay! Always, always, Molly will take care of you!"

Rhoda was deeply touched. This was the cry of the famished motherhood of a dying race. She put her soft cheek on Molly's shoulder and she could no longer see the sun, for her eyes were tear-blinded. Kut-le, standing on the other side of the camp, looked at the picture with deepening eyes; then he crossed and put his hand on Rhoda's shoulder.

"Dear one," he said, "you must eat your supper, then we must take the trail."

Rhoda looked up into the young man's face. She was exquisite in the failing light. For a moment it seemed as if Kut-le must fold her in his arms; but something in her troubled gaze withheld him and he only smiled at her caressingly.

"Before you eat," he said, "come to the edge of the camp and look through the glasses."

Rhoda hurried after him, and stared out over the

desert. A short distance out, vivid in the afterglow, moved two figures. She distinguished the short wiry figure of Porter, the gaunt figure of DeWitt, walking with determined strides. Waiting till she could command her voice, Rhoda turned to Kut-le. He was watching her keenly.

"Will they pick up our trail? Are the poor things badly lost?"

"Billy Porter lost! I guess not! And I gave him enough hints so that he ought to join Newman in another twenty-four hours."

Rhoda smiled wanly.

"Sometimes you forget to act like a cold-blooded Indian."

Kut-le gave his familiar chuckle.

"Well, you see, I've been contaminated by my long association with the whites!"

And so again the nights of going. During her waking hours, Rhoda spent the greater part of her time considering arguments that would have weight with Kut-le when the struggle came which she knew was imminent.

If she had suffered before, if the early part of her abduction had been agony, it had been nothing in comparison with what she was enduring in putting Kut-le aside for DeWitt. And, after all, she had no final guide in holding to her resolution save an instinct that told her that her course was the right one. All the arguments that she could put into words against inter-race marriage seemed inadequate. This instinct which was wordless and formless alone remained sufficient.

And with the ill logic of womankind, through all her arguing with herself there flushed one glad thought. Kut-le knew that she loved him, knew that she was suffering in the thought of giving him up! His tender, half sad, half triumphant smile proved that, as did his protective air of ownership.

Rhoda noticed one condition of her keeping to her decision. She was very firm in it at night when the desert was dim. But in the glory of the dawns and the sunsets, her little arguments seemed strangely small. Sitting on a mountainside one afternoon, Rhoda watched a rain-storm sweep across the ranges, across the desert, to the far-lying mesas. Normally odorless, the desert, after the rain, emitted a faint, ineffable odor that teased the girl's fancy as if she verged on the secret of the desert's beauty. Exquisite violet mists rolled back to the mountains. Flashing every rainbow tint from its moistened breast the desert lay as if breathing the very words of the Great Scheme.

Suddenly to Rhoda her resolution seemed small and futile, and for a long hour she revelled in the thought of belonging to the man she loved. And yet as night descended and the infinite reaches of the desert receded into darkness, the spell was broken and the old doubts and misery returned.

And so again, the nights of going. But the holiday aspect of the flight was gone. Kut-le moved with a grim determination that was not to be misinterpreted. Rhoda knew that they were to reach the Mexican border with all possible speed. The young Indian drove the little party to the limit of its endurance. Rhoda avoided talking to him as much as she could and Kut-le, seeming to understand her mood, left her much to herself.

On the fourth day they camped on a cañon edge. After Rhoda had eaten she walked with Kut-le to the far edge and looked down. The cañon was very deep and narrow. Some distance away, near where it opened on the desert, lay a heap of ruins.

"Is that another pueblo?" asked Rhoda.

"No, it's an old monastery. Part of the year they have a padre there. I wish I knew if there was one there now."

"Why?" asked Rhoda suspiciously.

"Don't bother your dear head," answered Kut-le. Then he went on, as if half to himself: "There's been an awful lot of fooling on this expedition. Perhaps I ought to have made for the Mexican border the very night I took you." He looked at Rhoda's wide, troubled eyes. "But no, then I would have missed this wonderful desert growth of yours! But now we are going straight over the border where I know a padre that will marry us. Then we will make for Europe at once."

The morning sun glinted on the pine-needles. Old Molly hummed a singsong air over the stew-pot. And Rhoda stood with stormy, tear-dimmed eyes and quivering lips.

"It can never, never be, Kut-le!"

"Why not?"

"We can't solve the problems of race adjustment. No love is big enough for that. I have been civilized a thousand years. You have been savage a thousand years. You can't come forward. I can't go backward."

"You know well enough, Rhoda," said Kut-le quietly, "that I am civilized."

"You are externally, perhaps," said the girl. "But you yourself have no proof that at heart you are not as uncivilized as your father or grandfather. Your stealing me shows that. Nothing can change our instinct. You know that you might revert at any time."

Kut-le turned on her fiercely.

"Do you love me, Rhoda?"

Rhoda stood silently, her cleft chin trembling, her deep gray eyes wide and grief-stricken.

"Do you love me—and better than you do DeWitt?" insisted the man.

Suddenly Rhoda lifted her head proudly.

"Yes," she said, "I do love you, better than any one in the world; but I cannot marry you!"

Kut-le took her trembling hands in his.

"Why not, dear one?" he asked.

Still the sun flickered on the pine-needles and still Molly hummed over her stew-pot. Still Rhoda stood looking into the eyes of the man she loved, her scarlet cheeks growing each moment more deeply crimson.

"Because you are an Indian. The instinct in me against such a marriage is so strong that I dare not go against it."

Kut-le's mouth closed in the old way.

"And still you shall marry me, Rhoda!"

"I am a white woman, Kut-le. I can't marry an Indian. The difference is too great!"

Kut-le turned abruptly and walked to the cañon edge, looking far out to the desert. Rhoda, panting and half hysterical, watched him. The moment which she had so dreaded had arrived, and she found herself, after all her planning, utterly unprepared to meet it save with hackneyed phrases.

It seemed a long time that Kut-le stood staring away from her. At last Rhoda could bear the silence no longer.

THE RUINED MISSION

She ran to him and put her trembling hand on his arm. He turned his stern young face to her and her heart failed her.

"O Kut-le! Kut-le!" she cried. "If you won't help me to do right, who will? It's not right for us to marry! Just not right! That's all I know about it!"

Kut-le put both hands on her shoulders.

"Look here, Rhoda. What you call the 'right' instinct is just the remnant of the old man-made race hatred in you. It's just a part of the old conceit of the Caucasian."

Rhoda stirred restlessly, but Kut-le held her firmly and went on.

"I tell you, if we're not to go mad, we've got to believe that great things come to us for a purpose. There is no human being who has loved who does not believe that love is the greatest thing that has been given to man. The man who has loved knows that the biggest things in the world have been done for the love of woman. Love is bigger than nations or races. It's *human*, not white, or black, or yellow. It's above all we can do to tarnish it with our little prejudices. When it comes greatly, it comes supremely."

He lifted the girl's face and looked deeply into her eyes.

"Rhoda, if it has come as greatly to you as it has to me, you will not pause for any sorrow that your coming to me may cost you. You will come, in spite of everything. I believe that if in your smallness and ignorance you refuse this gift that has come to you and me, you will be outraging the greatest force in nature."

Rhoda stood sorrow-stricken and confused. When the deep, quiet voice ceased, she said brokenly:

"I haven't lived in the desert so long as you. The way does not lie so clear to me. If only I had your conviction, I too could be strong and walk the path I saw unhesitatingly. But I see no path!"

"Then," said Kut-le, "because I see, I'll decide for you! O Rhoda, you must believe in me! I have had you in my power and I have kept the faith with you. I am going to take you and marry you. I am going to make this gift that has come to you and me make us the big man and woman that nature needs. Tonight we shall reach the padre who will marry us."

He watched the girl keenly for a moment, then he again turned from her deliberately and walked to the edge of the cañon, as if he wanted her to come to her final decision unbiased by his nearness. But he turned back to her with a curious expression on his face.

"Come and take a good-by look, Rhoda! Your friends are below. I hope it will be some time before we see them again!"

Rhoda went to him. Far, far below, she saw little dots

of men making camp beyond the monastery near the desert. Suddenly Rhoda sank to her knees with a cry of longing that was heart-breaking.

"O my people! My own people!" she sobbed, crouching upon the cañon edge.

Kut-le watched the little figure with inscrutable eyes. Then he lifted the girl to her feet.

"Rhoda, are you going to eat your heart out for your own kind if you marry me? Won't I be sufficient? It hadn't occurred to me that I might not be!"

"You haven't given up your people," answered Rhoda. "You are always going back to them."

"But you aren't really giving them up," urged Kut-le. "It really is I who make the sacrifice of my race!"

"And that is the reason for one of my fears," cried Rhoda. "I am afraid that some day you would find the price too great and that our marriage would be wrecked."

"Even if I went back for a few months each year, would that make you unhappy?" asked Kut-le.

"Kut-le!" exclaimed Rhoda. "I am not talking of externals. I mean that if your longing for your own kind made you lose your love for me. Oh, I can't see any of it straight, but I am afraid!"

"Nonsense, Rhoda! I fought that battle long before I knew you. There is absolutely no danger of my reverting. I am going to spend the rest of my life among the whites even if you shouldn't marry me, Rhoda. Rhoda, I wish I had had time to let you grow to it fully!"

Rhoda stood rigidly. Molly, sensing trouble, hovered restlessly just out of earshot.

"If you married DeWitt," Kut-le went on, "could you forget me? Forget the desert? Forget our days and nights? Forget my arms about you?"

"Oh, no! No!" cried Rhoda. "You know that I shall love you always!"

"And will DeWitt want what you offer him?" Kut-le went on, mercilessly.

Rhoda winced.

"I wish," said Kut-le huskily, "you never will know *how* I wish that you had come to me freely, feeling that the sacrifice was worth while!"

Rhoda looked at him wonderingly. After all the weeks of iron determination, was the young giant weakening, was his great heart failing him!

"I had thought," he went on, "that you were big enough to stand the test. That after the travail and the heart scourging, you would see—and would come to me freely—strong enough to smile at all your regrets and fears. That thought steeled me to put you through the torture. But if now, at the end, you are coming to me

THE RUINED MISSION

only because you must! Rhoda, I don't want you on those terms."

Rhoda gasped. She felt as one feels when in a dream one falls an unexpected and endless distance. The relief from the pressure of Kut-le's will that had forced her on, for so long, left her weak and aimless.

Yet somehow she found the strength to say:

"Kut-le, we must give each other up! I love you so that I can let you go! Oh, can't you see how I feel about it!"

Again Kut-le looked far off over vista of mountains and cañon. His eyes were deep and abstracted, as if he saw into the years ahead with knowledge denied to Rhoda. Then he turned to Rhoda and searched her face with burning gaze. He eyed her hair, her lovely heart-broken face, her slender figure. For a moment his face was tortured by a look of doubt that was heart-shattering. He lifted Rhoda across his chest in the old way and held her to him with passionate tenderness. He laid his face against hers and she heard him whisper:

"O my love! Love of my youth and my manhood!" Then he set her very gently to her feet. "Don't cry," he said. "I can't bear it!"

Rhoda threw her arms above her head in an abandonment of agony.

"Oh, I cannot, cannot bear this!" Then she added more calmly: "I suffer as much as you, Kut-le!"

Again the look of unspeakable grief crossed the young Indian's face, but it immediately became inscrutable. He led Rhoda along the cañon edge.

"Do you see that little trail going down?" he said.

"Yes," said Rhoda wonderingly.

"Then go!" said Kut-le quietly.

Rhoda looked up at him blankly.

"Go!" he said sternly. "Go back to your own kind and I will go on, alone. Don't stop to talk any more. Go now!"

Rhoda turned and looked at Cesca squatting by the horses, at Molly hovering near by with anxious eyes. Never to make the dawn camp, again—never to hear Molly humming over the stew-pot! Suddenly Rhoda felt that if she could have Molly with her she would not be so utterly separated from Kut-le.

"Let Molly go with me!" she said. "I love Molly!"

"No!" said Kut-le. "You are to forget the desert and the Indians. Go now!"

With awe and grief too deep for words, Rhoda obeyed the young chief's stern eyes. She clambered down the rough trail to a break in the cañon wall, then, clinging with hands and feet, down the sheer side. The tall figure, beautiful in its perfect symmetry stood immovable, the face never turning from her. Rhoda knew that she never was to forget this picture of him. At the foot of the cañon wall she stood long, looking up. Far, far above, the straight figure stood in lonely majesty, gazing at the life for which he had sacrificed so much. Rhoda looked until, tear-blinded, she turned away.

CHAPTER XXI

THE END OF THE TRAIL

THE cañon was sandy and rough. Rhoda could see the monastery set among olive-trees. Beyond this where the cañon opened to the desert she knew that the white men's camp lay, though she could not see it.

She had no fear of losing her way, with the cañon walls hemming her in. She still was sobbing softly to herself as she started along the foot of the wall. She tramped steadily for a time, then she stopped abruptly. She would not go on! The sacrifice was too much! She looked back to the cañon top. Kut-le had disappeared. Already he must be only a memory to her!

Then of a sudden Rhoda felt a sense of shame that her strength of purpose should be so much less than the Indian's. At least, she could carry in her heart forever the example of his fortitude. It would be like his warm hand guiding and lifting her through the hard days and years to come. Strangely comforted and strengthened by this thought, Rhoda started on through the familiar wilderness of the desert.

This, she thought, was her last moment alone in the

desert, for without Kut-le she would never return to it. She watched the gray-green cactus against the painted rock heaps. She watched the brown, tortured crest of the cañon against the violet sky. She watched the melting haze above the monastery, the buzzards sliding through the motionless air, the far multi-colored ranges, as if she would etch forever on her memory the world that Kut-le loved. And she knew that, let her body wander where it must, her spirit would forever belong to the desert.

Rhoda passed the monastery, where she thought she saw men among the olive-trees. But she did not stop. She gradually worked out into an easy trail that led toward the open desert.

The little camp at the cañon's mouth was preparing to move when Jack Newman jumped excitedly to his feet. Coming toward them through the sand was a boyish figure that moved with a beautiful stride, tireless and swift. As the newcomer drew nearer they saw that she was erect and lithe, slender but full-chested and that her face—

"Rhoda!" shouted John DeWitt.

In a moment, Jack was grasping one of her hands and John DeWitt the other, while Billy Porter and Carlos shook each other's hands excitedly.

"Gee whiz!" cried Jack. "John said you were in

superb condition, but I didn't realize that it meant this! Why, Rhoda, if it wasn't for your hair and eyes and the dimple in your chin, I wouldn't know you!"

"Are you all right?" asked DeWitt anxiously. "Where in the world did you come from? Where have you been?"

"Were you hurt much in the fight?" cried Rhoda. "Oh!" looking about at the eager listeners, "that was the most awful thing I ever saw, that fight! And Billy Porter, you are all right, I see. How shall I ever repay you all for what you have done for me!"

"Gosh!" exclaimed Porter. "I'm repaid just by looking at you! If that pison Piute hasn't made monkeys of us all, I'd like to know who has! How did you get away from him?"

"He let me go," answered Rhoda simply.

The men gasped.

"What was the matter with him!" ejaculated Porter. "Was he sick or dying?"

"No," said Rhoda mechanically; "I guess he saw that it was useless."

"And he dropped you in the desert without water or food or horse!" cried DeWitt. "Oh, that Apache cur!"

"No! No!" exclaimed Rhoda. "He dropped me not far from here. We saw the camp and he sent me to it."

The men looked at each other incredulously. Jack

Newman's face was puzzled. He knew Kut-le and it was hard to believe that he would give up what he already had won. DeWitt spoke excitedly.

"Then he's still within our reach! Hurry up, friends!"

Rhoda turned swiftly to the gaunt-faced man. Then she spoke very distinctly, with that in her deep gray eyes that stirred each listener with a vague sense of loss and yearning.

"I don't want Kut-le harmed! I shan't tell you anything that will help you locate him. He did me no harm. On the contrary, he made me a well woman, physically and mentally. If I can forgive his effrontery in stealing me, surely you all will grant me this favor to top all that you have done for me."

Porter's under lip protruded with the old obstinate look.

"That fellow's got to be made an example of, Miss Rhoda," he said. "No white that's a man can stand for what he's done. He's bound to be hunted down, you know. If we don't, others will!"

Rhoda turned impatiently to DeWitt.

"John, after all our talk, *you* must understand! *You* know what good Kut-le has done me and how big it was of him to let me go. Make them promise to let him alone!"

But there was no answering look of understanding in DeWitt's worn face.

"Rhoda, you haven't any idea what you're asking! It isn't a question of forgiveness! You don't get the point of view that you ought! Why, the whole country is worked up over this thing! The newspapers are full of it. Just as Porter says, the Apache's got to be made an example of. We will hunt him down, if it takes a year!"

So far Jack Newman had said nothing. Rhoda looked at him as if he were her last hope.

"Oh, Jack!" she cried. "He was your friend, your dearest friend! And he sent me back! Why, you never would have got me if he hadn't voluntarily let me go! He is wonderful on the trail!"

"So we found!" said DeWitt grimly.

But Rhoda was watching Jack.

"Rhoda," Jack said at last, "I know how you feel. I know what a bully chap Kut-le is. This just about does me up. But what he's done can't be let go. We've got to punish him!"

"'Punish him!'" repeated Rhoda. "Just what do you mean by that?"

"We mean," answered DeWitt, "that when we find him, I'll shoot him!"

"No!" cried Rhoda. "No! Why he *sent me back!*"

The three men looked at Rhoda uncomfortably and at each other wonderingly. A woman's magnanimity is never to be understood by a man!

"Are you tired, Rhoda?" asked DeWitt abruptly. "Do you feel able to take to the saddle at once?"

"I'm all right!" exclaimed Rhoda impatiently. "What are your plans?"

DeWitt pointed out across the sand to the cañon wall. A line of slender footprints led through the level wastes as plainly as if on new-fallen snow.

"We will follow your trail," he said.

There was silence for an instant in the little camp while the men eyed the girlish face, flushed and vivid beneath the tan. As it had come when DeWitt had rescued her, the old sense of the appalling nature of her experience was returning to her again. With sickening clarity she was getting the men's view-point. The old Rhoda would have protested, would have fought desperately and blindly. The new Rhoda had lived through hours of hopeless battle with circumstance. She had learned the desert's lesson of patience.

"I have thought," she said slowly, "so much of the joy of my return to you! God only knows how the picture of it has kept me alive from day to day. All *your* joy seems swallowed up in your thirst for revenge. All right, my friends. Only, wherever you go, I go too!"

Billy Porter shook his head with a muttered "Gosh!" as if the ways of women were quite beyond him.

"I think you had better ride on to the ranch with Car-

THE END OF THE TRAIL

los," said DeWitt, "while we take up Kut-le's trail. This will be no trip for a woman."

"You're foolish!" exclaimed Jack. "We'll not let her out of our sight again. You can't tell what stunt Kut-le is up to!"

"That's right!" said Porter. "It'll be hard on her, but she'd better come with us."

"Don't trouble to discuss the matter," said Rhoda coolly. "I am coming with you. Katherine probably sent some clothing for me, didn't she?"

"Why, yes!" exclaimed Jack. "That was one of the first things she thought of. She sent her own riding things for you. She spoke of the little silk dress you had on and said you hadn't anything appropriate in your trunks for the rough trip you might have to take after we found you."

Jack was talking rapidly, as if to relieve the tension of the situation. He undid a pack that he had kept tied to his saddle during all the long weeks of pursuit.

"We can rig up a dressing-room of blankets in no time," he went on, putting a bundle into Rhoda's hands.

Rhoda stood holding the bundle in silence while all hands set to rigging up her dressing-room. She felt suddenly cool-headed and resourceful. Her mind was forced away from her own sorrow to the solution of another heavy problem. In the little blanket tent she unrolled the bundle and smiled tenderly at the evidence of Katherine's thoughtfulness. There were underwear, handkerchiefs, toilet articles and Katherine's own pretty corduroy divided skirt and Norfolk jacket with a little blouse and Ascot scarf.

Rhoda took off her buckskins and tattered blue shirt slowly, with lips that would quiver. This was the last, the very last of Kut-le! She dressed herself in Katherine's clothes, then folded up the buckskins and shirt. She would keep them, always! When she came out from the tent she stepped awkwardly, for the skirts bothered her, and Jack, waiting near by, smiled at her. At another time Rhoda would have joined in his amusement, but now she asked soberly:

"Which horse is for me?"

"Rhoda!" cried DeWitt, "I really wouldn't know you! I thought I never could want you anything but ethereal, but—Jack! Isn't she wonderful!"

Jack grinned. Rhoda, tanned and oval-cheeked, and straight of back and shoulder, was not to be compared with the invalid Rhoda.

"Gee!" he said. "Wait till Katherine sees her!"

Rhoda shrugged her shoulders.

"My pleasure in all that is swallowed up by this savage obsession of yours."

John De Witt led out Rhoda's pony.

THE END OF THE TRAIL

"You don't understand, dear," he said. "You *can't* doubt my heavenly joy at having you safe. But the outrage of it all— That Apache devil!"

"I do understand, John," answered Rhoda wearily. "Don't try to explain again. I know just how you all feel. Only, I will not have Kut-le killed."

"Rhoda," said DeWitt hoarsely, "I shall kill him as I would a yellow dog!"

Rhoda turned away. The line of march was quickly formed. Porter led. Carlos closed the rear. DeWitt and Newman rode on either side of Rhoda. They were not long in reaching the trail down the cañon wall. Here they paused, for the rough ascent was impossible for the horses. The men looked questioningly at Rhoda but she volunteered no information. She believed that Kut-le had left the camp at the top long since. If for any reason he had delayed his going, she knew that he had watched every movement in the white camp and could protect himself easily.

"We can leave Carlos with the horses," said Porter, "while we climb up and see where the trail leads."

Rhoda dismounted, still silent, and followed Porter and DeWitt up the trail, Jack following her. The trail had been difficult to descend and was very hard to ascend. There was a dumb purposefulness about the men's movements that sickened Rhoda. She had seen too much of men in this mood of late and she feared them. She knew that all the amenities of civilization had been stripped from them and that she was only pitting her feeble strength against a world-old instinct.

Her heart was beating heavily as they neared the top, but not from the hard climb. She was inured to difficult trails. There was a sheer pull, shoulder high, at the top. The four accomplished it in one breathless group, then stood as if paralyzed.

Sunlight flickered through the pines. Molly and Cesca prepared the trail packs. And Kut-le sat beside the spring, eying his visitors grimly. He looked very cool and well groomed in comparison with his trail-worn adversaries.

DeWitt pulled out his Colt.

"I think I have you, this time," he said.

"Yes?" asked Kut-le, without stirring. "And what are you going to do with me?"

"I'm going to take about a minute to tell you what I think of you, and give you another minute in which to offer up some sort of an Indian prayer. Then I'm going to shoot you!"

Kut-le glanced from DeWitt to Rhoda, thence to Porter and Newman. Porter's under lip protruded. Jack looked sick. Both the men had their hands on

THE END OF THE TRAIL

their guns. Rhoda moistened her lips to speak, but Kut-le was before her.

"Are you a good shot, DeWitt?" he asked. "Because I know that Jack and Porter are sure in their aim."

"You'll never know whether I am or not," replied DeWitt. "You'd better be thankful that we are shooting you instead of hanging you, as you deserve, you cur! You'd better be glad you're dying! You haven't a white friend left in the country! All your ambition and hard work have come to this because you couldn't change your Indian hide, after all! Now then, say your prayers! Rhoda, cover up your eyes!"

Kut-le rose slowly. The whites noticed with a little pang of shame that he made no attempt to touch his gun which lay on the ground beside him.

"You'd better let Jack and Billy shoot with you," he said quietly. "You won't like to think about the shot that killed me, afterward. It isn't nice, I've heard, the memory of killing a man!"

"I'm shooting an Indian, not a man!" said DeWitt. "Say your prayers!"

The spell of fear that had paralyzed Rhoda snapped. Before Jack or Billy could detain her she ran to DeWitt's side and grasped his arm.

"John! John! Listen to me, one moment! Look at me! In spite of all, look, see what he's made of me, for you to reap the harvest! Look at me! I beg of you, do not shoot him! Let him go! Make him promise to leave the country. Make him promise anything! He keeps promises because he is an Indian! But if you have any love for me, if you care anything for my happiness, don't kill Kut-le! I tell you I will never marry you with his blood on your hands!"

A look curiously hard, curiously suspicious, came to DeWitt's eyes. Without lowering his gun or looking at the girl, he answered:

"You plead too well, Rhoda! I want this Indian to pay for more torture of mine than you can dream of! Get back out of the way! Are you ready, Kut-le?"

Rhoda's slender body was rigid. She moved away from DeWitt until she could encompass the four men in her glance. With arms folded across her arching chest she spoke with a richness in her voice that none of her hearers ever could forget.

"Remember, friends, you have forced me to this! You had me safe, but you thought more of revenge than you did of my safety! John, if you kill Kut-le you will kill the man that I love with all the passion of my soul!"

DeWitt gasped as if he had been struck. Newman and Porter stared dizzily. Only Kut-le stood composed. His eyes with the old look of tragic tenderness were fastened on the girl.

"Are you going to shoot him now, John?"

"Rhoda!" cried DeWitt fiercely. "Rhoda! Do you realize what you are saying?"

"Yes," said Rhoda steadily. "I realize that a force greater than race pride, greater than self love, greater than intelligence or fear, is gripping me! John, I love this man! He and I have lived through experiences together too great for words. He had me in the hollow of his hand but he sent me back to you, his enemy. You say that you love me. But you would not listen to my pleading, you would not grant me the only favor I ever asked you, the granting of which could not have harmed you."

Her listeners did not stir. Rhoda moistened her lips.

"Kut-le—— Think what he sacrificed for me. He gave up his dearest friendships. He gave up his honor and his country and risked his life, for me. And then when he thought the sacrifice would prove too great on my part, he gave me up! I ask you to give him his life, for me. Because, John, and Billy Porter, and Jack, I tell you that I love him!"

"My God!" panted DeWitt. "Rhoda, don't! You don't know what you're saying! Rhoda!"

Rhoda looked off where the afternoon sun lay like the very glory of God upon the chaos of range and desert. Almost—almost the secret of life itself seemed to bare itself to the girl's wide eyes. The white men watched her aghast. There was a desperate, hunted look in DeWitt's tired face. Rhoda turned back.

"I know what I'm saying," she replied. "But I tell you that this thing is bigger than I am! I have fought it, defied it, ignored it. It only grows the stronger! I know that this comes to humans but rarely. Yet it has come to me! It is the greatest force in the world! It is what makes life persist! To most people it comes only in small degree and they call *that* love! To me, in this boundless country, it has come boundlessly. It is greater than what you know as love. It is greater than I am. I don't know what sorrow or what joy my decision may bring me but—John, I want you to let Kut-le live that I may marry him!"

DeWitt's arm dropped as if dead.

"Rhoda," he repeated, agonizedly, "you don't know what you are saying!"

"Don't I?" asked Rhoda steadily. "Have I fought my fight without coming to know the risk? Don't I know what atavism means, and race alienation, and hunger for my own? But this which has come to me is stronger than all these. I love Kut-le, John, and I ask you to give his life to me!"

Still Kut-le stood motionless, as did Jack and Porter. DeWitt, without taking his eyes from Rhoda's, slowly, very slowly, slipped his Colt back into his belt. For a long moment he gazed at the wonder of the girl's exalted face. Then he passed his hands across his eyes.

"I give up!" he said quietly. Then he turned, walked slowly to the cañon edge, and clambered deliberately down the trail.

Jack and Billy stood dazed for a moment longer, then Porter cleared his throat.

"Miss Rhoda, don't do this! Now don't you! Come with us back to the ranch. Just for a month till you get away from this Injun's influence! Come back and talk to Mrs. Newman. Come back and get some other woman's ideas! For God's sake, Miss Rhoda, don't ruin your life this way!"

"When Katherine knows it all, she'll understand and agree with me," replied Rhoda. "Jack, try to remember everything I said, to tell Katherine."

"*I* tell her!" cried Jack. "Why can't you tell her yourself? What are you planning to do?"

"That is for Kut-le to say," answered Rhoda.

"Rhoda," said Jack, and his voice shook with earnestness, "listen! Listen to me, your old playmate! I know how fascinating Kut-le is. Lord help us, girl, he's been my best friend for years! And in spite of everything, he's my friend still. But, Rhoda, it won't do! It won't work out right. He's a fine man for men. But as a husband to a white woman, he's still an Indian; and after the first, that must always come between you! Think again, Rhoda! I tell you, it won't do!"

Rhoda's voice still was clear and high, still bore the note of exaltation.

"I have thought again and again, Jack. There could be no end to the thinking, so I gave it up!"

Kut-le's eyes were on the girl, inscrutable and calm as the desert itself, but still he did not speak.

Billy Porter wiped his forehead again and again on a cloth that bore no resemblance to a handkerchief.

"I can't put up any kind of an argument. All I can say is I don't see how any one like you could do it, Miss Rhoda! Just think! His folks is Injuns, dirty, blanket Injuns! They scratch themselves from one day's end to the other. They will be your relatives, too! They'll be hanging round you all the time. I'm not a married man but I've noticed when you marry a man you generally marry his whole darn family. I—I—oh, there's no use talking to her! Let's take her away by force, Jack!"

Rhoda caught her breath and instinctively moved toward Kut-le. But Jack did not stir.

"No," he answered; "I've done all the chasing and trying to kidnap that I care about. But, Rhoda, once and for all I tell you that I think you are doing you and yours a deadly wrong!"

"Perhaps I am," replied Rhoda steadily. "I make no pretense of knowing. At any rate, I'm going to stay with Kut-le."

"For heaven's sake, Rhoda," cried Jack, "at least come back to the ranch and let Katherine give you a wedding. She'll never forgive me for leaving you this way!"

Porter turned on Jack savagely.

"Look here!" he shouted. "Are you crazy too! You're talking about her *marrying* this Apache!"

Jack spoke through his teeth obstinately.

"I've sweated blood over this thing as long as I propose to. If Rhoda wants to marry Kut-le, that's her business. I always did like Kut-le and I always shall. I've done my full duty in trying to get Rhoda back. Now that she says that she cares for him, it's neither your nor my business—nor DeWitt's. But I want them to come back to the ranch with me and let Katherine give them a nice wedding."

"But—but—" spluttered Porter. Then he stopped as the good sense of Jack's attitude suddenly came home to him. "All right," he said sullenly. "I'm like DeWitt. I pass. Only—if you try to take this Injun back to the ranch, he'll never get there alive. He'll be lynched by the first bunch of cowboys or miners we strike. Miss Rhoda nor you can't stop 'em. You want to remember how the whole country is worked up over this!"

Rhoda whitened.

"Do you think that too, Jack and Kut-le?"

For the first time, Jack spoke to Kut-le.

"What do you think, Kut-le?" he said.

"Porter's right, of course," answered Kut-le. "My plan always has been to slip down into Mexico and then go to Paris for a year or two. I've got enough money for that. I've always wanted to do some work in the Sorbonne. By the end of two years I think the Southwest will be willing to welcome us back."

Nothing could have so simplified the situation as Kut-le's calm reference to his plans for carrying on his profession. He stood in his well-cut clothes, not an Indian, but a well-bred, clean-cut man of the world. Even Porter recognized this, and with a sigh he resigned himself to the inevitable.

"You folks better come down to the monastery and be married," he said. "There's a padre down there."

"Gee! What'll I say to Katherine!" groaned Jack.

"Katherine will understand," said Rhoda. "Katherine always loved Kut-le. Even now I can't believe that she has altogether turned against him."

Jack Newman heaved a sigh.

"Well," he said, "Kut-le, will you and Rhoda come

THE END OF THE TRAIL

down to the monastery with us and be married?" His young voice was solemn.

"Yes," answered Kut-le, "if Rhoda is agreed."

Rhoda's face still wore the look of exaltation.

"I will come!" she said.

Kut-le did not let his glance rest on her, but turned to Billy.

"Mr. Porter," he said courteously, "will you come to my wedding?"

Billy looked dazed. He stared from Kut-le to Rhoda, and Rhoda smiled at him. His last defense was down.

"I'll be there, thanks!" he said.

"There is a side trail that we can take my horses down," said Kut-le.

They all were silent as Kut-le led the way down the side trail and by a circuitous path to the monastery. He made his way up through a rude, grass-grown path to a cloistered front that was in fairly good repair. Here they dismounted and waited while Kut-le pulled a long bell-rope that hung beside a battered door. There was not long to wait before the door opened and a white-faced old padre stood staring in amazement at the little group.

Kut-le talked rapidly, now in Spanish and now in English, and at last the padre turned to Rhoda with a smile.

"And you?" he asked. "You are quite willing?"

"Yes," said Rhoda, though her voice trembled in spite of her.

"And you?" asked the padre, turning to Jack and Billy.

The two men nodded.

"Then enter!" said the padre.

And with Cesca and Molly bringing up the rear, the wedding party followed the padre down a long adobe hallway across a courtyard where palms still shaded a trickling fountain, into a dim chapel, with grim adobe walls and pews hacked and worn by centuries of use.

The padre was excited and pleased.

"If," he said, "you all will sit, I will call my two choir-boys who are at work in the olive orchard. They are not far away. We are always ready to hold service for such as may wish to attend."

He disappeared through the door of the choir loft and returned shortly, followed by two tall Mexican half-breeds, clad in priceless surplices that had been wrought in Spain two centuries before. They lighted some meager candles before the altar and began their chant in soft, well-trained voices.

The padre turned and waited. Kut-le rose and, taking Rhoda's hand, he led her before the aged priest.

To the two white men the scene was unforgetable.

The dim old chapel, scene of who could tell what heart-burnings of desert history; the priest of the ancient religion; standing before him the two young people, one of a vanishing and one of a conquering race, both startlingly vivid in the perfection of their beauty; and, looking on, the two wide-eyed squaws with aboriginal wonder in their eyes.

It was but a moment before Kut-le had slipped a ring on Rhoda's finger; but a moment before the priest had pronounced them man and wife.

As the two left the priest, Jack kissed Rhoda solemnly twice.

"Once for Katherine," he said, "and once for me. I don't understand much how it all has come about, but I know Kut-le, and I'm willing to trust you to him."

Kut-le gave Jack a clear look.

"Jack, I'll never forget that speech. If I live long enough, I'll repay you for it."

"And an Indian keeps his promises," said Rhoda softly.

Billy Porter was not to be outdone.

"Now that it's all over with, I'll say that Kut-le is a good fighter and that you are the handsomest couple I ever saw."

Kut-le chuckled.

"Cesca, am I such a heap fool?"

Cesca sniffed.

"White squaws no good! They—"

But Molly elbowed Cesca aside.

"You no listen to her!" she said.

"O Molly! Molly!" cried Rhoda. "You are a woman! I'm glad you were here!" And the men's eyes blurred a little as the Indian woman hugged the white girl to her and crooned over her.

"You no cry! You no cry! When you come back, Molly come to your house, take care of you!"

After a moment Rhoda wiped her eyes, and Kut-le, who had been giving the old padre something that the old fellow eyed with joy, took the girl's hand gently.

"Come!" he said.

At the door the others watched them mount and ride away. The two sat their horses with the grace that comes of long, hard trails.

"Maybe I've done wrong," said Jack. "But I don't feel so. I'm awful sorry for DeWitt."

"I'm awful sorry for DeWitt," agreed Porter, "but I'm sorrier for myself. I'm older than DeWitt a whole lot. He's young enough to get over anything."

When they had ridden out of sight of the monastery, Kut-le pulled in his horse and dismounted. Then he stood looking up into Rhoda's face. In his eyes was the same look of exaltation that made hers wonderful. He put his hand on her knee.

"We've a long ride ahead of us," he said softly. "I want something that I can't have on horseback."

Rhoda laid her hand on his.

"You meant it all, Rhoda? It was not only to save my life?"

"Do you have to ask that?" said Rhoda.

"No!" answered Kut-le simply. "You see I waited for you. I knew that they would bring you back. And if you had not spoken, I would rather have died. I had made up my mind to that. O my love! It has come to us greatly!"

Then, as if the flood, controlled all these months, had burst its bonds, Kut-le lifted Rhoda from her saddle to his arms and laid his lips to hers. For a long moment the two clung to each other as if they knew that life could hold no moment for them so sweet as this. Then they mounted and, side by side, they rode off into the desert sunset.

THE END